VACATION FRIENDS
A THRILLER

CHRISTY BARRITT

CHAPTER
ONE

YOU SHOULDN'T HAVE WALKED into a place you weren't supposed to be.

When you did and you realized your mistake, you should have looked away.

But you didn't.

Instead, you became suspicious and hostile.

You confronted me.

Then you made a threat.

I've put entirely too much into this to let someone like *you* ruin it.

This isn't my fault. It's *yours*. It's all because you didn't mind your own business.

I saw it in your eyes. Saw how you were going to wreck everything.

Now it's come down to this. I never planned on taking such drastic measures. But you've left me no choice.

I shrug my shoulders and continue down the path to the beach as darkness hangs overhead, making me feel as if I'm tucked under the black cloak of an evil, ominous deity.

At least the nighttime disguises my face and what I'm about to do.

You're waiting by the water, just as I told you to.

But do you think I asked you to meet so we could make a deal?

I regret to inform you that isn't the case.

I can't pay you off. No amount of money would be enough for your silence.

Instead, I have other ways of handling things.

As I approach, you turn toward me. Something flickers in your brown eyes—greed.

You're slimy—that much is obvious.

But I hadn't anticipated you being this much of a problem.

"You wanted to meet?" you begin, the start of a smirk on your face.

You're in your mid-twenties and only five foot four. Your build is hefty but not muscular. You're too much of a desk jockey. Your brown hair is dark and thick, always perfectly styled with a side part.

You think you're smarter than you really are.

You think you're smarter than I am.

I'm going to prove you wrong. I'm going to prove a lot of people wrong.

"Yes, I wanted to meet," I tell you, grateful for the

darkness and that no one else is around. But I have to act quickly because in the blink of an eye that can change. "I want to explain myself."

"There's no explaining what I saw." You definitely smirk now, your double chin emphasizing your cocky expression—but in a repulsive way. "You and I both know it. You'll do anything to get ahead. So why don't you just get to the point?"

You're clearly hoping for a payout here.

You greedy little idiot.

I need to set you straight.

Before I can second-guess myself, I pull the gun from the pocket of my dark sweatshirt. Too bad I can't use it. Shooting you would be easy. But then your death won't look like an accident. Plus, someone might hear the bullet firing through the air. Even though the roar of the waves is loud, I fear the gunshot would be louder.

Still, it's a good scare tactic to ensure I get what I want.

Your eyes widen as your cockiness disappears. Your hands shoot into the air, palms facing me as fear dawns on your face. "No, please don't! I'll keep your secret."

Like I'd believe that one . . . "Secrets come at a price."

"I was being stupid. I'm sorry!" You back up, the edges of your sweatpants doused by the water.

I follow you as you back farther into the ocean, not caring about the fact that my own pants are getting wet.

I'll think of an excuse for that later. I'm good at

making excuses. Coming up with stories. Making people believe me.

You have the power to stop me from getting what I deserve. And I can*not* let that happen.

As I continue toward you, you take several more steps into the waves.

You're panicking.

Good.

The next instant, you turn and begin to run into the ocean.

You dive beneath the surface, desperate to get away.

If you really want to do things this way . . .

I stuff the gun into my waistband.

Then I easily catch up with you as you surface.

I grab your shoulders and pounce on you.

Your head goes under the water.

A wave hits us. We tumble and roll, but I hold on.

When I surface again, I slam your body down.

Your head hits one of the rocks barely visible above the waterline.

Even in the dark, I see blood trickling from your temple.

Your body goes limp, and you stop fighting.

Which is just what I want.

I shove your body farther out into the water, face down.

I don't have to do anything else. The ocean will take care of this problem for me.

I watch your body floating in the moonlight.

Then I begin to walk back to shore.

I glance at the resort where I'm staying this week.

The place is pure paradise.

I can't wait to enact everything I have planned. I've been meticulous in my preparations.

Now you can't get in my way.

My first obstacle has been taken care of and checked off my list.

But I have many other tasks to complete in order to reach my goal.

I turn around once more and see your body floating in the water, the soft moonlight hitting your white shirt as waves toss you around.

"Farewell, Jared," I whisper. "I'm sorry things had to end this way."

But I'm not really.

I smile at the thought.

Then I slither through some brush until I reach the resort.

It's time to enact the rest of my plan.

The next step is for me to look like I have no idea what just happened.

I know something you need to know. Someone is out to get you. I need to explain in person and not through text. Meet me at 5:30 a.m. on the beach. Tell no one—trust no one. Delete this message.

MADDIE WATERS LAY BACK in bed and read the text again.

Meet a stranger in an unfamiliar place at that early hour?

She shivered as she glanced out her patio doors to the dark sky blackening the outside of her suite.

The message sounded so ominous.

How could she ignore words like that? However, the person who'd sent the text wasn't in her contacts and didn't leave a name—which raised some major red flags. Why wouldn't someone want her to know his or her name? Maybe they were hiding something.

Based on the message, that was *definitely* true.

When she'd received the text at eleven p.m. last night, she'd responded asking who sent it. There'd been no answer, and that was five hours ago.

She hadn't been able to sleep since then.

Should she go find out who wanted to meet her? Find out what this person knew? Or would that be stupid—practically a death wish?

Maddie wasn't sure. But her curiosity was strong . . . especially in light of everything that had happened recently. Did this have something to do with her past? With the secret she'd kept hidden for more than a decade?

What if someone knew? If they wanted to expose her?

Her head spun at the thought of it.

Should she tell Josh, her fiancé, about the message? Maddie already knew what he would say. He'd tell her that going to the beach at such an early hour to meet an unknown person would be stupid, that no one in their right mind would be foolish enough to do something like that.

But Maddie was the type who liked answers. Who loved justice. Who wanted to get to the bottom of things. It was why she'd taken a job investigating elder abuse.

Righting wrongs ignited a fire inside her.

Her gut told her to keep this message quiet, just as the sender had warned.

At five a.m., she climbed out of bed and pulled on a sweatshirt and some running shorts. She threw her curly, dark hair into a ponytail and slipped on her flip-flops.

Then she left her suite at the resort where she'd be staying for the next five days as a part of a corporate retreat for Josh's company. She padded down the hallway, a chilly breeze brushing through the open windows.

This place was paradise. She should feel safe. But she didn't.

Especially because of that text. But even before that . . .

The words of a woman she'd run into at the Lihue airport slammed into her mind.

Visitors come here with the mindset that nothing bad happens on vacation. But this island is dangerous. Things get wild quickly. Don't think that being on vacation will insulate you or put you in a protective bubble. Letting down your guard can mean the difference between life and death.

The words had been chilling. Josh had overheard part of the woman's rant and ushered Maddie away before she could listen to more. The woman had stood outside near baggage claim, almost acting like a sidewalk prophet.

A breeze sweeping through the hallway brought with it the sweet scent of orchids and another floral aroma Maddie couldn't name.

She loved the open-air buildings here in Kauai. They were so different from New York, where she currently lived. The crowded city made her feel like she was living in a box. Trapped. Unable to breathe.

She'd been determined to leave when she'd met Josh.

Her lips twisted into a frown as she glanced down at the engagement ring on her hand.

This was a big week for him. He would most likely be named CEO of tech giant Benchmark. He was currently acting as interim CEO, and most people thought he was a shoo-in.

As soon as this trip was over, Maddie would call things off with Josh for good, she promised herself as she hurried toward an exterior door. There was no hope of saving their relationship. She'd been in denial about it for too long now, hoping something would change.

But it wouldn't.

She swept those thoughts aside and stepped outdoors. An intricately paved walkway and sparkling turquoise pools greeted her. Palm trees surrounded the massive resort, and the roar of waves filled the air as the water crashed in the distance.

Maddie had never been anywhere like this before.

She imagined what it might be like to come here

with friends. With people she could actually enjoy the resort with. Where she could cut loose and have some fun—something she hadn't done in months.

Nothing had been the same in her life since her Poppy died. He'd been such a support and source of joy in her life. His death had shaken her to the core.

Instead, she was here with Josh.

Maddie held back a grimace.

She couldn't stand here and revel at the view.

Curiosity urged her onward.

She hurried across the pathway, down some steps, and across another path. Finally, her feet hit the sand, and she cut through some bushes and between several large boulders until she reached the beach.

A shiver raked through her.

Even though the grand resort stretched behind her, being out here on the beach before sunrise felt isolated. The waves were so loud, strong . . . overpowering.

She scanned her surroundings but saw no one.

Where was the person who'd sent her this message? He or she had said to meet at 5:30.

Maddie's watch showed she was right on time.

Wait . . . there *were* a couple of surfers farther down the beach. And a couple of people jogged a trail in the distance, barely visible except for the light from the softly glowing moon above.

She shivered.

Had coming out here been a mistake? Probably.

But she was already here.

She would wait a few more minutes.

Maddie glanced at the waves as they crashed on the shore. Black rocks bordered the sand, and a cliff rose in the distance. When she'd arrived on Sunday, she'd been warned about how dangerous the cliffs were with the jagged rocks poking out of the ocean below. Many people had lost their lives being too adventurous and careless near the cliff edges.

She'd be staying far away.

Maddie squinted as she stared at the ocean.

Something caught her eye as it floated in the water. What was that? It wasn't a dead mammal of some sort, was it? She'd heard about whales and dolphins occasionally washing up on the beach. Was that what she was looking at?

She crept closer and let out a gasp.

That wasn't a whale, she realized.

That was a . . . man.

Just then, he lifted his head and yelled something.

Yelled for help.

Maddie's adrenaline surged, and her heart began to thrash in her chest.

She glanced around. No one else was close enough to help.

Only her.

She reached for her phone.

It wasn't in her pocket.

She must have left it in her room. What a terrible mistake!

She glanced at the ocean again. She couldn't let the man die!

Taking a deep breath, she rushed toward the water. A wave nearly took her out before she was even ankle-deep.

But she didn't stop.

If she could get past this line of shore break, maybe she could reach the man.

Despite her fear, something compelled her to keep moving forward. If there was any chance she could help . . . she couldn't leave him there to die.

Another wave hit her, and she fell back. Water engulfed her.

As it passed, she stood, coughing to expel the salty water from her lungs.

She only had a few seconds until the next wave crashed. She needed to move faster.

But wave after wave knocked her down. The undercurrent tugged at her legs. Water filled her mouth—her lungs—as she fought to get to the man.

Her strength waned as the ocean sucked away all her energy.

Even if she reached the man, she wasn't sure she could make it back to shore with him.

The man's face bobbed from the dark water again.

"Help . . ." he gasped, his voice barely discernable over the waves.

Maddie lunged through the water trying to grab him, but a wave pulled him farther away.

If only she could get closer . . .

His head dipped up again, and his eyes widened as he saw her. Was that recognition that flickered in his gaze?

"You . . ." he croaked.

Was this the man she was supposed to meet?

"Someone . . . murder . . ."

Her blood went icy cold at the word "murder." Was he trying to tell her someone had attempted to murder him? That his current state of distress wasn't an accident?

She reached for him, but he disappeared beneath the water again.

A cry escaped from deep inside her as another wave engulfed her.

She had to get out of the ocean. Maddie was no match for its strength. She wasn't sure why she'd ever thought she could rescue this man.

Now they were both going to die.

As she tried to stand, the water knocked her down again. The waves tossed her around like a ragdoll.

Tears of despair pressed at her eyes.

She couldn't give up. She wasn't helpless. She had to keep trying.

Using all her remaining energy, she stood once more. Just as she took a step back to shore, another wave pounded her.

She toppled forward.

Before she could gain her footing, an invisible force began to drag her under, drag her deeper into the ocean.

She was caught in a riptide.

Paradise, she realized, might become her grave . . . just like that woman at the airport had warned.

MADDIE'S ARMS flailed as she tried to fight the ocean and get back to the surface.

But it was no use. She was no match for the mighty Pacific.

She would become another vacation statistic.

No, don't think like that. Keep trying. You're stronger than this.

That was right. She couldn't give up. She couldn't give in without a fight.

As a second wind hit her, she fought to get to the surface and draw in a breath.

To survive.

Finally, she managed to resurface.

But her arms felt as if weighted ropes were attached. For every inch she swam closer to shore, the current pulled her back nearly a foot.

The ocean pulled her under again.

This was it. She was done. She couldn't fight anymore.

Just then, arms swooped beneath her.

As her face rose above the surface, water spurted from her mouth. Her lungs gurgled.

Through blurry eyes, a man appeared in the darkness above her.

The man murmured something. Maybe, "It's going to be okay. I'll get you out of here."

Between the ocean and the water jostling in her ears, she couldn't be sure.

She coughed more, desperate to dispel the saltwater from her body.

Waves still pummeled her, though not as violently now. Instead, her body rocked back and forth with the waves as the man swam with her to shore.

Could anyone survive these waves?

Or would both she and her savior become a vacation statistic?

And what about the man she'd tried to save? Where was he now?

Finally, the rocking stopped.

Everything went still as her body splayed against something wet and grainy.

Sand.

She coughed again, and water spurted from her mouth.

Maddie didn't have time to recover. She needed to

tell the man who'd saved her about the other man in the ocean.

She forced herself to sit up, still wheezing and breathless. She raised a shaky arm and pointed toward the rocks jutting from the water. "A man . . . out there . . . needs . . . help."

Her vision cleared in time for her to see her rescuer's eyes widen with alarm. "Someone else is in the ocean?"

Maddie nodded before having another coughing fit.

"Stay with her," the man lifted his head and muttered.

A woman dropped to her knees beside her and grasped Maddie's hand. "It's going to be okay. You're going to be fine. Paramedics are on the way."

Paramedics? That meant the police might come also.

The cops were the last people Maddie wanted to see.

But she didn't have the strength to argue.

Besides, all she could think about was that man.

The guy drowning in the ocean was the one who'd wanted to meet her, wasn't he? And he'd said something about murder.

She assumed he'd been talking about himself.

But what if . . . what if he was talking about her?

She'd felt lately as if death was stalking her.

Maddie coughed again, more water gushing out. The woman beside her pounded on her back.

She'd come so close to losing her life. Thank God that this man had seen her when he did. That he'd been a good swimmer. That she hadn't swallowed too much water.

"My name is Adrienne." The woman beside her patted Maddie's back again. "The man who pulled you out is my boyfriend, Brody. I'm so glad you're okay. I know that had to be scary."

Maddie hardly heard the woman. Instead, her gaze searched the dark water. "Is Brody okay?"

"He's a great swimmer. He was a surfing champion before he had to grow up and get a real job. He should be fine."

That made Maddie feel a little better. But the ocean had claimed some of the best, and the waves on the south shore were especially dangerous.

More commotion sounded near the water.

"What's happening?" Maddie blinked, trying to figure out what was going on. But her vision was still blurry.

"Brody . . . he's pulling someone out of the water."

Maddie's heart beat harder. "Is the man alive?"

"I . . . I don't know. Was he alive when you saw him? Let me see if I can get an update for you. Can I leave you alone?"

"Yes, of course. Please, go. I'm fine." Maddie leaned back on her palms, still trying to steady her breathing.

Adrienne ran toward Brody, sand flying behind her feet.

As she left, another woman appeared beside Maddie. Maybe she was one of the spectators who'd gathered.

Everyone seemed to materialize from nowhere, but Maddie wasn't complaining.

She'd be dead right now if Brody hadn't seen her. She felt certain of it.

"I thought you shouldn't be alone," the woman muttered.

That was kind of her. "Thank you."

Maddie turned back to the scene. The sun was beginning to rise beyond the cliffs, smearing pinks and oranges in the sky—and allowing her to see a little more.

She watched as Brody and Adrienne leaned over the man, trying to revive him. Another man joined them.

"Do you think he's dead?" Maddie's voice cracked as she asked the question.

"I . . . I don't know. I'm better with computer things than I am with medical things. But they're still doing CPR."

Four paramedics rushed through the shrubs and onto the scene, a stretcher between them.

Maddie tried to stand.

When her jelly-like legs started to collapse on her, the woman beside her grabbed her arm. "I can help."

With the stranger by her side, Maddie managed to find her balance. Together, the two of them crept closer to the man who'd been pulled from the water. She wanted to get a better look at his face.

But it was still dim outside, and too many people stood around him.

Maddie prayed the man survived. But in her gut, she knew the prognosis wasn't good.

As she paused near the group, someone beside her did a double take.

It was the man who'd saved her, she realized.

"Brody, right? Thank you." Maddie's voice sounded raw as she turned toward him. "You saved me."

"I'm glad I got here when I did."

Gratitude filled her. This man had risked his life to help her. He was truly a hero.

She continued to watch as the paramedics worked on the man sprawled on the beach, but she knew their efforts were futile.

The man from the ocean was dead.

Now the police would come. They'd probably want to question her.

A knot grew in her stomach.

The police were the last people she wanted to speak with.

One day, she knew her past would resurface. That people would find out the truth.

When they did, life as Maddie knew it would be over.

———

Several seconds later, Maddie turned as she heard someone in the distance calling her name. "Madison . . . are you okay?"

She recognized the deep voice right away.

Josh. He was one of the only people who called her Madison. He said it sounded more sophisticated than Maddie, the name she preferred.

She should be relieved to hear her fiancé's voice, but she wasn't.

Could it be because she wondered if he was trying to kill her?

The thought still startled her. But she couldn't deny the truth in the question.

Weird things had been happening over the past couple of weeks. The gas leak in her apartment. If she'd flipped on a light switch . . . she shuddered, not wanting to think about that scenario.

Josh had worked on her hot water tank. Had he purposefully nicked the gas line?

Then her tire had blown out while she was driving to a charity event in the Hamptons. Thankfully, she'd managed to pull to the side of the road in time. Again, Josh had just checked out the pressure in her tires the night before.

Maddie suddenly felt like she was part of one of those *Final Destination* movies. Especially when she coupled those facts with the reality that she'd almost been killed three months prior.

Then there was what happened today in the ocean . .

Maddie knew the thoughts were ridiculous. Death

wasn't chasing after her. But she couldn't deny her worries either.

As Josh paused on the sand beside her, his handsome face came into view. "What were you even doing out here at this time of the morning?"

She swallowed hard, not ready to tell him about the text. "I just wanted some fresh air and to maybe catch the sunrise. I couldn't sleep."

When she'd first met him, she'd thought he looked like Josh Lucas from the actor's *Sweet Home Alabama* days. Yes, she did have an affection for rom-coms and thrillers from the nineties and early two thousands.

She and her Poppy had spent hours watching their favorite movies together after he'd become bedridden, and she often thought of people by how they resembled actors or actresses from those movies. Weird quirk, yes. But she'd done it for so long that it was a habit now.

Her Josh had the same sandy blond hair and classic good looks as Josh Lucas. Except her Josh was more refined. He had the perfect barely there beard. Every hair was in place. His clothes were expensive and chosen by a stylist. He was the consummate businessman.

"I'd gone to grab some coffee when I heard there was an incident at the beach. Then you didn't answer your phone." Josh studied her face, concern in his gaze. "I had a bad feeling and rushed right down."

"I'm fine," Maddie insisted. "A man in the ocean needed help and—"

"You thought *you* could help him?" he interrupted, the concern in his voice replaced with a snort.

She gritted her teeth.

Josh was famous for interrupting people. Not just her, but his employees also.

Maddie found it disrespectful. When she'd brought up the subject once, Josh had laughed it off. He'd said life was too short to waste time with drawn-out conversations when he could just get right to the point. He had the gift of forgetting about the oyster in order to get to the pearl—his words.

She swallowed hard, trying to push down her resentment. "I couldn't just stand there and do nothing."

His eyes flickered with judgment. "Who is the guy anyway? Do you even know him?"

"No . . . I don't know who he is. Or . . . was." Her throat burned as she made the correction.

"He didn't survive?"

"I don't think so." She glanced back and saw that paramedics had stopped CPR and now stood in a circle around the man.

She'd tried to help. She'd almost lost her life by doing so.

But it looked like it was all for nothing.

Heaviness pressed on her at the thought.

MADDIE QUICKLY SCANNED the people around her.

Josh was here, of course.

Then she saw Brody. The man was probably in his early thirties with wavy blond hair that fell around his face. His skin was tan. His wet T-shirt and shorts showed a sculpted, broad physique, and his accent sounded Texan. He had a Matthew McConaughey vibe.

Adrienne stood beside him. She was a petite blonde with long hair, bright eyes, and a toothy smile. She wore white jogging shorts and a fuchsia tank top. If Maddie was going to continue making comparisons with actors, then she'd say Adrienne looked a little like Sarah Michelle Gellar.

The other woman—she'd overheard someone call her Bree—had a light brown complexion and long, dark hair. She wore leggings with hiking boots and a white shirt with an emu on it and the words "Do I Look Emused?" Threaded bracelets lined her wrists, and a crocheted headband stretched across the top of her head. Actress: Selma Hayek—if Selma was a crunchy hipster who liked emus.

Maddie instantly liked the woman—mostly because Maddie was a closet fan of emus also. Not many people could say that.

Josh's gaze slid to Brody, who still stood on the other side of Maddie. Josh raked his gaze over the man before turning up his nose as if deeming Brody unworthy.

A surge of protectiveness rose in her. "Josh, this is Brody, the man who saved me. I would be dead if not for him."

Realization washed over Josh as he extended his hand. "I see. Thank you so much for what you did."

"It's no problem." Brody straightened, his shoulders squaring. "Adrienne and I were out jogging when I saw something happening in the water. I'm glad I was here when I was. Just a few minutes difference—"

"So am I. Of course, I would've saved her myself had I known she was going to be out here so early." Josh pulled out his wallet and brought out two one hundred-dollar bills. "Please, take this as a thank-you."

Horror washed over Maddie.

He wasn't really doing this . . .

But he was.

Brody stared at the money before shaking his head.

"I, uh . . . I couldn't possibly take that. I was just trying to be a decent person."

"It's good to know there are still good people out there." Josh offered a stiff smile. "Now, if you'll excuse us, I'm going to take Maddie to get some water. If anyone needs to talk to her, she'll be over there with me." He pointed toward one of the patios where lounge chairs were stretched.

Maddie wasn't ready to move yet, but Josh pulled her away.

She glanced back one last time at the paramedics as they continued to stand around the man she'd tried to save. But the man's body remained lifeless.

Heaviness pressed on her chest.

Josh kept an arm around her as he led her back to the resort. He stopped by a lounge chair near the saltwater lagoon and nudged her into one of the seats.

"I'll be right back with that water," he promised.

Maddie nodded, grateful to have some space from him.

She wished when she'd tried to call off their engagement that she hadn't let Josh convince her otherwise. He'd begged her to wait to make any big decisions until after this retreat. He needed her by his side for the big event.

She watched Josh as he walked away, anxiety knotting her stomach. As soon as this trip was over, Maddie would call it quits between them. That was all there was to it.

The two of them weren't a good fit.

As for this week . . . well, it was important to Josh to maintain his image, and part of that image was having Maddie at his side. He needed to be the picture of stability.

That was what he'd told her.

He worked for Benchmark, a technology company that was the innovator behind a line of computers, phones, and tablets, to name a few. They'd developed products that rivaled—if not excelled—those of Apple. This week they planned to announce their newest project. Whatever it was, there had been a lot of buzz—but very few details—floating out there about it.

Four thousand people were employed at their New York headquarters. Of those, fifty had come on this corporate retreat, along with spouses or a plus one. They were board members and the top innovators—the core players in the company.

Meetings were scheduled. Excursions set up. A luau and concert planned. The event would conclude with a gala where the new CEO would be named and Benchmark's newest product would be launched.

It should be the perfect week in paradise.

So why did a feeling of dread swirl in Maddie's stomach?

———

"I thought that was you over here." Adrienne appeared beside her.

Maddie forced a smile and tried to push away her heavy thoughts. "It's me."

"I just wanted to check on you one more time," Adrienne said. "Are you sure you're okay? That had to be so scary out there."

Maddie nodded, still embarrassed that people were making such a big deal over her. "I'll be fine. My fiancé went to get me some water."

Adrienne nodded at the empty seat beside her. "Do you mind?"

"Go right ahead." Maddie rubbed a hand across her face and felt the wet hair on her forehead, the gritty sand on her cheek.

She must look like a mess.

But at least she was alive.

"I'm here for the Benchmark retreat also," Adrienne continued.

"Oh, are you? My fiancé—"

"Is Josh Harding, and you're Maddie Waters," Adrienne finished before shrugging sheepishly. "I know. Not to sound weird, but when you work for Josh Harding, you kind of know about his personal life."

His personal life, which really meant his trophies. He delighted in shiny things. Flashy cars. Big houses. Beautiful women.

Or *a* beautiful woman. Her.

However, Maddie had suspected on more than one

occasion that Josh had cheated on her. But she'd found no proof. It was probably just her paranoia talking. Of the three men she'd seriously dated in her twenty-eight years, the first two had been unfaithful. It seemed to be a pattern in her life.

She didn't want to simply lump Josh into that category. But there were some strange absences of time in Josh's schedule that made her curious.

Then there was the night she'd accidentally run into him on the way home from a work event. When he'd given her a kiss on the cheek, Maddie had thought for sure she'd smelled perfume on him.

And it wasn't *Maddie's* honeysuckle perfume. This one smelled fancy, like silk and crystal.

"What a crazy way to start this, right?" Adrienne said.

"That might be an understatement." Maddie closed her eyes, still trying to comprehend everything that had happened. The text, the meeting that didn't happen, trying to save the man.

Being saved herself.

Adrienne leaned closer and lowered her voice. "By the way, who was the man who died? Do you know who he was?"

"I have no idea. I never really saw his face. It was too dark."

"It's so tragic . . ." Adrienne rubbed her arms. "I wonder how often terrible things like that happen here in paradise, you know? Do things like this usually get swept under the rug in order not to scare tourists off?"

She didn't know how to respond. But the woman at the airport . . . Maddie couldn't stop thinking about what she'd said.

Letting down your guard can mean the difference between life and death.

It was almost as if her words had been an omen.

CHAPTER
FIVE

MADDIE LIKED ADRIENNE, she decided. The woman wasn't as pretentious as most people Maddie had encountered on this retreat.

She remembered her earlier thought. Remembered how she'd imagined how fun it would be to come on vacation at this resort with a friend.

Maybe Maddie could make the best of this trip.

Maybe she could make friends.

Vacation friends.

"Aloha, Adrienne," a deep voice said behind her. "I've been looking for you."

Maddie glanced over her shoulder, and Brody's eyes filled with recognition when he saw her. He gave her a nod as he stood beside Adrienne.

Maddie sat up straighter, her mind scrambling through what she should say. She finally settled on,

"Thank you again. You could have been killed yourself."

Adrienne stood and rested her hand on his chest, her eyes beaming. "That's Brody for you. Always selfless."

"It's a good thing you both were out jogging," Maddie said.

"Adrienne insisted we get some exercise. If not for her, I would have still been sleeping. She's probably the one you should be thanking." His Texas drawl saturated each word.

"I certainly appreciate the fact you were both out so early," Maddie said.

Brody smiled stiffly. Was it because of Maddie's praise or because of Adrienne's hand on his chest? Maddie wasn't sure.

Two other people headed their way—Bree with her emu shirt and the man Maddie had seen doing CPR.

"We thought we'd join the party." Bree offered a soft grin. "But really, my boyfriend and I were out hiking on the cliffs of Shipwreck Beach when we heard something happening. We rushed over to make sure everything was okay. This is my boyfriend, Fowler Johnson."

Everyone said hello to the man, who had dark, wavy hair to his chin and oversized glasses—a Johnny Galecki vibe.

Adrienne and Fowler seemed to recognize each other from the office, though they didn't appear to know each other very well.

The sound of someone singing off-key filled the air. "Cheeseburger in Paradise."

They all turned and saw a man walking near the pools, a beer in his hand.

"A little early for drinking," Brody muttered with a frown.

"A little early for us to hear him singing so off-key," Adrienne quipped.

They shared a chuckle.

The man paused, raised his bottle in the air, and when he started to walk again, he stumbled into a line of chairs. A loud clatter filled the air.

He quickly straightened and glanced around as if to make sure no one had seen. Then he continued walking, singing off-key again.

"Should we help the guy?" Bree asked.

"It looks like he's headed to his room," Brody said. "I think he'll be okay. We just need to make sure he doesn't fall into one of the pools."

Maddie liked these people, she realized. She appreciated how they'd been selfless this morning on the beach. They'd gone out of their way to help strangers. It was something Maddie didn't see very often.

She hadn't realized how much she craved basic kindness. But she did.

Being around them now felt like a balm to a wound she didn't know she had.

She'd felt all alone as she tried to integrate into Josh's world.

But maybe it was time to change that.

———

A moment later, Josh returned with a bottle of water. He paused when he reached the group, and his gaze flickered—almost suspiciously—from Adrienne to Brody to Bree to Fowler and then back to Maddie.

Josh handed her the water, and Maddie took a long sip.

Then he glanced back at Fowler. "Hey, man. Good to see you."

Fowler clearly worked for him. Maddie hadn't been sure who in this group was with the company and who was a plus one.

"You too." Fowler nodded.

"Good morning, Mr. Harding." Adrienne suddenly sounded more professional, her shoulders looked more squared and her composure more uptight.

Josh observed Adrienne for a moment, a flicker of recognition in his gaze. "Remind me of your name again?"

"Adrienne Peters." She extended her hand with a smile. "I work in event planning for your company. I'm actually just an assistant in the department, but I hope to be more one day. All that to say, I understand why you don't recognize me. It's such a large company that I'm sure you can't get to know everyone."

Some people would sound like a suck-up saying those words. But somehow Adrienne sounded sincere.

"I *thought* you were familiar. Good job with this retreat. I think it's going to be wonderful." His gaze moved to Brody. "The two of you are here together?"

"That's right." Adrienne grinned. "Brody is my plus one."

"They're all heroes." Maddie told Josh. "Brody pulled me from the water, Adrienne and Bree stayed with me to make sure I was okay, and Fowler did CPR on the man who drowned. They're all—"

"You're all lifesavers—truly." Josh shifted. "I'd love to take the four of you out to dinner tonight as my way of saying thank you for looking after my beautiful fiancée."

"You don't have to do that." Brody waved the idea off.

"I insist," Josh said. "It's the least I can do. I can make reservations tonight at Terrapin."

Adrienne's eyes widened. "When I talked to the resort yesterday, they said it takes months to get reservations there."

"I can pull a few strings." Josh shrugged as if it weren't a big deal.

That was how it worked when people were rich. They could get things that others couldn't.

Adrienne raised her eyebrows, making it clear she was impressed. "If you insist, then that sounds perfect.

I'd love to try that restaurant out—and to get to know everyone better as well."

"We'd love to join you," Fowler said with a slow, thoughtful nod. "You've done a great job since you took over as interim CEO. It would be an honor."

Dinner with this group tonight *did* sound intriguing, Maddie thought as she twisted her engagement ring on her finger.

She'd been on her own yesterday since Josh had meetings. She'd gone on a shopping excursion—alone— where she'd grabbed some lunch from a food truck. The sushi hadn't agreed with her, and she'd spent most of the rest of the day in the bathroom.

It had been miserable on more than one level.

She now had something to look forward to and something else to think about.

Something other than the fact that she believed her fiancé might be trying to kill her and the realization that the man she'd tried to save—and who'd possibly sent her that text—was dead.

CECILIA SUBCONSCIOUSLY TAPPED her fork on the white linen tablecloth as she waited.

She glanced at her watch again.

Fifteen minutes late.

Only five minutes ago she'd told herself that ten minutes was as long as she would wait.

Anything beyond that amount of time was just fooling herself.

When she'd met Ryan Fielding at the grocery store—in the produce section, of course—he'd seemed like an upright guy who knew how to pick a piece of ripe fruit and carry on a decent conversation. So when he'd asked her to dinner, Cecilia had agreed.

She'd told him they could meet at the restaurant. There was no need for him to pick her up.

She'd had so many bad experiences with men, and she was trying to do better. To set more boundaries. To be more selective about who she dated and who knew where she lived.

Her friends had said she was looking too hard for a man.

But she wasn't. Just because men asked her out didn't mean she was looking hard or that she even wanted a husband or someone to take care of her.

Having good conversation and someone else paying for her meals seemed a good option.

Except she always fell for the wrong guys. The ones who were controlling. Who only wanted one thing. Who didn't appreciate her for the right reasons.

She glanced at her watch one more time, hating how self-conscious she felt.

Twenty minutes had passed.

That was it. She needed to go. Staying any longer was just humiliating.

She stood and placed her napkin on her plate. She would go back to her apartment, cook some ramen, and change out of her red dress into some sweats and a T-shirt.

As she stepped away from the table, the waitress—a serious woman in her fifties with her hair pulled back into a tight bun—suddenly appeared in front of her. "Good evening, ma'am. Are you ready for your bill?"

"I didn't order anything," Cecilia reminded the waitress.

Her expression remained cool. "We have a minimum reservation fee."

A minimum reservation fee? She'd never heard of such a thing. Then again, her idea of a nice dinner was Applebee's.

"But I didn't even make this reservation . . ." Cecilia explained. Certainly this woman would hear what happened and back off. Anyone with some common sense would.

"I understand. But here's your check." The waitress handed her a slip of paper. "Our tables are in high demand, so we charge for each reservation."

Cecilia's eyes widened when she saw the amount on the bill. "It cost *that* much *just* to reserve a table here?"

"That's right." The waitress frowned. "People who come into establishments like this usually understand the intricacies of fine dining."

She heard the underlying tone in the woman's voice.

Cecilia didn't belong in places like this.

But sixty dollars for a reservation fee seemed excessive. "That's my entire pay after working a day at Balderston's Department Store."

The waitress's expression remained unchanged. "I understand, but that's not my problem."

Cecilia needed that money. Sixty dollars could buy her groceries for a week. Her pantry wasn't even stocked with anything expensive—mostly ramen, spaghetti noodles, jars of marinara sauce, and a few cans of tuna.

"I didn't eat any food." She worked hard to keep her voice calm, to not get wound up or cause a scene.

"So I don't feel as if I need to pay for simply being here."

"Unfortunately, that's not the way it works." The waitress popped her hip out, clearly becoming impatient.

The woman had to have other tables to oversee, other patrons to serve. Couldn't she just move on?

Ryan. This was his fault. If he'd just shown up, then Cecilia wouldn't be in this position right now.

She should have known the man was too smooth for his own good. What man took that much time picking out an apple?

"Do I need to get my manager?" The waitress's voice turned from cool to almost angry.

Cecilia glanced around. Other restaurant patrons—the rich elite who frequented high-brow places like this—were already starting to stare. She couldn't blame them. She knew she was creating a scene, even though that hadn't been her intention.

"Ma'am?" the waitress prodded as she waited for her answer.

"You don't need to get your manager because I'm not paying for it," Cecilia repeated, crossing her arms. The fact that these people thought she should pay sixty dollars just for the privilege of sitting at one of their tables was ridiculous.

"I'm afraid that's not going to work." The waitress's words sounded clipped and tight.

Cecilia heard the judgment in her tone, and she

didn't appreciate it. She might not be rich, but that didn't mean—

"Here you go," a deep voice cut into the conversation. "This should cover the ridiculous cost you have for simply entering this establishment. Now, if you'll please leave this nice woman alone. She seems to be the only one here with any common sense."

Cecilia's breath caught as she looked up at the man who'd interceded for her.

In his thirties. Dark hair. A nice suit.

He screamed affluence.

The waitress actually flushed as she took the money from him and nodded. "Thank you, sir."

"And I will *not* be giving this establishment my business anymore, not if this is the way you treat your customers."

"Mr.—"

He held up his hand to stop her mid-sentence. "Please don't say anything else. I've heard enough. Have a good evening."

He took Cecilia's arm and led her outside.

They paused under a bright-red awning. Two valets worked on the sidewalk, and a tuxedoed host greeted restaurant patrons. A red carpet stretched like a ribbon to the front door, intending to make restaurant guests feel like stars.

Unless you were the *wrong* guest. Then everyone working at the restaurant made you feel like trash.

"I'm sorry they treated you like that," the man told Cecilia.

Cecilia's heart still pounded in her ears.

It wasn't often that people stood up for her. Usually, they liked to use her. Liked to embarrass her. To throw her away. Especially men.

"You didn't have to do that. If you give me a few weeks, I can pay you back." Cecilia didn't want to be under anyone's thumb. Didn't want to owe anyone anything.

"Don't be ridiculous. I only paid that wretched woman so she'd stop making a scene back there. You didn't deserve that." He paused and observed her, his voice soft as if he didn't want to embarrass her.

Cecilia pushed a curl behind her ear. "I don't know what to say."

"You don't have to say anything. I don't like when people are mistreated."

"You're one of the good guys, huh?"

A movie star-worthy grin spread across his face. "I *try* to be one of the good guys."

They began to walk side-by-side down the bustling New York City sidewalk, naturally falling into step beside each other.

"I'm Garrick, by the way."

"I'm Cecilia."

She shivered at the chilly early October breeze, and Garrick took his jacket off and placed it over her shoulders.

"Can I walk you to your car? I know I'm old-fashioned, but something about the city at night always makes me more cautious."

"I took the subway," she explained.

"The subway also makes me nervous." He let out a chuckle.

"It's not that bad." If she were being honest, she'd admit she didn't like taking the subway alone either, especially at night.

Two weeks ago, her friend had been attacked while waiting for the train to come. Her purse had been stolen, and the man might have done more if it hadn't been for two cops that strolled up. They'd chased the man, but he'd gotten away.

Now Cecilia couldn't get those images out of her head. Images of her friend shaking and crying. Unable to sleep at night. Afraid to go out alone again.

"Are you from this area, Cecilia?" Garrick's voice pulled her from her thoughts as they slowly walked down the sidewalk, almost as if purposefully wanting more time to draw out the conversation.

"No, I came here two years ago."

"What brought you to the city?"

"I know it's going to sound cliché, but I wanted to be an actress. On Broadway."

When that hadn't worked out, Cecilia had worked on some other skills to try to earn money. She'd settled on working retail.

"You certainly have the looks for Broadway."

Her cheeks warmed. "Thank you. But looks aren't enough. I should have known that."

"Sometimes these things take time."

Something about his tone filled her with a moment of hope, like maybe she still had a chance. Like maybe her future wasn't confined to working at a department store selling clothing that cost more than she made in a month to rich women who turned their noses up at her.

She peered up at him and offered a grateful smile. "I appreciate your confidence in me."

"I'm just telling the truth."

They continued down the street, ignoring the throngs of people sharing the sidewalk. The savory scent of garlic and roasted tomatoes from a nearby Italian restaurant filled her nostrils, mingling with the odd odor of the city that she'd never quite been able to identify. Sewage? Subway gases?

She wasn't sure.

They reached the subway and paused.

"I'd offer to give you a ride home, but I have a feeling you're not the type who will take a ride with a stranger—which is only smart."

She gave him a soft smile. "You're right. I try not to do that."

"Could I at least pay for a taxi for you?" He tilted his head as he waited for her response.

"Then I might feel like I owe you something."

"But you wouldn't," he told her. "This city can eat people up and spit them out. I know it seemed like that when I first moved to New York. It's the least I can do to help someone out."

"No strings attached?" She studied his face looking for any signs of ulterior motives.

"No strings attached."

Cecilia glanced at the steps leading to the subway and considered how much nicer it would be to take a taxi.

But taking the subway was just one way of taking care of herself, of not depending on anyone else. She liked standing on her own two feet.

"I appreciate the offer, but I'm going to catch a train back to my place instead."

"I understand." He didn't seem surprised.

"Thank you again." Cecilia gave him another smile.

"Any time."

She glanced at him one more time before heading down the steps.

It was strange. She wanted so badly for the man to ask for her phone number. Or for him to give her his.

But then it would seem as if his kindness was done just as a matter of hitting on her, because he wanted something in return.

That might have changed Cecilia's overall image of him.

She *had* glanced at his left hand as they spoke.

No ring.

How was it possible for a man like that to be single

still? He had it all. Looks, charisma, kindness. If she had to guess, money.

She knew from working at the department store what expensive clothes looked like. His suit was *definitely* expensive.

She would *never* be his type.

In fact, she needed to forget about this encounter and move on with her life.

She needed to stay away from highfalutin men. Men like Ryan, who'd stood her up. Men like Garrick, who certainly had his pick of women.

In fact, if Cecilia were smart, she'd get out of this city ASAP.

But making good decisions had never been her specialty.

CHAPTER
SEVEN
NOW

THE REST of the day was a blur as Maddie tried to keep up with her obligations, which included breakfast with Josh and a few board members and a shopping trip with several "spouses" from upper management.

Maddie was still shaken from everything that had happened early this morning. Plus, she couldn't stop thinking about that text she'd received.

Had the man who'd died sent it to her? Had he been the one she was supposed to meet? It was the only thing that made sense.

And who exactly was the man? Did he have a family mourning him right now?

She did her best to hide the tremble still raking through her body as she went about the day.

Maddie had become quite good at acting like the person Josh wanted her to be. There were certain expectations that came with dating a man in his position.

Maddie considered herself a blue-collar woman. She hadn't grown up with the need to impress people—which was one reason she'd become a social worker. But now that her role had changed, being presentable was required.

She was, however, looking forward to tonight's dinner, looking forward to hanging out with people who were "ordinary" instead of rising superstars of the corporate world.

Most of the people she'd met through Josh were skilled at climbing the career ladder. They put on the right facade in order to get the promotions and accolades they wanted. They schmoozed and befriended the right people by keeping up appearances.

In other words, they knew how to play the game.

Maddie had never been one to be fake.

Adrienne, Brody, Bree, and Fowler seemed more like her kind of people.

The kind she'd grown up around.

At six o'clock, she met Josh in the hallway so they could walk to dinner together at the restaurant.

He gave her an approving glance. "You look beautiful."

She ran her hand down the knee-length, coral-colored sheath dress. The pale color showed off her tan skin and dark hair.

"Thank you. You don't look too bad yourself." She grinned.

Josh did look striking in his black slacks and pale

pink T-shirt. Looks were never one of his weaknesses—though he often mentioned how much his ears bothered him. He thought they stuck out too much. They'd never bothered Maddie, however.

He took her hand, and they started toward the lobby.

Before they reached it, he paused and tugged her to a stop.

"What's going on?" she asked.

"I wanted to let you know that I found out a few hours ago that the man who died in the ocean worked for Benchmark," he leaned close as he told her, his voice low.

That man had been with the company?

How tragic, she mused. How very, very tragic.

———

"His name was Jared Kline," Josh continued. "He was Darla Bowman's executive assistant. She personally paid his way because she needed his assistance with part of the presentation she's doing. Usually assistants don't come."

Darla Bowman was the Assistant Director of Development. Maddie had never cared for the woman, and Darla had made it clear she didn't care for Maddie either.

It might have something to do with the fact Darla used to date Josh—right before he dated Maddie, actually. Maddie wasn't sure what had happened between the two of them. She'd never asked.

She only knew that Josh had said several times that it was a bad idea to mix work and pleasure. His eyes always darkened when he said the words as if he had personal experience.

Even though Josh and Darla were cordial to each other, Maddie could always feel the tension simmering between them when they were in the same space.

"I'm sorry to hear he worked for Benchmark," Maddie finally said. "I know this is a big loss for you all."

"It is, indeed."

She thought again about that text she'd received.

I know something you need to know. Someone is out to get you. I need to explain in person and not through text. Meet me at 5:30 a.m. on the beach. Tell no one—trust no one. Delete this message.

Knowing what she did now, should she mention the text to Josh?

No, Maddie decided. He had enough on his mind. Another part of her wanted to hold tightly to her secret until she had more information.

Just then, Josh's phone buzzed, and he glanced at the screen.

His gaze darkened.

"Everything okay?" Maddie resisted the urge to look over his shoulder at the screen to see for herself.

He nodded, but his eyes remained dark. "It's fine. Just some work stuff."

He slipped his phone back into his pocket.

But Maddie didn't believe him. He'd been preoccupied with something lately, and he wasn't opening up to her.

She was certain her fiancé had some type of secret.

That fact left her feeling unsettled.

CHAPTER
EIGHT

MADDIE WASN'T ready to let the subject drop yet. "You don't look fine."

Josh waved her off, a flicker of annoyance in his gaze. "It's nothing."

Maddie wondered if his bad mood had something to do with Derek Bonner.

Josh had fired Derek two weeks ago, and the man had gone ballistic. He'd made threats and caused a scene, so much so that security had to escort him out of the building.

Josh didn't talk about it a lot, but Maddie knew the incident bothered him.

Unhinged former employees had a way of doing that.

She'd overheard a conversation between Josh and Benchmark's Vice President of Technology, William Wright, last week. Josh had said something about proprietary information Derek had. He was worried the man might do something foolish with it.

The company could sue Derek if he did. But by then it would be too late. The information would already be out there.

Plus, a new startup company called Blue Engineering had burst onto the tech scene in the past several months. Josh was worried about the hoopla surrounding them. Worried how their new innovations might ultimately affect Benchmark.

Maddie didn't envy his job. The stress from it consumed him at times.

She studied his tight, serious expression as they walked.

He was distracted by something internal—most likely, thoughts about his job.

As he always was.

This wasn't the future Maddie saw for herself.

But right now, they had a dinner to attend.

Maybe meeting with Adrienne, Brody, Bree, and Fowler was just what she needed.

———

All the dinner guests were waiting for Maddie and Josh at Terrapin when they arrived.

They sat at a table on a private terrace overlooking the ocean. A lush waterfall cascaded from manmade rocks on one side, and the hotel's swimming pools—lit a gentle turquoise—glimmered on the other.

The restaurant truly was stunning, and Maddie had heard the food was even better.

Adrienne wore a black dress—a bodycon—and Brody donned a blue Hawaiian shirt with rows of pink and green surfboards across it.

Bree had some type of breezy beige linen dress on, and Fowler wore khaki shorts that seemed too tight and too short.

Both were stunning couples.

For some reason, Maddie felt a ripple of nerves as she sat down across from the group.

"I'm so glad you all could make it," she murmured.

"We're honored that you invited us." Adrienne grinned, showing a row of shiny white teeth. The fact they weren't all perfectly straight seemed to indicate she hadn't come from money either. "Thank you."

"It's the least I could do." Josh flicked his hand at the menu. "Please, choose anything you'd like to eat. It's my treat."

He said the words dismissively, as if he were the king doing a favor for his underlings.

Maddie resisted an eye roll. Typical Josh.

They all ordered and made chitchat, mostly about the resort, until their food was served. She discovered that Fowler worked in finance for the company and that Bree worked cybersecurity for a major hotel chain. This was the first time all of them had been to Hawaii.

Maddie was ready to bypass the generic talk, however, and chat about something deeper.

There was nothing she hated more than surface-level conversations.

She took a bite of her macadamia-crusted mahi—which tasted like a flavor explosion on her tongue. No wonder this restaurant was booked for months in advance. Between the expertly prepared food and the view, it was perfect.

"So, where are you all from?" Maddie started at a lull in the conversation.

"Puerto Rico," Bree said. "But I moved to Florida when I was only three."

"Detroit," Fowler said.

"I'm from Georgia," Adrienne said. "Brody is from Texas."

"I'm actually from Nebraska," Maddie said. "It gets a bad rep for being boring, but I think the heartland is a wonderful place."

Brody nodded slowly. "I agree. There's no place quite like it."

"You ask me, I can't imagine why anyone would want to live anywhere besides the Big Apple," Josh piped in. "I was raised there, and I don't think it gets any better."

Another reason they shouldn't get married, Maddie mused. "There's something about wide open spaces that makes me feel like I can breathe."

"Maybe you two can have a summer home in the Midwest after you're married," Bree suggested.

"Maybe." The idea didn't seem that bad to Maddie. Better the Midwest than the Big Apple. City life didn't fit her personality.

"I wouldn't count on it." Josh paused with his fork, laden with tuna, in mid-air. "Real estate should be an investment, and I don't see that location as being a wise place to spend a lot of money. People are moving away from those areas, which will make real estate there less valuable."

Maddie resisted an eye roll. That was what everything boiled down to for Josh, wasn't it? Money.

Some things were more important than a financial portfolio.

Maddie glanced at Adrienne and saw the woman's face had gone pale.

Maddie followed her friend's gaze in time to see someone disappear around the corner.

She looked back at Adrienne, curiosity pulsing inside her. "Everything okay?"

Brody glanced at Adrienne and then rushed to his feet. "If you'll excuse me, I'll be right back."

Maddie narrowed her eyes.

Based on the tension in the air, Adrienne had seen something that spooked her.

It appeared danger was waiting around every turn here at this retreat.

And today was only the second day.

MADDIE'S THOUGHTS remained on whatever was happening with Adrienne and Brody.

Adrienne, however, didn't offer any information, though Maddie gently prodded.

She didn't want to be pushy. Maddie knew what it was like when people were nosy, and she preferred sharing things in her own time. She would give Adrienne that respect also.

Her new friend remained tense until Brody returned.

He sat back in his chair and placed his napkin in his lap, acting as if he'd just come from the restroom or something else mundane. "Sorry about that."

Adrienne stared at him as if waiting for an explanation. Actually, almost everyone at the table did.

Finally, he shrugged and said softly, "I thought I saw someone. No one was there."

Adrienne's face remained pale, but she nodded. "That's good news."

"Everything okay?" Josh's gaze flicked between the two of them.

"It's fine." Adrienne waved a hand in the air as if the whole incident was no big deal, but her shaky arms showed her nerves. "It's just my ex . . . he's been a little obsessive since I called things off. He's made some threats, and I'm just a little paranoid."

Alarm coursed through Maddie. "That's terrible. Did you tell the police?"

Adrienne nodded. "I did—back in New York. But I think he's been watching me. I'm nervous he might have followed me here."

"Maybe you should tell security here at the hotel so they can keep an eye out," Fowler said.

"It's probably just me being paranoid." She placed a hand on Brody's shoulder. "And I have Brody to watch out for me. He's better than any hotel security."

"I don't know about that." Brody shrugged off the compliment.

"Listen to him being humble." Adrienne cast him a look. "But he was Special Forces for the Navy for six years. He knows how to handle himself in high-stress situations."

"What are you doing now?" Brody now had Josh's full attention.

"I work private security. Wanted a more flexible schedule."

"If you're ever looking for another job, let me know." Josh leveled his gaze with Brody. "We could always use new people in our security department. Most people don't realize what a cutthroat business the tech world is. Innovators in this field stand to make billions—and that's reason enough for some people to go to extreme measures."

"I can imagine that's true." Brody nodded slowly as if carefully choosing his words. "If I ever decide to look for a new job, I'll find you."

"You do that." Josh said before sighing and placing his napkin on his plate. "Well, this has been a lot of fun. I may need to charge you guys with taking care of my fiancée while I'm busy with other events."

Maddie nearly spit out the sip of water she'd just taken. "I'm sorry, but I don't need a babysitter."

"That's not what I meant. You just seem to have a series of unfortunate events happening around you lately. Maybe someone needs to keep an eye on you until this streak of bad luck is over." Josh gave her a pointed look.

Maddie's cheeks heated. She was a grown woman. She didn't need people to talk about her like this—especially when she was sitting right here.

"She's more than welcome to hang out with us whenever she wants." Bree winked.

Relief relaxed her shoulders, if even just slightly.

At least her new friends weren't looking at her as if

she were a freak—which was how Maddie felt at the moment.

"Speaking of which," Josh glanced at his watch, "I need to run. I have a meeting with HR about Jared. We need to figure out how to handle the incident."

His words sounded callous enough that Maddie's stomach knotted.

This wasn't a PR nightmare. A man had died. His family would grieve.

But this wasn't the time to point that out.

"Feel free to stay as long as you would like, darling. I can handle this." He leaned forward and gave her a quick kiss on the cheek.

Part of Maddie felt as if she should leave anyway.

The other part of her wanted to stay.

To have some real conversation.

About something other than Josh's job.

Maddie watched him walk away and then turned to the rest of the group. "Don't let me keep you if you have other things to do."

"I think we're free for the rest of the night," Brody said.

"Please, don't feel obligated," Maddie pleaded.

"Not at all." Bree waved her hand through the air to brush off the thought. Her bracelets—mostly leather and beads—clanked together at the movement. "You seem normal, unlike most of the people here."

Maddie smiled. "I get that. I never feel like these people are my type of people."

Adrienne's eyes widened. "Me either! But I love my job, so I'm forced to conform."

"I totally understand."

Maddie and Adrienne exchanged a smile, the kind forged by a natural, unexplainable bond.

Maybe this trip wouldn't be so terrible after all, Maddie mused.

But she still had to figure out if her fiancé was trying to kill her.

———

Maddie and her new friends continued to talk as they finished their meal.

Maddie discovered she had a lot in common with them. They were each from blue-collar backgrounds, three out of the five of them named pizza as their favorite food, and none of them wanted to grow old in New York City.

They'd also discovered they were all doing at least two excursions together. And, of course, Bree and Maddie both liked emus. Bree even did a great impression of them, mimicking the grumbling sound the animal made.

They'd all had a good laugh at that—except for maybe Fowler, who only rolled his eyes. If Josh had been here, Maddie wouldn't have been able to cut loose like this. He took himself too seriously.

Maddie had never felt like she fit in with the corporate types. She was a pizza and football kind of girl who liked to let down her hair. These people—Josh's people—were all about climbing corporate ladders, playing golf, and talking about their portfolios.

At a lull in their conversation, voices from the group sitting on the balcony next to them drifted across the water and caught Maddie's ear—everyone else's as well, it seemed. They all leaned closer to hear.

"I still can't believe Jared is dead," a woman said.

Maddie thought she recognized the woman's voice from one of the corporate events she'd taken part in.

"That's Nancy," Adrienne whispered. "She's the head of sales at Benchmark."

So, yes, Maddie had seen her before.

"Is she saying that man worked for Benchmark?" Adrienne whispered.

"That's what Josh told me earlier," Maddie said. "I guess you didn't recognize him?"

Adrienne and Fowler both shook their heads.

"There are so many people at the office, we can't possibly know everyone," Adrienne explained.

That made sense.

"I can't believe he's dead either," the woman with Nancy said. "He hated the water. I can't figure out why he'd want to go swimming. And why so early? It doesn't make any sense to me."

"I know! Besides, he'd never let loose like that. He was a workaholic."

"I heard one of the police officers talking." Nancy

leaned closer to the woman across the table. "They found Jared's cell phone, and there was a strange text message on it. They're trying to track down the person he sent it to."

Maddie froze. Though she'd suspected he might have sent that text, this could be a confirmation.

But why would Jared have sent her that message?

Maddie didn't like the unsettled feeling in her stomach. Jared hadn't been out on the beach for no reason. He hadn't simply gone on a predawn swim wearing sweatpants and a T-shirt.

So what had happened leading to his death?

CHAPTER
TEN

TEN MINUTES LATER, Bree and Fowler stood, saying they needed to turn in for the evening.

Maddie considered whether or not she should wrap up this conversation and return to her room when Adrienne's phone buzzed.

She glanced at the screen and frowned. "If you'll excuse me a moment."

She paced from the table, phone to her ear.

As she did, Maddie glanced at Brody and flushed.

She hated the reaction, but the man *had* saved her life, so maybe the response was completely normal. Perhaps she was experiencing a touch of savior complex with him.

Or maybe it was like your body craving a nutrient you were deficient in.

She craved security that Josh couldn't—or wouldn't—give her.

As she glanced at Brody, another surge of attraction gripped her.

Why did she feel drawn to this man? The feelings were inappropriate.

She was engaged. And Brody had a girlfriend.

She wasn't the cheating type.

She shoved her feelings down. Just because she felt attracted to the man didn't mean she would act on that temptation.

For now, she would simply try to keep boundaries in place.

She was curious, however. There was something interesting about the interactions between Adrienne and Brody.

Something that felt stiff.

Maddie couldn't put her finger on exactly what was bugging her. Perhaps the two of them had simply gotten into a disagreement before dinner. Maddie had found herself in that position many times before.

She shouldn't read too much into it.

"I think it was a valiant effort you made out there this morning when you tried to save that man."

She came back to the present at the sound of Brody's voice.

"Thank you. Maybe it wasn't the smartest move, but thank you." She shifted. "So you were special forces? I always imagine those guys being super intense."

Brody seemed almost too easygoing.

"A lot of people think that," Brody said. "The truth is, you have to be a little crazy. I think that fits me. Crazy in a good way . . . at least, I hope. As a matter of fact, my friends used to call me Easy Go Crazy Bro."

She smiled at the nickname. "I guess that's where your background in surfing comes from? The crazy side?"

"If I could have made a living at it, I would have. But I needed a more stable career, so I joined the military. In some ways, it was more stable. But when I nearly lost my leg on my last mission, I decided that was it for me."

"Almost lost it?"

He pulled his fully intact leg out from under the table. "Someone must have been watching out for me."

She smiled at his words and wondered if he believed in a higher power. That made her instantly like him.

Brody shifted. "We talked about a lot tonight, but you never said what do you do for a living."

"Up until the past six months, I worked for the state investigating elder abuse."

His eyebrows shot up. "Is that right?"

She nodded. "My granddad was mistreated while in a nursing home, and I vowed I would fight to put more protections in place to stop the same thing from happening to others."

"Sounds noble."

"I suppose. I mean, yes, it is noble," she corrected. "It's also very hard to live on the salary from that job in

New York City. Josh convinced me to take a job in fundraising for a nonprofit that helps the elderly instead."

"That also sounds noble."

"I have to admit that I miss being on the battlefield." She shrugged. "Who knows? Maybe one day I'll go back to my old job."

"It helps to be passionate about what you do."

Which was why she sometimes wished she hadn't listened to Josh and made the job switch.

Maddie swallowed hard and decided to change the subject. "And you work security?"

Brody nodded. "I do. I love it. The job gives me freedom to experience new places and meet new people—like on this trip."

"I'm certainly glad you're on this trip. I might not be here right now if you weren't."

He pressed his lips together in a solemn expression. "I'm just glad I was there at the right time."

So was she. So was she.

Maddie stared at him another moment, hoping her gratitude showed in her gaze.

———

Adrienne returned to the table and apologized for taking the phone call.

"Work?" Brody asked.

"Yes. It was Logan, one of my colleagues in event

planning. We were just hashing out a few details about tomorrow's schedule."

"How many are on your team?" Maddie asked.

"Just three. We did most of our planning before-hand, and the resort has been great about heading up the excursions and evening activities. But we still need to be around to oversee things. If anything goes wrong, then we're to blame and our heads are on the chopping block. No one wants that." She cut her eyes, as if half-joking and half-serious.

"I can imagine." Maddie knew Josh was difficult to work for.

She'd shown up at the office one day in time to see him raking his administrative assistant over the coals. Apparently, she'd written down the wrong time for an important meeting.

When Maddie had talked to him about it afterward, he said greatness was found in the details.

He claimed that was what made him good at his job —that he demanded excellence from the people around him. Sometimes Maddie wondered if he took that to the extreme, however.

"Maddie Waters?" someone asked beside her.

She looked up to see a man with dark hair, graying at the temples, standing beside her. If fifty-something Anthony Hopkins was Polynesian, he would look like this man.

Something about his posture and button-up shirt

indicated he wasn't here on the company retreat. He looked too tired and his clothing too cheap.

"Yes?" She swallowed hard, a bad feeling already simmering in her gut.

"I'm Detective Kalani with the Kauai PD." His gaze was as hard and unyielding as his voice. "I need to ask you a few questions."

Maddie sat up straighter. "Questions about what?"

"About Jared Kline."

Her heart pounded harder. "Yes, of course. I don't know how much I can tell you, however. I didn't know the man."

His expression remained stony. "Would you like to go somewhere private?"

She glanced at Adrienne and Brody and decided that she'd like to stay here with her new friends. Somehow, she felt more secure with them. "No, I think I'm fine here."

"Very well then." He pulled out Josh's empty seat and slowly lowered himself into it. He carefully placed his wrists on the table and glanced around. Then he turned back to Maddie. "I'll just jump right in. You said you didn't know Jared. Is that correct?"

The man's tone was lackluster, as was his expression. But she had the feeling that behind those dull eyes was someone perceptive and quick.

She already had the feeling that his man didn't like her. She'd become an expert at picking up on undertones of accusation. She sensed those now.

"That's right," she finally answered. "My fiancé is the acting CEO for the company, but I don't work at Benchmark. I only know a handful of employees."

"I understand. So you just happened to see Jared in the water this morning?"

"Correct. I went out to get some fresh air. I thought I saw something unusual in the ocean. When I took a closer look, I realized a man was struggling in the surf. He called out in distress, so I tried to help him."

"And then?"

"And then . . . the waves overtook me." She glanced at Brody. "Thankfully, a former military guy was nearby because it turned out the rescuer needed a rescuer."

"And you're that former military guy?" The detective glanced at Brody.

"Yes, sir. By the grace of God, I was in the right place at the right time."

Maddie shifted, her gut telling her there was more to this conversation than the detective was letting on. "What's all this about? Jared's death was an accident, right?"

His expression remained unreadable. "A few things have come up that we're looking into."

"Like what?" The question came out before Maddie could stop it.

She knew it wasn't any of her business and that it wouldn't be appropriate for the detective to share. But she felt personally involved in this, even if she wasn't.

She had, however, nearly lost her life trying to save the man.

Should she tell the detective what he'd said to her as waves pummeled them? At least, what Maddie had *thought* he said? Something about murder?

Probably.

She rubbed her throat, suddenly anxious. "When I tried to rescue him, he was still lucid. He . . . well, I thought he said something about murder."

Everyone around her went silent.

Finally, Detective Kalani asked, "Something about murder?"

"It was garbled, and the waves were loud, and my adrenaline was pumping. But he looked at me and muttered the word 'murder.' And before you ask, I have no idea why."

Kalani didn't react with surprise, like Maddie thought he might. His deadpan expression remained.

Instead, he asked, "What's your cell phone number, Ms. Waters?"

She rattled it off.

He nodded slowly. "We found Mr. Kline's phone earlier. Not long before he died, he sent a message to an unknown number. We traced that number back to you."

The blood drained from her face. It *was* Jared who'd sent her that message.

"Do you want to rethink what you told me earlier?"

She snapped her attention back to the detective. "What? Why would I do that?"

"Why would a man you don't know text you a message like that? Maybe it spooked you and . . ."

Maddie shook her head, maybe a little too quickly. "I have no idea why he sent me that message. I didn't even know it was him for sure until now."

"Then why did you go to meet him?"

"I was curious about what he meant."

"What if he said something you didn't like and you decided to silence him? What if you were in the water, not to rescue him but to drown him?"

She gasped at the absurdity of the detective's words. "You've got this all wrong."

"He was heard arguing with someone on the beach about thirty minutes before you found him." The detective's gaze never left her. "Were you that person?"

Panic raced through her as the detective's implications hit her. "I wasn't arguing with Jared earlier. It's like I said, I didn't know him. I'd never met him before. I'm still not sure why you think his death was anything other than an accident."

"We're just exploring every possibility."

"I had nothing to do with his death. Nothing." Maddie sliced her hand through the air as she shook her head, trying to drive home the truth in her statement.

"One more thing. A piece of paper was found in his room." He paused, possibly for dramatic effect before finishing with, "Your name was scribbled on it."

Maddie sucked in a breath. "What? Why would my name be on a paper in his room?"

"That's what we're all wondering." The detective's words sounded pointed as he stood. "I'll be in touch if I have more questions."

Maddie knew what that meant.

She was a suspect.

Panic raced through her, quickening her pulse.

How was this even possible?

CHAPTER
ELEVEN

I WATCH EVERYONE AROUND ME.

How can I not? I need answers.

Jared's death didn't go as I planned, thanks to Little Miss Perfect.

Now I must do recon.

Until this evening, I hadn't known Jared had texted Maddie. What an idiot.

Did he think I wouldn't find out?

Why had he planned it so close to the time we were meeting?

The man had no common sense. If he was going to try to play in the big league, he should have thought things through a little more.

I'd bet all the money in my bank account that he'd been planning on trying to get money from Maddie also.

I'm just glad he's out of the way. People that dumb don't deserve to live.

I've been listening to all the chatter around me.

And I'm so glad I'm close enough to hear the detective talking to Maddie now.

Does he think she killed Jared?

I resist a smile at the thought.

That turn of events would be so poetic. It would fit right into my plan.

In some ways, Jared may have helped me. *Thank you, Jared.*

Unfortunately for those around me, I'm not done yet. I have more lessons to teach.

I'm going to need to keep my eye on Maddie.

Four days. Four days until my grand finale—if I can wait that long.

I nearly salivate at the thought of it.

This is going to be one incredibly fun vacation.

I'm going to show everyone that paradise doesn't exist.

"WHAT IS THE DETECTIVE TALKING ABOUT?" Adrienne whispered as she watched Detective Kalani exit the restaurant.

Maddie blinked, her head pounding with a sudden headache. The detective's words kept playing over and over again in her mind.

Why in the world was Maddie's name found on a piece of paper in Jared's room? It didn't make sense.

And the way the detective had looked at her . . . panic fluttered in her chest, the feeling growing stronger by the second.

She glanced up and realized Adrienne and Brody were waiting for her response, confusion—and concern —on their faces.

She swallowed hard before saying, "Late last night, I got a text from an unknown number. The message said we needed to talk, that there were things I needed to know, but the sender couldn't type them on the phone."

"Things about what?" Brody shifted forward, all his attention on Maddie.

"I have no idea. I thought maybe it was the wrong number. I texted back asking who it was, but I never got a response." She paused and drew in a shaky breath. "I went to meet this person, and when I got there, I thought I'd been stood up. Then I saw that man in the water and knew I had to help. I wasn't sure if it was the person who'd sent the text or not. But I couldn't just stand there and do nothing."

A cry lodged in Maddie's throat. She quickly took a sip of water to drown it before the sound escaped.

Adrienne placed a hand on Maddie's back. "I can only imagine how stressful this must be for you. But you have an alibi for last night and this morning, right? Josh? He should be able to verify that wasn't you arguing with Jared."

That familiar feeling of dread swirled in Maddie's gut, the one she experienced every time she had to explain herself. She wasn't ashamed of her new convictions, but she did hate the judgment she usually received from people.

"Josh and I aren't actually staying in the same room," Maddie explained, keeping any emotion out of her voice. "It's a long story."

She didn't want to get into it now. Didn't want to see the assumptions in their eyes.

Josh wasn't happy about the arrangement.

But three months ago, Maddie had been in a car accident. She'd survived, but her whole life had flashed before her eyes when she was stopped in traffic on a bridge and the car behind her barreled into her.

Her Camry had burst through the guardrail and teetered precariously on the edge of the bridge for what felt like hours.

Rescuers had warned Maddie not to move, had told her that one shift in the weight could send the vehicle toppling.

Her anxiety had skyrocketed, and she'd been certain she would die.

Then the unthinkable happened.

Her car plunged over the edge.

Maddie had watched the water slowly cover her windows as her car sank into the river.

She'd seen news programs that showed her what to do in those types of situations. But at that moment, her mind had gone blank.

That was when she'd cried out to God. She begged that if He saved her, she would change.

A few seconds later, a diver had appeared on the other side of her window.

She'd been rescued.

Afterward, she'd realized just how short life was, and she knew she needed to get herself in order.

She'd found an old Bible that had belonged to her

granddad and had begun to read it. All the values she'd grown up with had flooded back to her.

Maddie was tired of living for herself, by her own set of rules. Her personal pursuit of happiness hadn't worked for her so far. When she'd faced death, she'd had an awakening.

She knew she needed to make some changes.

That included not staying overnight with Josh anymore—not until they were married.

Josh hadn't been happy when she'd told him about her new convictions—and, in return, her new boundaries. He'd actually ridiculed her, said she was becoming a religious zealot.

She'd decided to pretend he hadn't said the words.

People in the business world, for the most part, weren't religious. Christianity in particular was a sign of weakness, of a less educated and backward-thinking individual. At least, that had been Maddie's experience while in New York.

She rubbed her chest, trying to ease the tension there. "If Josh hears about this . . ."

"What do you mean?" Brody squinted as he stared at her.

A flash of self-consciousness hit her. She shouldn't have said her thoughts aloud. She hadn't intended to, but the words had slipped out.

"He's obsessed with this whole event going perfectly," Maddie explained. "So when he found out one of his employees died, he wasn't happy. But if he finds out

that his *fiancée* might be a suspect in the man's death . .
."

She let out a long breath as nausea swirled inside her. She didn't even want to think about his reaction.

"Hopefully, he'll be supportive of you and not try to make you feel worse about this whole situation." Brody's voice tightened. "It sounds like you're just an innocent bystander in it all."

"I *am* innocent. I'd like to think Josh would support me. But I have a bad feeling in my gut."

"If there's anything we can do for you . . ." Adrienne frowned as she peered at Maddie.

"I appreciate that." Maddie paused, her thoughts still muddled. But now a new determination mingled with her confusion. "I don't know this Jared guy, but why would someone want to murder him?"

And why would he have her name handwritten on a scrap of paper in his room? Why would he send her that message? How did he get her phone number?

She had so many questions.

Perhaps the biggest was: What did he know that Maddie didn't?

Nothing made sense.

"That's a good question." Brody tilted his head thoughtfully, his gaze appearing equally as curious. "This certainly isn't the start I wanted for our retreat."

"We're going to make sure this is the very best event Benchmark has ever thrown," Adrienne assured him. "Nothing is going to ruin it. I'm sure everything will be fine. Anyone can see you're not a killer."

"I appreciate that." But Maddie's words sounded lackluster, even to her own ears.

"We won't tell Josh what that detective said," Adrienne continued. "He doesn't need to know, right?"

"There's nothing to really know," Maddie muttered.

Although, if Josh were to find out the detective had questioned her—and maybe even suspected her—from someone other than Maddie, he'd be angry. Really angry.

The detective didn't appear to be looking at other suspects. Maybe he was. But something about the way he spoke with Maddie made her think his mind was made up.

That he was looking only at her.

Maddie swallowed hard as a realization hardened in her gut.

She needed to find out more information before Jared's murder was pinned on her.

She had no other choice.

———

Brody and Adrienne had wanted to walk Maddie back to her room, but she insisted she would be fine.

She didn't tell them how wobbly her legs felt.

Instead, she thanked them again and said she'd see

them tomorrow. Then she started to head back to her room.

It was surprisingly dark outside.

She wasn't sure why that left her feeling spooked. Everything that had happened was messing with her mind.

Her heels tapped against the stone pavers as she cut through the pool area to get to her room.

People still played in the water, and the joyful sound of laughter floated toward her—a sound she couldn't relate to at the moment. It was so carefree and full of happiness.

A footfall sounded behind her, and she turned, expecting to see another resort patron walking behind her.

The path was empty.

A chill crept up her spine.

Was Maddie hearing things?

She picked up her pace.

This was all too much. Especially considering her past . . . Kevin's family had been making threats against her for years. Would they choose this retreat to retaliate? If they knew she was engaged to Josh, would they try to extort money?

This wasn't the first time those questions had fluttered through her mind.

Her throat tightened. She didn't want to think through those possibilities right now. Instead, she forced herself to push the thoughts aside, to not inch back in time.

After being saved on the beach this morning, she'd been given a new lease on life, and while she could learn from the mistakes of her past, she didn't want to dwell on them. Those thoughts always dragged her down and brought waves of anxiety that tried to serve as a constant companion.

As she crossed a small bridge, the noise sounded again—another footfall.

Someone *was* behind her. She was sure of it.

She glanced over her shoulder, trying to be subtle.

Again, there was no one.

Was this person following her and trying not to be seen?

Goosebumps spread across her arms.

She should have accepted Adrienne and Brody's offer to walk her back to her room.

But she'd never anticipated this.

She glanced at the door leading into her wing of the resort just ahead.

She was almost there. Only twelve feet or so.

Fear made her want to dart inside. Instead, she forced herself to walk. She couldn't afford to draw any attention to herself.

Inside, she decided to take the stairs. The elevator was too risky.

She was huffing by the time she reached her floor.

Now, only a few more turns and then she'd be at her room.

She'd be safe.

Fear crept over her, making her skin crawl.

Maddie didn't see anyone watching her. But she felt unseen eyes.

What if this person tried to kill her like they'd killed Jared?

No . . .

She couldn't let this continue while she was here. She might lose her mind if she did.

Tomorrow, maybe Maddie should talk to Darla Bowman and find out more about Jared. See if she could figure out why the man might have Maddie's name written on a paper in his room. See if she could figure out who Jared might have been arguing with on the beach before his trip into the ocean.

The only way to possibly clear her name was to find answers.

Yes, that was what she would do. She'd use her skills to find the truth.

She continued to hurry toward her room.

Tomorrow. Tomorrow Maddie would find some answers. Tonight it was too late.

As she turned a corner, something jostled behind her —almost as if the person following her had accidentally bumped the table where some plants had been displayed.

Her heart pounded in her ears.

She wasn't losing her mind. Someone *was* following her.

Self-preservation kicked in, and she took off in a jog. No one else was near to see her, to judge her.

Finally, she reached her room. Her arms shook as she held up her wristband to the lock.

The mechanism turned.

She threw the door open and practically fell inside. Wasting no time, she slammed the door and leaned against it as she tried to get hold of herself.

A paper on the floor caught her eye.

What was that? Correspondence from the hotel?

Maddie knew management slipped notices under the door sometimes if they had a maintenance project coming up or when it was time to check out—which it wasn't.

Still, she hesitated before reaching for it.

Then she opened the folded slip.

Words were typed there.

Someone you know has CRUEL INTENTIONS. I'd be careful.

CHAPTER
THIRTEEN

THEN

A WEEK HAD PASSED, and Cecilia was still thinking about Garrick.

He seemed to have stepped directly out of her dreams and into her real life.

Only he was just a blip on her timeline, someone she'd talked to for a few minutes one evening and whom she'd never see again.

Besides, it was probably as she'd assumed. The man most likely already had a girlfriend. What kind of man like that didn't?

She straightened some of the expensive suits hanging on the racks at Balderston's, each one silky and luxurious.

She hadn't heard from Grocery Store Ryan since he stood her up. She really wanted to give the man a piece of her mind for leaving her at that restaurant to foot a bill she didn't even know would exist.

Then again, if Ryan *had* shown up, Cecilia might not have met Garrick.

And Garrick had nicely occupied her thoughts for the past seven days.

She needed to stop though. What were the odds she'd ever see the man again?

"If it isn't the woman from the restaurant," a deep, gravelly voice said behind her.

Cecilia turned a little too quickly, instinctively knowing who it belonged to. But she also feared she was only hearing what she wanted to hear. Making things up in her mind.

When her eyes confirmed that it was Garrick standing there, her eyelids began to flutter, and her heart swelled. "Garrick . . . fancy seeing you here."

"I need to get some new clothes for a fundraiser tonight. How fortuitous that I happened to show up at the very place where you're employed."

"How fortuitous," she repeated.

He pointed to the suits beside her. "Do you mind?"

Cecilia shook her head quickly, hating how flustered she felt. "Right. Of course. Do you remember your measurements?"

"I've been working out so I'm hoping those numbers may have changed slightly." He ran a hand down his chest as if checking his muscles. "Would you mind measuring me?"

Why did her cheeks heat at the thought of touching

him? Of being that close? She was a professional. She took measurements all the time.

But never for someone like Garrick.

She swallowed hard. "Of course."

They stepped toward the angled, three-paneled mirrors that stood on a platform amidst the suits.

Cecilia pulled the measuring tape from her pocket and faced the mirrors. "Raise your hands, please."

Her throat tightened as she slipped her arms around Garrick to measure his chest. His waist. His hips.

Just touching him caused electricity to shoot through her. Slipping her arms around him proved how muscular he was. How fit. That he was a man who took care of himself.

And he smelled just as she imagined he might.

Like evergreen.

Like expensive, lux evergreen.

Like expensive, lux evergreen as it grew in the Alps.

The kind you might experience while on a luxurious vacation where no expense was spared.

She swallowed hard and reminded herself to keep her thoughts in check. Then she wrote down his measurements and showed him.

Satisfaction filled his gaze. "I've lost inches around my waist and gained some around my chest. Just what I was hoping for."

Yes, a physique like his *did* require care and commitment. He seemed like the type who gave attention to the things most important to him—his job, his money, his body.

She cleared her thoughts and tried to focus. "So what exactly were you thinking of? Something sleek and elegant? Or something more casual?"

"It's for a charity event. What do you think?" He glanced over his shoulder at her.

Cecilia observed him and tried to picture what she would pick for him.

She grinned as an idea hit her. "I know the perfect suit. Come with me."

Garrick followed her to the other side of the men's department, and she pulled out a black Dior suit. Slim cut and sharp. Expensive.

"How about this one?" She held it up. "It would look great with a pale blue tie to stay casual or a striking red if you wanted to make more of a statement."

His eyes sparkled. "You've got a good eye. Let me try it on."

He grabbed it and disappeared into the changing room. When he emerged several moments later, Cecilia's jaw nearly dropped open. He looked even better than she had imagined.

"What do you think?" He stared at himself in the mirror, brushing lint off one of the shoulders.

"I think it's perfect. I don't even think it needs to be altered. It's like this suit was made just for you."

"I was thinking the same thing." He observed himself another moment in the mirror and then nodded with approval. "Pick out a tie for me—your choice since you've got excellent taste—and then I'll take it."

Satisfaction filled her. She'd picked the pale blue one. It would look fantastic with his eyes.

"Great," she murmured. "Then I can ring you up."

Garrick followed her to the register. Her hands shook as she scanned the tags. The price of these suits never failed to amaze her. How could people pay this much for one outfit?

He paused and tilted his head as he watched her before asking, "Do you have plans tonight?"

His words startled her, and Cecilia looked up to see Garrick looking at her with a twinkle in his gaze. He was asking about her plans for tonight?

"Just the normal," she finally said. "Nothing too fun."

"What do you think about going to this fundraiser with me?" The twinkle in his eyes turned to a glimmer of hope.

Cecilia tried to shake off her shock at his offer. Had she heard him correctly? How did she even respond?

Cecilia finally settled on, "I think there's no way I can afford a dress that would match this suit."

"Then I'll buy you one." His eyes sparkled as he said the words.

Cecilia quickly shook her head, trying not to let the seed of hope grow inside her. "I couldn't let you do that."

"It wouldn't be *me* doing a favor for *you*. You would

be doing the favor for me. It's pretty awful having to sit through these events by myself."

She tilted her head. "And you're telling me that you don't have anyone else to go with?"

Garrick slowly shook his head back and forth. "I mean, I *suppose* I could find another date. But none of them interest me. Not like you." He paused and tilted his head. "Is that too forward?"

The truth was, Cecilia loved how he didn't hold back.

But something inside her still made her hesitate. "I don't know . . ."

"What's stopping you?"

What *was* stopping her? It was a great question. Cecilia wasn't sure about the answer, other than the fact that this man was completely out of her league. She wouldn't even know how to handle herself around the people she would need to rub elbows with.

"I just feel like I would embarrass myself," she admitted, deciding to be honest. "My idea of a dressy event is buying a secondhand dress to wear to a backyard wedding."

He chuckled, the sound deep and heartwarming. "I like that. And I don't particularly like hanging out with highbrow people either. I actually grew up dirt poor."

Her eyebrows flew up. "You're joking?"

"I'm not."

"So if I were to go with you and if I were to say

something uncouth in front of these very important people, you wouldn't be humiliated?"

"You could never humiliate me." His gaze caught hers. There wasn't even a hint of doubt in his voice.

Cecilia's cheeks flushed again. This man knew exactly what to say, didn't he?

She swallowed hard. "You said the event is tonight?"

"Yes, seven o'clock. Would you have time to get a dress before then?"

"I *suppose* I could look after work to see what I could find."

His eyes glimmered with delight. "Yes. Do that. Put it on my tab."

Her eyebrows flew up this time. "Your tab?"

"That's right. I'll let the manager know you have my permission so everything is on the up and up."

She opened her mouth, but her argument wouldn't leave her lips.

"Where should I pick you up?" Garrick continued.

Cecilia swallowed hard, momentarily wanting to forget her rule of having people not pick her up on the first date. It would be so much easier if Garrick simply swung by her place.

He must have seen her hesitation. "Cecilia, you can trust me."

Her heart pounded faster as he said those words.

She believed him.

She rattled off her address. However, when he saw where she lived, he was going to change his mind about her. Her apartment was in a bad area of town, but it was all she could afford.

Drug dealers liked to hang out on street corners, as well as prostitutes. Graffiti marked one side of her building, and the train rattled nearby, sometimes waking her at night.

"Perfect." He flashed another movie-star grin. "I will see you at seven."

Then he grabbed her hand and planted a firm but slow kiss on top of it.

Tingles ran up and down her entire body.

Cecilia couldn't wait for tonight.

FIRST THING IN THE MORNING, Maddie slipped out of her room.

She was still shaky as she remembered Jared. As she remembered being followed back to her room.

As she remembered that note someone had left beneath her door. What did that message mean? And why had the words "cruel intentions" been in all caps?

The threat didn't make sense, but it had definitely left her on edge.

She prayed today would be a better day. One without mishaps. One where she realized she'd been overthinking all of this. One without any drama or reasons for her to feel paranoid.

She had a feeling that was wishful thinking.

Benchmark was hosting a breakfast buffet in the conference room downstairs. She'd told Josh she would meet him there.

If she was vacationing by herself, she would have worn sweats and a tank top to breakfast. But not while she was here with Josh. He'd told her those kinds of clothes weren't suitable for someone dating the future CEO of Benchmark. She needed to dress for success.

For that reason, she'd donned a bright green sundress and sandals. This look would be her basic uniform while she was here—unless she was going to the beach, on an excursion, or to the gala at the end of the week.

After breakfast, she'd go back to her suite and change into something more appropriate for the UTV ride through the mountains. From what she understood, the outing was dusty, and red dirt would cover her from head to toe afterward.

She made her way down the long, winding hallways of the resort until she reached the expansive, lush lobby. Marble columns rose at strategic places, massive windows displayed the ocean and palm trees, and exotic trees laden with parrots grew in an arboretum in the center.

Maddie turned and headed into the large conference room.

Once inside, she paused and took another moment to stand in awe of the huge open windows that stretched at least twenty feet into the air. A koi pond, complete with swans, shimmered on the other side of the windows.

The scene was serene and awe-inspiring.

Maddie wasn't sure if she'd ever been in such a beautiful hotel before. Part of her felt like she'd be quite content to live here forever.

She pulled her gaze from the scenery and glanced at the crowd. Probably thirty people from Benchmark were already here dining. But she didn't see Josh yet.

Her gaze stopped on Darla.

Just the person she wanted to talk to.

Maddie had seen Darla before at past company functions, and the woman was icy, to say the least. Not exactly the warm and friendly type.

But Maddie would take her chances right now—especially if the payoff meant putting her mind at ease.

She hadn't gotten much sleep last night. She had too many things on her mind. Too much to think about.

Besides the scares she had, she'd also thought a lot about the conversation she'd had with Detective Kalani. That encounter had left a knot in her stomach.

The man thought she might have something to do with Jared's death. What if he continued to think that? If he continued to pursue evidence that might point to her as a killer?

Maddie's head swam at the thought.

She grabbed a plate before getting behind Darla in line.

When the woman glanced back at her, Maddie plastered on a smile. "Aloha. Darla, right?"

The woman was tall with impossibly long legs, dark hair styled in a pixie cut that totally worked for her heart-shaped face, and dark-rimmed glasses that made her look both sexy and smart. Actress: Natalie Portman.

Darla looked her up and down before saying, "You're Josh's fiancée."

"I am." Maddie took a spoonful of scrambled eggs and put them on her plate. "Are you enjoying yourself here so far?"

"Who wouldn't at a place like this?" She paused near some salmon, and her gaze swept the room with an arrogant smirk that made Maddie feel as if her question was stupid.

"I agree."

They continued down the line, and Maddie spotted some fried rice with kimchi. Was this a Hawaiian thing? It looked interesting.

Maddie hesitated before venturing with, "I'm really sorry to hear about Jared. I heard you worked with him."

"Don't you mean *he* worked with *me*?" Darla cut her a look, her eyes a little narrower than before. "It's all such a shame. He was bright and full of potential."

"Was it like him to go out so early to the beach?"

Darla sighed. "How would I know? I only knew him on a professional level. I have no idea what he did in his personal time."

There it was again. That snobbishness. That hierarchy of importance where people in leadership were at the top and everyone else was well below them—and not as worthy.

Maddie could hardly stand it.

"Something must have been going on with him lately," Darla continued, spooning some fruit onto her plate. "He sent me a bunch of emails that didn't make any sense."

Her breath hitched. "What kind of emails?"

She pursed her lips as if annoyed by the fact that Maddie kept talking. "Like I said, ones that didn't make sense. Maybe Jared was drunk or something. All I know is what he wrote wasn't coherent."

What if those emails had something to do with his death? Had Darla told the detective this?

Even more, did those emails have anything to do with the message Jared had sent Maddie? The reason he'd wanted to meet her on the beach?

She was about to ask more questions when a hand squeezed her side.

She turned to see Josh behind her, a fresh plate of fruit in his hand.

"I was wondering if you'd come down yet." He displayed a wide but shallow grin.

Maddie raised her plate, which only had eggs and kimchi fried rice on it. "Just got here."

"The food looks delicious." He turned to Darla, his expression tightening. "Good morning, Ms. Bowman."

Darla plastered on a fake smile. "Good morning to you also, Mr. Harding."

It was hard to ignore the awkwardness pulling taut

between them. Was it always like this for these two? Even at the office?

Either way, it looked like this conversation was done for now.

She wished she had a way of finding out more about those emails. But she didn't—not without sounding suspicious, at least.

The truth was that Darla didn't care enough about those who worked for her to find out anything about them outside of work.

As Josh led her to a table, Maddie tried to let those thoughts drift out of her mind.

———

Maddie tried to make polite conversation during breakfast as Josh talked business to those around him at the table.

As people stood to get seconds, Josh's shoulders sagged—almost as if he were exhausted from being "on." Instead of talking to her, he glanced at his phone.

He frowned.

"Everything okay?" she asked.

He shoved the phone back into his pocket. "Yes, of course. Just trying to stay on task for the retreat. Jared's death has been a PR nightmare."

Despite his words, she felt certain there was *something* more he wasn't telling her.

His mood could go back to what happened with

Derek. Was Josh concerned the man might show up here in Hawaii for some type of revenge or something?

The possibility didn't seem likely.

Then again, neither had finding a drowning man on her first morning here.

Maddie excused herself to get some juice. But as she walked by the omelet bar, a conversation between two Benchmark employees waiting in line caught her ear. Though the two men spoke in low tones, she could make out some of what was being said.

"I'm not sure Josh is going to make the cut," one of them said.

Her eyes widened. Had she just heard him correctly?

Maddie wished she knew who the man was who'd said that. But she was nearly certain both men were on the board. In other words, they were decision-makers.

"Nico, on the other hand, has been very impressive," the other man said in a hushed tone.

Nico Rankin was another vice president at Benchmark. He was older than Josh—in his early fifties—and he'd been at the company for a couple of decades. He'd been the righthand man of Josh's father—who'd started the company.

"Let's face it. Personally, Josh is a failure—just like his dad," the first man said.

Just like his dad? What did that mean? Maddie had always liked Mr. Harding. For the most part, at least. Like his son, he was hard to get to know. Driven.

Focused. But he'd been kind to her, even if it was in a very standoffish way.

"He's not very personable," the second man said. "If he wants to be named CEO, he really needs to rally support somehow. Thankfully there was a clause in his father's trust that made it clear the board could choose someone different if his son wasn't qualified or could ruin the company."

Josh had made it sound like he was a shoo-in for this new job.

Did he know Nico might be named instead? Did he know about the clause? He had to . . . right?

Maddie wasn't sure, nor was she sure she should bring it up. It seemed like a touchy subject.

As the men's omelets were served, she grabbed her juice and made her way back to the table.

Just as Maddie took her last sip, Josh turned toward her. "Our excursion is leaving in twenty minutes. I suppose we should go meet the rest of the group."

"That sounds perfect. I just need to change first."

But really, the only thing she was looking forward to was knowing that Adrienne, Brody, Bree, and Fowler would be on this tour with her also.

Those four might just be her sanity—not only on this excursion, but on this entire trip.

MADDIE LINGERED on the edge of the crowd in the massive lobby as people split up for various excursions on the island. Josh had said he didn't care what they did so Maddie had picked the things that interested her.

Today they were riding a side-by-side on mountain trails. She was much more comfortable on land than in the air or in the water, which was what primarily made up the rest of the outings. She figured she'd ease herself into these adventures.

She observed the group going with her as she waited for her new friends to show up.

She didn't recognize anyone else.

Her gaze stopped on a leggy brunette standing in the middle of a circle of people, entertaining them with a story.

The woman had long, shapely legs that were highlighted by tiny jean shorts. The black halter top she wore emphasized her ample bosom. Her hair was wild, falling all the way to her waist. Actress: Rachel Bilson.

She was definitely the type of woman who garnered attention.

As Maddie glanced at Josh to see what he was doing now, she noticed his gaze was also on the bombshell.

Familiar questions began to pummel her again.

Was Josh cheating on her? Should she even have to ask herself that question?

Maddie wasn't sure. She wasn't even sure if her suspicions were fair. After all, she was still planning on breaking up with him when this retreat was over. And being upset over that was like the pot calling the kettle black since just last night she'd been marveling over how handsome Brody was.

"Maddie . . . we were hoping to run into you before the excursion began," a feminine voice said.

She looked over and saw Adrienne and Brody had arrived, backpacks slung over their shoulders and hiking boots on their feet.

Relief filled her.

"I'm here and ready for some adventure." Maddie put as much enthusiasm into her voice as she could muster. However, she'd already had all the excitement she needed for the week.

"Glad to hear it." Adrienne's gaze trailed toward the buxom brunette. "That's Logan."

She must have seen Maddie gawking at the jaw-dropping beauty.

"We work together," Adrienne explained. "She's the kind of woman you basically want to hate because she's so beautiful, bubbly, and everyone loves her."

Maddie could see where that would be true. She wasn't usually the jealous or envious type, however.

"It looks like Logan is a part of our group today," Maddie said.

"She is." Adrienne clucked her tongue. "Everything is always fun when she's around."

Funny that Adrienne had said that because Maddie and Josh had gotten into a fight only a couple of weeks ago, and Josh had told her she took things too seriously and needed to loosen up.

That was fresh coming from a Type A workaholic. What he really meant was that socially she was too introverted for him. That her new boundaries were irritating. That she was too much her own person.

Maybe Josh needed a woman like Logan. The thought was honest, not born out of bitterness or jealousy.

Just then, Logan clapped to get everyone's attention. "Okay, it's time to load up. I hope everybody's ready to have some fun!"

The crowd cheered.

But not Maddie.

This would be an interesting excursion for sure.

That earlier conversation she'd overheard about Josh still lingered in her mind.

People didn't think Josh was likable. He might not be named CEO. If not, he would be devastated.

Then there was Jared's death. And Kalani's suspicion of Maddie as the killer. And the note someone had left her.

This dream trip hadn't gone at all like she'd imagined. In fact, it felt more like a nightmare.

———

At the Kauai Adventures Basecamp, the group gathered around Hilo, their guide, as they were given instructions about how to operate the side-by-side. Josh claimed he'd driven UTVs plenty of times and checked his phone, citing something urgent.

Typical Josh.

Logan was on this trip, as well as Darla, board member Tom McLemore, and head of technology William Wright. She didn't recognize anyone else.

When Hilo finished, everyone climbed into their respective vehicles and pulled bandanas over their mouths so they wouldn't breathe dust. Josh had insisted on driving, which was fine with Maddie. She sat in the passenger seat and snapped her seatbelt in place.

All the perfunctory warnings they'd been given before leaving did nothing to make her feel better. It seemed as if the guides had to go over every possible scenario of what could go wrong.

Now all those situations lingered in Maddie's mind: Tipping over. Driving off a cliff. Ramming the vehicle in front of them.

The possibilities seemed endless.

"Let's ride!" Hilo called.

Josh looked over at her and grinned, looking like a little boy at Christmas. "Are you ready for this?"

"Ready as I'll ever be."

He pulled the bandana over his face, pressed the accelerator, and let out a whoop as they zoomed away.

Brody and Adrienne's side-by-side was near the front of the group, Bree and Fowler were behind them, and Maddie and Josh had been placed closer to the back.

As the ride went on, Maddie found herself relaxing as they bumped along on the trail. Lush mountains loomed above them. Jungle foliage swept by on either side. On occasion, she got a glimpse of the sparkling Pacific in the distance.

Maybe yesterday had been a fluke. Maybe it wasn't a sign of how horrible this trip would be.

Maybe being in Kauai would be a good thing.

The group stopped as they reached a particularly treacherous area of the trail. Hilo had already explained that this downhill section was steep with a ten-foot drop-off on one side. For that reason, they would all go down vehicle by vehicle.

They waited their turn.

As they did, Maddie's phone buzzed. She glanced at the screen. It was a message from an unknown number.

Jeepers Creepers.

She squinted. Jeepers Creepers? What did that mean?

How odd.

Before she could ruminate on it too long, Josh said, "It's our turn. Hold on!"

He pressed the accelerator, and the side-by-side lurched forward, headed down the steep trail.

Halfway down, a bang split the air.

The side-by-side tilted toward the embankment beside her.

Maddie gasped and clutched the grab bar in front of her to steady herself.

Had a tire blown? That was her best guess.

"What the . . ." Josh muttered as the UTV careened out of control. His face reddened as he gripped the wheel, his shoulders locked in place as he struggled to steer.

His efforts didn't seem to do any good.

She and Josh headed straight for the drop-off.

Josh took one of his hands off the wheel and unbuckled his seatbelt.

Maddie gaped at him. What was he doing? He needed both hands on the wheel right now.

"Jump!" he yelled.

The next instant, he launched himself out of the side-by-side and landed with a roll on the side of the trail.

As soon as he did, the vehicle barreled toward the cliff at a frightening speed . . . Maddie still inside.

CHAPTER
SIXTEEN

PANIC RACED THROUGH MADDIE.

The UTV bumped down the mountain out of control. If it continued in this direction, it would plunge off the cliff within seconds—taking Maddie with it.

How could Josh have jumped out and left her? Hadn't the guide said always stay in your vehicle?

Now she was here on the passenger side. Unable to reach any of the pedals. Barely able to reach the steering wheel.

Maddie grabbed the wheel and tugged it, struggling to veer the vehicle back onto the path.

The rest of the group stood at the bottom of the hill, watching with wide eyes and ready to dive out of the way—whenever they figured out which direction that would be.

Their guide yelled something, but Maddie couldn't make out his words.

She only hoped that everyone moved before she crashed into them.

Unless she rammed into a tree first.

Or went off the cliff.

None of the possibilities seemed good.

Someone began sprinting up the trail toward her. Brody.

No . . . what if she hit him?

She gestured wildly for him to get out of the way.

But that didn't slow him down.

He reached her, let the side-by-side pass, and then jumped onto the back.

A moment later, looking like a stunt driver, he climbed through the top and lowered himself into the driver's seat.

Just as the vehicle began to edge toward the cliff again, Brody slammed on the brakes.

With a lurch, they came to a dead stop.

Red dust flew around them as Maddie's heart pounded out of control.

Was she really safe? Had Brody just saved her?

Shock consumed her until nothing made sense.

Brody peered at her, pulling the bandana from his mouth. "Are you okay?"

Was she? She wasn't sure.

Her world still spun.

She blinked as she tried to comprehend what had just happened.

Maddie really was safe, wasn't she?

Thanks to Brody.

She nodded slowly, still feeling in a stupor. "Yes . . . I think so."

The rest of the group surrounded them, questions flying.

Then Josh appeared at her door. "Madison! Why didn't you jump out when I told you to?"

Wait . . . was he blaming this on her?

Their guide had said to always stay in their vehicles. Besides, Maddie had nowhere to jump except straight for the drop-off. What had Josh expected?

She opened her mouth to respond, but she didn't even know what to say.

Before she could answer, Hilo pushed past Josh, opened her door, and helped her out.

But Maddie was trembling so bad she doubted she'd be able to stand on her own two feet. Instead, she leaned on the UTV.

It wasn't so much the physical danger she'd barely avoided that had her shaky.

It was the fact Josh had jumped out and left her. He'd abandoned her in a dangerous situation.

She could have died as a result.

What kind of fiancé did that?

———

After the dust had died down, Hilo squatted on the trail to examine the vehicle. "This tire has been tampered with. I don't know how that's possible. I inspected them each myself before we left."

Maddie's heart vaulted into her throat at his words.

She stepped to the side of the trail for a better look. Sure enough, the tire was slashed.

Her heart beat harder in her ears.

Was this a terrible accident? Or had someone done this on purpose?

She glanced at the group around her. At her new friends. Then at Josh. Logan. Darla. Tom.

Had one of them been so desperate to get rid of either Maddie or Josh that they'd tried to take them out this way?

And what was the deal with Josh jumping out of the side-by-side and leaving her to fend for herself? How dare he blame it on her.

Maddie still fumed over that fact. He had a lot of nerve.

Hilo had already given him a stern lecture about it, but Josh had looked unconvinced that he'd done anything wrong.

Typical Josh. *Leaders don't project weakness.* Another one of his sayings. She personally thought that vulnerability led to relatability, which led to people actually wanting to follow those in charge.

"We're going to need to have you checked out," Hilo said as he turned toward Maddie.

"I'm fine," she insisted, waving him off.

He nodded to her arm. "You got a little scratched up. We should have it checked out, just to be on the safe side. I'll have another driver come by to take you and your fiancé back to the base camp and then to a local clinic."

She glanced at her skin and saw the cuts. With adrenaline rushing through her, she hadn't even noticed. She must have scraped by some bushes and rocks.

She wanted to argue again, to refuse the treatment. But she could see by the look in the guide's eyes that he wouldn't change his mind.

Finally, she nodded.

When she glanced at Josh to get his reaction, she saw his gaze was on Logan again.

Her throat tightened.

She understood why he might be attracted to the woman. She was captivating. But did he have to be so obvious? And did he have to do this right now, of all times?

Maddie shifted her gaze to Brody. He was studying her from a distance. What was that behind his gaze?

She wasn't sure.

Concern? Or was there something more? Suspicion maybe?

He was former special forces. Maybe he was seeing something in this situation that she couldn't see herself.

Either way, she was happy to be walking away from this incident alive.

She didn't plan on going on any more UTV tours.

Not just this week, but ever.

JOSH HAD SAID little during the ride to the clinic. Every so often, he'd looked at Maddie and shook his head as if this was all her fault. She had words she wanted to unleash on him, but she held back. She was too angry to talk to him right now.

At the clinic, a doctor cleaned up her cuts and put bandages on them as she sat in a private room that smelled of rubbing alcohol and lemon disinfectant. She was given the all-clear to go and told that her accident could have been much worse.

He didn't have to tell her that. She already knew. Her life had flashed before her eyes.

As the doctor had worked on her, Josh had stared at his phone as if being here bored him. Once in a while, that strange, mysterious look fluttered through his gaze —one that was full of secrets.

Enough was enough.

As soon as the doctor left the room and as they waited for a nurse to bring some paperwork, Maddie turned to him. "What's going on?"

"Nothing." He looked surprised that she'd spoken as he slipped his phone into his pocket.

Her hands dug into the thin pad of the examination table. "You seem preoccupied, and please don't tell me you're not because I know you are. Every time you look at your phone, you practically age ten years."

He sighed and ran a hand over his face. Maddie waited for him to deny her statement again.

To her surprise, he said, "I didn't want to burden you with anything. But the truth is I think we may have a corporate spy at the retreat."

"What?" Certainly, Maddie hadn't heard him correctly. Of all the things she'd thought he might say, that wasn't one of them. "Are you serious?"

"I'm serious. I think someone here works for a competitor, and they're trying to get their hands on proprietary technology we're developing."

"Why would you think that?" That was a big accusation to make without some serious evidence to back it up.

"There's scuttlebutt in the tech world that Blue is developing something new also and that it's similar to the new product we're about to announce. Our plans for this new technology are top secret. The only people who know the details are top-level executives." He ran a hand over his face. "I've had a bad feeling in my gut for a while about this."

"Are you sure it's not just fear talking?" She shifted on the crinkly paper covering the examination table.

A flash of irritation flitted through his gaze. "Six months ago, I found out someone we'd hired was using a false name. That they worked for Blue. That they were trying to work their way into the good graces of one of our VPs to find out information."

"What?" Why hadn't Maddie heard about this? If there was one thing Josh loved talking about, it was work.

"We kept the incident under wraps," Josh explained. "Obviously, we fired the mole. Even though we pressed charges, we've been able to keep what happened quiet. We don't want people to lose confidence in our company, so we decided to keep the matter quiet instead."

She supposed that made sense. "So you think Blue still might be trying to get their hands on the details of this product so they can create their own version? And you think this new corporate spy could be someone who's here as a spouse or plus one?"

"We vet everyone we hire so I can't see it being someone on the inside. But just in case, I'm having one of my guys dig deeper into the couples on the retreat. I want to know how long they've been together, what their past jobs were, if they have a criminal record."

Maddie's eyebrows flew up. "You're really taking this seriously, aren't you?"

"Yes, of course." His expression hardened as his mind seemed to shift to work problems.

Brody's image filled her mind. He was someone's date. So was Bree. Could someone like Brody or Bree be a corporate spy?

Maddie just couldn't see either of them being guilty. They seemed like salt of the earth people, not the viciously driven types.

"I also have people tracking Derek."

Josh's statement jerked Maddie from her thoughts. "Derek, the man who was fired? Why are you having him followed?"

His gaze continued to darken. "I need to make sure he doesn't follow us here to start trouble. Right now, he's still in New York, so we should be good. But I can't take any chances."

Maddie tried to control her reaction, to not appear dumbfounded at his paranoia—and that was exactly what she felt like: dumbfounded. Derek would have to be really angry and unhinged to come here to Kauai and exact revenge.

Josh's theories sounded outlandish, but maybe they weren't. She knew the stakes were high.

"I had no idea you were this worried about this new proprietary technology," she finally said.

Josh locked his gaze on hers. "There are people who would *kill* to get their hands on it. We stand to make billions if the launch is as successful as we believe it will be."

His words stretched through the air until a chill shimmied through her.

The tech world really *was* a cutthroat business, wasn't it?

But was it cutthroat enough that someone was willing to turn innocent people into casualties?

Maddie knew the answer to that question was a resounding yes.

———

Maddie arrived back at the resort, unable to shake her embarrassment. Word of what happened had probably already spread throughout everyone attending the event.

Truly, she shouldn't have come to Kauai. She should have pulled the Band-Aid off and broken up with Josh before the event—and not let him persuade her otherwise.

She'd been trying to do the right thing, but the lines felt murky. Though she wanted to spare Josh any heartache, maybe delaying the inevitable was only making things worse.

She paused in the lobby and glanced in the mirror. Her eyes widened at her reflection.

Red dirt coated her hair and skin. Her pink shirt now looked orange. Bandages covered her right bicep, and numerous scrapes could still be seen.

Why hadn't Josh told her how horrible she looked?

"You're back!" a female voice called.

Maddie turned to see Bree and Fowler walking toward her holding slushy tropical drinks with pineapple wedged on the rims. They'd both cleaned themselves up since the UTV ride and looked presentable.

Maddie, on the other hand, looked as if she'd just been rescued from underneath rubble after an earthquake. She didn't usually care about appearances, but her looks right now would draw entirely too much attention.

Bree peered at her with concern. "Are you okay? We've been worried."

"I'm fine." Maddie waved a hand in the air, trying to make it seem like the accident hadn't been a big deal. "Just embarrassed."

"There's nothing to be embarrassed about." Fowler frowned and pushed his glasses up on his nose. "That's terrible what happened to your side-by-side."

It was . . . but equally as terrible was the fact that her fiancé had bailed and left her to fend for herself.

Maddie kept those words silent.

"I should have reacted quicker." She shook her head, realizing how lame her words sounded. She was just making excuses for Josh, and she hated herself for it.

Fowler stepped closer and lowered his voice. "Look, I'd want to know this if I were in your shoes."

"Know what?" A wrinkle formed between her eyes.

Fowler shifted. "There's a video of the incident going around."

"What?" Maddie's voice rose, and she glanced around to make sure no one had heard her. She glanced at Bree for confirmation, and her friend nodded.

"Who took a video?" she whispered.

"I heard it was that woman Logan—the pretty brunette," Bree said.

"Logan?" Maddie repeated. "But in order for someone to take a video of that, they'd almost have to know what was going to happen in advance."

As she said the words, sick realization pooled in her stomach.

Had Logan known? Had she done this in order to have Josh for herself?

Someone *could* have slashed the tire, though their guide gave no indication of that. He seemed to think they'd brushed against a sharp rock or something.

"She said she was filming the excursion to use in a promotional video and just happened to have her camera on Record when your tire popped and you started careening down the hill," Bree said.

"Is she showing it to people?" Please say no . . .

Bree frowned, and Maddie had her answer.

"Thanks for letting me know." Maddie let out a long breath.

She'd have to think more about that later. She was certain Josh would be furious if he found out one of his employees was showing people a video of what he'd done. It would make him look bad.

"Anyway," Maddie murmured. "To change the subject . . . are you guys going to be at the luau tonight?"

"Of course." Bree perked up. "We wouldn't miss it."

"I'm going to save seats for everyone, okay?" Maddie said. "You two—along with Adrienne and Brody—are the only ones who seem normal at this whole event, and I'm going to lose my mind if I have to plaster on a fake smile very much longer."

"We would absolutely *love* to sit with you," Bree said.

"Perfect."

When she looked up and saw Detective Kalani walking into the resort, she knew her injuries and that video were the least of her problems.

MADDIE EXCUSED herself from Bree and Fowler, not wanting them to be close as she talked to the detective. She had a feeling he was still hunting for information.

"Aloha," he started as they paced through the lobby beside each other. "I was hoping to run into you."

Maddie continued walking. "Is that right?"

"I received more information from one of our witnesses that I wanted to talk to you about." His voice remained placid and unreadable.

"The witness who saw two people out on the beach the night Jared died?" she clarified.

"Yes. She's the one."

"And?" Maddie could hardly breathe as she waited to hear what the detective would say.

"It turns out she saw one of the two people who'd

been on the beach return to the west wing of the resort a few minutes after the argument."

"Okay . . ." Her steps faltered. Where was he going with this?

The detective paused and locked gazes with her. "I understand you're staying in the west wing."

Maddie's eyebrows shot up. "I am. But so are a lot of other people. Was it a woman or a man?"

Kalani offered half a shrug. "The witness isn't sure. It was too dark outside to tell."

She crossed her arms, determined to keep her panic at bay.

Was she making too many assumptions about this investigation? It was driving her crazy that the detective was so difficult to read.

"Why do I feel like you're insinuating I had something to do with this?" she finally asked.

He remained unreadable. "We're trying to figure out what happened. Mr. Kline had some strange bruising on his shoulders, bruising that doesn't fit with him being slammed into the rocks by waves. The marks almost look like hands left them."

Maddie's outrage turned into shock. "So you think someone shoved Mr. Kline's head into a rock and then let the ocean do the rest of the work?"

"That's one of our working theories. The bruising. The conflict he was having with someone right before he died. And the fact your name was written down on a paper in his room . . ."

Her throat tightened as fear tried to strangle her, making it hard to breathe. She reminded herself to keep her composure. "It's like I told you, I have never talked to the man."

Kalani reached into his pocket and pulled out a photo. The image was of two people standing next to each other at baggage claim at the airport.

Maddie was one of them.

The other was . . . a man who looked vaguely familiar with his stout built and dominant double chin.

"Do you recognize the man in this photo?" Detective Kalani studied her, his gaze sharp and piercing.

He was watching for any sign she was lying, wasn't he? Panic fluttered through her as she realized where Detective Kalani was going with this.

She swallowed hard before asking, "Is that Jared?"

He narrowed his eyes. "You're telling me you didn't know what he looked like?"

"I only have a vague idea. It was dark when I tried to pull him out of the ocean."

"Do you remember this conversation?" he asked. "The video this snapshot was taken from shows you talking with him."

"My conversation with that man lasted all of five seconds. We were waiting for our luggage, and I happened to say something about how different it was to be in an open-air airport."

"That's all there was to that conversation?" He cocked his head skeptically.

"Yes, that's all." Her muscles ratcheted tighter.

"But you're verifying that you *did* talk to Jared?" he continued to press.

"I did talk to him." Maddie swallowed hard, trying not to show her panic. But she knew this looked bad, even if the conversation had been innocuous. "But I didn't know who he was at the time. The conversation we had wasn't significant. We were two strangers passing at the airport and making small talk."

She, however, knew based on the look in Detective Kalani's eyes that he didn't believe her.

But an idea hit her. "Have you checked the resort's keycard entries? You can see who came and went during the night."

His gaze remained unchanged. "We're looking into that."

"Good. Then you'll see it couldn't have been me."

At least in theory that was true.

She couldn't be blamed for Jared's murder. She would do everything in her power to make sure that didn't happen.

———

Maddie couldn't let panic take hold. She'd been in tough situations before. She would be in them again.

The important thing was to keep a cool head, even when the heat turned up.

She stared Detective Kalani square in the eye, ready to make her case. "I'm innocent."

He didn't break eye contact as he said, "You're not leaving the resort before this retreat is over, are you?"

Her heart pounded in her ears, each beat deafening as the implications of what he was saying washed over her. "No. I'm staying until the end."

"Good. Make sure it stays that way." He gave her a pointed look.

Before she could say anything else, Josh stepped through the front doors and strode toward them. He'd been talking to a couple of colleagues outside.

He paused beside Maddie and planted a quick kiss on her temple. The sweet gesture was a contrast to his earlier sharp words and selfish actions. Was he simply putting on a good show for anyone watching? Most likely.

He looked at the detective, and his brow scrunched. "Everything okay here?"

"Yes, the detective was just asking for some more details about what happened with Jared," Maddie quickly said before Kalani could answer.

"That's still crazy to think about." Josh snaked an arm around her waist. "That could have really turned out so differently."

Her first urge was to stiffen, but she reminded herself to stay loose and not draw any attention.

"But I'm glad it didn't," Josh continued, his voice softening. "I'm glad you're still here."

Yes, he'd had a total mood shift from earlier.

Maddie stole a glance at the detective, wondering what he was thinking. At least he hadn't indicated to Josh that she might be a suspect.

Not yet.

But she was on borrowed time.

The fact remained that if the detective began to dig deep enough into her past, he'd have even more reasons to suspect her as a killer.

Maddie didn't want anyone to know certain things about her history. No one would ever look at her the same way if they found out. They wouldn't even take time to hear her explanation.

"Well, I need to be going." Detective Kalani took a step back and nodded stiffly. "But I'll be seeing the two of you around."

"I need to get going also. I have another meeting." Josh glanced at Maddie. "But I'll see you at the luau later, right?"

"Wouldn't miss it." She forced a smile, trying to remain composed.

Then she watched as Josh walked in one direction and the detective in the other.

She needed to be alone a moment. To sort her thoughts—thoughts that raced wildly out of control.

Her arms trembled as she started back to her room. *Don't look anxious. And watch your step. People are looking for any reason to blame you for Jared's death.*

Finally, she reached her door, waved her wristband

against the lock, and heard a churning sound. She threw the door open and slipped inside.

But as soon as the door closed behind her, a white piece of paper on the floor came into focus.

Another one.

She carefully picked it up, dreading what she might see.

The typed words made her blood grow cold.

I know what you did that summer.

MADDIE SAT ON HER BALCONY, marveling again at the view from the fourth-floor suite. She stared at the ocean as she tried to process everything.

She'd hoped when she came here that she'd see at least one rainbow. But she hadn't seen any so far.

She didn't believe in signs, but if she did—this would seem like one.

After all, rainbows represented hope.

Her thoughts shifted back to more pressing issues.

Who had left this note? Why?

When the sender wrote, "I know what you did that summer," did that mean he knew about her secret? How would he—or she—have found out? Everything was sealed. She'd even been able to get a job with the state because of that fact.

She stared at the words.

Yes, she was touching the paper. She knew that

whoever had stuffed it under the door might have left fingerprints on it. But she didn't plan on taking this to the police, so it didn't matter. She avoided the police whenever possible.

Maddie found it interesting that this note had been typed—just like the one she'd received the night before.

Most people who came on these trips didn't bring a printer with them. Sure, there was a business area in the resort where people could use a printer, mostly for boarding passes and tickets or things of that sort. Someone *could* have printed the notes there.

But that seemed like a lot of trouble, and this person could have been seen.

She leaned back in her patio chair, her limbs suddenly heavy and knots forming across her shoulders.

She supposed someone could have printed these notes at home and brought the papers with them on the trip. That would have required a lot of preplanning—the thought of which was unnerving. If someone had been planning this for weeks, then she really was in trouble.

But the only reason she could think of that someone might want to print these notes was because they wanted to disguise their handwriting. But why would they do that . . . unless the sender feared Maddie might recognize the penmanship?

The thought startled her.

Really, the only person on this trip whose handwriting she might recognize would be Josh. But Josh wouldn't have had the opportunity to get back to the hotel after their excursion to leave this. As far as Maddie knew, he'd been talking to people ever since they returned from the clinic.

Plus, she couldn't see him sneaking into the business center to print something like this. It would be too risky.

Nothing made sense.

The warning left her feeling even more unsettled than before.

Maybe she could feign sickness and lock herself in the room for the rest of this trip. Or maybe she could switch her plane ticket and head back to New York.

But Detective Kalani had warned her not to leave.

That only left her with one other choice.

She had to buckle down and find answers herself. So far, she'd been casual.

But maybe she needed to take more aggressive measures.

Josh had said he was trying to pinpoint a possible corporate spy. She would ask him if he'd found out anything.

She would also keep an eye on everyone in attendance and see if anyone was acting suspicious.

Someone here was up to no good and was determined to either pull Maddie into things or to get her out of the way.

She couldn't let that happen. She'd worked hard to develop the life she had for herself.

No one was going to ruin it.

Though it was seventy-eight degrees outside, goosebumps popped over her arms. She rubbed her hands over her skin before pulling her arms tight across her chest and staring out at the ocean in the distance.

One thing was certain. Maddie had never felt so alone in all her life.

———

Maddie decided to take a walk. She didn't want to sit in her room until the luau. Plus, she'd never find answers that way.

Nearly as soon as she stepped out of her room, she ran into Brody. He looked—and smelled—freshly showered.

"Fancy seeing you here." She flashed a smile. "Where's Adrienne?"

"She wanted to rest a little." He fell into step beside her as she headed toward the lobby. "How are you doing?"

"I've been better," she admitted.

"That was a close call back there at the base camp."

"You can say that again. My life flashed before my eyes for a second time since I've been on this island. Thank you again for everything you did." Her throat burned as she said the words. Brody had been a real hero. Again.

"It was no problem." He nodded toward the hall-way. "You headed anywhere in particular?"

"Just stretching my legs and trying to clear my thoughts. I heard they're serving fresh fruit in the lobby and that it's delicious."

"Mind if I join you? I'm walking that way also. I need to pick up a few toiletries from the market."

"Not at all." She meant the words. She enjoyed Brody's company—probably more than she should. In fact, she found herself looking forward to seeing him and chatting with him.

That wasn't a good thing. But she could keep her feelings platonic.

"You know what I'm looking most forward to when I get home?" Brody casually tucked his hands into his black shorts, giving their walk the feel of a leisurely stroll.

"What's that?" They stepped outside to cut through the pool area. A fresh breeze tugged at her hair and linen pants, temporarily loosening her lungs.

"Eating Lucky Charms and watching cartoons."

Maddie slowed a step and chuckled. "Are you serious?"

"It's one of my favorite things to do on my days off."

She chuckled again. "I like that. Only I would be eating Cinnamon Toast Crunch instead. It's clearly the best cereal ever created."

"I think we need to have a face-off or take a poll before we can determine the winner on this."

They laughed again. She pictured the two of them eating cereal in a showdown. The image filled her chest with warmth.

She liked that idea.

A few seconds of silence passed before Brody asked, "This may seem like a weird question, but I'm curious why you moved to New York—if you don't mind me asking."

"Not at all." She slowed her steps again, this time on purpose. She wanted to draw out their conversation and for their walk not to be over too soon. "It was my Poppy's influence—Poppy was my granddad. He'd always wanted to live in New York but never could. He made me promise him before he died that I would live there for at least a year so I could experience it for him."

"And you kept your promise."

She nodded slowly. "I did."

"What about your parents?"

"My dad died when I was young, and my mom had to work a lot to make ends meet. That's how I got so close to my Poppy—he babysat. Then he became ill. Around that time, my mom remarried and seemed preoccupied with her new life. So I would sit with my granddad, and we'd watch movies together."

"Sounds like you had a strong bond."

"For sure."

"You even moved to New York for him."

She frowned at that part of the memory. "I did—though part of me dreaded it. One month before my time in the city was up, I met Josh and ended up staying."

Something flickered in his gaze when she said Josh's name.

"You miss the Midwest?" he asked.

Brody's change of subject didn't go unnoticed.

"Terribly." Maddie glanced at him. "You miss Texas?"

He shrugged, still looking laid-back with his hands tucked into his pockets. "I moved there because it's where I could find the most business doing private security. But my goal has always been to move somewhere with a slower pace one day."

They reached the lobby and paused.

"Thanks for walking with me," she told him. "It was fun."

"It was. I hope you find some of that tasty fruit you want."

She grinned and watched him walk into the market.

As she did, a TV blaring inside one of the resort's bars caught her eye.

A commercial that was a spoof of an old movie—*Urban Legends*—was on the screen.

She froze as her brain signaled some kind of realization in her.

I know what you did that summer.

Maddie hadn't been able to stop thinking about that note and what it might mean. And why the peculiar wording?

She closed her eyes.

Think, Maddie. Think. What are you missing?

She opened her eyes and straightened.

Wait . . . Cruel intentions. Jeepers creepers. I know what you did that summer.

Those were all titles—or plays on the titles—of some of her favorite nineties movies. Was that a coincidence?

It couldn't be.

Had she ever posted on social media that she liked nineties flicks? She didn't think so, but she couldn't be sure.

Who on this trip knew she loved movies from back then?

No one except Josh.

A lump formed in her throat at the thought.

He couldn't be behind this . . . right?

But she *had* seen him inspecting the side-by-side before they took off.

Would he have sabotaged the tires and risked his own safety? Then jumped out, hoping Maddie would be hurt?

She'd scolded herself for the ridiculous thoughts.

But maybe she shouldn't.

After all, what better way to build sympathy from board members than by having something happen to his fiancée?

Despite the warm breeze brushing through the open-air lobby, her blood went cold.

Did Josh think hurting her would ultimately get him

the job he wanted? He still hadn't even mentioned to her that he wasn't a shoo-in, that Nico was also being considered.

If not Josh, how would someone else have found out what movies she liked?

So many questions flooded her mind.

Maddie had to get to the bottom of this.

It was more important now than ever.

At the thought, goosebumps popped up all over her arms.

There it was . . . that feeling again.

The sense that she was being watched.

As she scanned the lobby again, she didn't see any eyes on her. But there were lots of people mingling here.

Her head began to spin when she realized that someone near her right now could be trying to harm her.

CHAPTER
TWENTY

THIS HAS BEEN MORE fun than I thought.

I've loved watching the panic and horror on people's faces.

Especially Maddie. She just seems so clueless.

So deserving of everything she has coming.

I haven't told anyone this—actually, I haven't told anyone anything. I'm not that dumb. Anyway, I haven't told anyone this, but I actually wrote out a list of possible ways I could wreak havoc. One never knows when you'll need an idea on the spur of the moment.

That's what sets me apart. I think these things through. I'm meticulous in my planning.

And I'm brilliant. Truly, I am. People have underestimated me my entire life.

One day they'll see.

It's much better if they discover these things on their own instead of me telling them.

It's a good thing I'm patient.

I sit in my room. On my phone, a movie plays. *She's All That.*

I wonder if Maddie likes this movie too. Yes, I know all about her little quirks. They're actually kind of endearing.

Knowing she likes the movies has made this all even more fun. There's nothing I like more than incorporating some creativity into my deeds.

Maddie and Josh are about to find out this is only the beginning.

I have so much more in store.

I will get my way, make my point, get what I want.

This whole retreat will be a disaster.

Josh won't be named CEO.

His product launch will be ruined.

There will be no happy ever afters.

I smile as I think about it all. I didn't think I'd enjoy this so much.

But I do.

Now I need to enact the next part of my plan.

CHAPTER
TWENTY-ONE

THAT EVENING, Maddie donned a blue Hawaiian dress with large turquoise and white flowers across it. It tied behind her neck and showed off her tanned shoulders and arms. She left her hair down, grateful it was long enough to cover the cuts and bruises on her arms.

She'd gotten to the event ten minutes early and had been greeted with a fragrant white and purple lei. Its floral scent was a nice contrast to the aroma of roasted pig also wafting through the air. In the background, a man played a ukelele and sang Hawaiian songs. The sun was just beginning to set, casting a pink hue across the sky.

She found a table near the front and saved seats for Josh and her friends, just as she had promised. She mingled with everyone as she waited, all the while keeping her eyes open for anyone acting suspiciously.

She knew the truth—there was a good chance the

person who knew her secrets worked for Benchmark. That they were attending this luau. That they could be watching her as well.

Her gaze stopped on Adrienne and Brody as they stepped into the dining area.

Adrienne looked gorgeous in a body-hugging, pink-flowered dress. Brody wore a breezy white button-up shirt and khaki shorts.

He glanced at her and smiled.

The sight of his grin made her heart flip-flop.

No, Maddie. That's not okay. No flip-flopping in your chest. Got it?

Several minutes later, everyone settled into their seats—everyone except Josh.

"Where's Mr. Harding?" Fowler asked from across the table.

Maddie tempered her voice before saying, "Rubbing elbows with important people. I didn't anticipate him sitting here with me very long. The way he's learned to schmooze, he really should go into politics."

"I guess trying to be CEO is great training for a political campaign." Adrienne flashed a smile.

Finally, someone who understood.

"Take advice from an emu and don't let yourself be ostracized." Bree chuckled at her own joke.

"That was pretty bad," Fowler murmured. "But nice effort."

Bree shrugged. "What can I say? I try."

A man got up front and began telling everyone about the history of luaus on the island.

When he finished, Adrienne leaned closer and whispered, "Say, is that detective still asking about Jared? I've been thinking about that all day."

A lump formed in Maddie's throat. "Yes. The police think Jared may have been," she swallowed hard before glancing around and then whispering, "murdered."

Adrienne gasped. "What? That's terrible. I thought it was just a fluke accident."

"So did I." She had no idea when she went outside yesterday morning that everything would change so drastically.

"You're not a suspect or something, are you?" Adrienne continued to study Maddie's expression, on the verge of looking horrified. "I mean, I heard what the detective told you yesterday, but I was hoping he was just testing the waters."

How did Maddie even answer that?

She scrambled for the right words to say. "Honestly, I don't really know what the detective is thinking."

"I'm sure it was just procedure when he talked to you." Brody's gaze met hers, his words reassuring.

"I hope so. Anyway . . . maybe we could talk about something else?"

"Absolutely." Adrienne seemed to snap from her inquisitive stupor. She straightened and glanced around, her eyes lighting. "Let's have some fun."

Maddie only wished it were that easy.

But having fun wasn't on her agenda . . . not when a killer was out there.

As her gaze drifted, Maddie spotted Nico talking with several board members. They all looked at him with admiration in their eyes.

Maybe Josh really was on shaky ground. He'd be devastated if he wasn't named CEO. Since his dad had started the company, Josh had been determined to take over one day, to follow in his father's footsteps.

So where was Josh now?

Her gaze traveled to the other side of the event area, and she spotted him.

He was leaning close to Darla, whispering something to her.

What was that about? Maddie didn't like the way both Darla and Josh glanced around after their quiet conversation. It was almost like . . . they were plotting something.

But what sense would that make?

Maddie didn't know. But she didn't like the unsettled feeling in her gut, a feeling that indicated a vast abundance of secrets cowered in corners here at this retreat.

And if there was one thing she knew about secrets, it was that they could get people killed.

TWENTY-TWO

JUST AS MADDIE HAD ANTICIPATED, Josh was hardly present to sit beside her.

She was a work widow. Though they weren't married, the concept was still the same.

Actually, maybe *vacation widow* would be a better term.

At events like this one, there was no time to hang out together. She'd mostly gotten used to being alone and finding people to chat with. But she was glad to have found Adrienne, Brody, Bree, and Fowler.

Maddie's group had already been through the buffet line. They'd tried some of the world-famous poi Hawaii was known for. She discovered she wasn't a fan of purplish pudding.

She did, however, go back for seconds on the pork barbecue and macaroni salad.

As she waited for the rest of the group to return to

the table, she took a bite of creamy pasta. She scanned the area again. Again, her gaze stopped on Josh.

This time, he was talking to Logan, who wore a body-hugging white dress.

Maddie's shoulders tightened.

"You're not worried about him, are you?"

She snapped her attention to Adrienne, who'd come back to the table and had clearly seen her watching Josh.

Maddie tried to neutralize her expression. "No, the only thing Josh wants is to be named CEO. That's his primary goal in life right now."

Adrienne frowned. "I guess you haven't done too much wedding planning then?"

Maddie glanced at the two-carat engagement ring on her finger. She hadn't wanted something this large, but for Josh, it was another trophy to add to his collection. That was how she'd always seen it, at least.

"No, I guess I haven't," Maddie answered. "No rush, right?"

Brody quietly joined them again, giving them space to finish their conversation.

"It was a shame what happened to his dad." Adrienne stabbed a piece of her Lomi Lomi Salmon.

"It really was. Everyone thought he was as healthy as a horse." Two months ago, he'd dropped dead while working late in the office. He'd had a massive heart attack, one that had left Josh and his brother, Sam, fatherless, and Lynn, Josh's mother, a widow.

"Josh seems like a no-brainer for the position," Adrienne continued.

"That's what everyone says."

A member of the event team waved to Adrienne from a few tables over.

"Excuse me a minute," Adrienne muttered.

She scurried to her coworker, leaving Maddie and Brody sitting at the table.

She glanced at Brody and shoved down another rush of attraction.

Inappropriate, Maddie. Do better.

She swallowed hard before asking, "Are you having fun?"

"Hawaii is an amazing place."

"That didn't answer my question."

Brody laughed. "I can't complain. How about that?"

"I guess that works." But Maddie was still curious about his relationship with Adrienne. Something between the two of them didn't seem quite right. They weren't especially affectionate with each other, nor did they exchange warm glances.

Then again, people probably said the same thing about her and Josh. They were often rather stiff together.

"How about you?" Brody shifted in his seat as he turned toward her.

Maddie pushed her hair behind her ear as she considered what to say. "I don't like being paraded around. I guess you could say I'm not in my element here."

"That's a hard position to be in."

She suddenly realized what a drama queen she sounded like and let out an embarrassed laugh. "Listen to me. I'm sorry. I don't know why I said that."

"Nothing wrong with being honest."

Her cheeks flushed at his sincere comment.

Why was she letting this man have this effect on her?

Her thoughts shifted—scrambled really—as an idea hit her. This man had been special forces.

Maybe Brody could help her sort through some of the thoughts and ideas she'd been playing with. After all, investigating elder abuse was different than investigating a homicide. She had some of the skills and experience, but this was still bigger than what she'd previously handled.

She could certainly use someone in her corner, a second set of eyes to help her navigate this and someone to bounce ideas off of.

"Listen, this is going to sound weird," she started, turning toward him. "But hear me out. Please."

Brody's eyes narrowed with curiosity. "Okay."

She told him how she was a suspect in Jared's death and how she needed to clear her name.

"I need help," she finished. "Would you—"

"Hey, guys! Sorry I took so long." Adrienne appeared by their table.

Maddie clamped her mouth shut, promising herself she'd finish this conversation later.

Just as that thought settled in her mind, her phone buzzed. It was a text from an unknown number reading.

Don't be CLUELESS.

She glanced around.
Was the person who'd sent this watching her now?
No one appeared to be looking at her.
Despite that, her insides began to quake.

———

As the skies turned dark, the show following the luau started. Maddie sat with her group in some comfortable seats and watched as the history of Hawaii played out in front of them, demonstrated by song and dance, along with narration and even a fire dancer.

However, it was hard for Maddie to concentrate after she'd gotten that text.

It had used the word clueless, which was the title of another old movie she'd watched with her Poppy. Someone knew enough about her to know what movies she liked.

The thought was unnerving, to say the least.

The show ended. Watching it had been good for Maddie. She needed to get her mind off things, if only for a few minutes. However, she knew as soon as the show was over that her ponderings would return.

She had to figure out what was going on. She couldn't let herself get distracted.

And eventually, she needed to finish the conversation she'd started with Brody. He could offer some valuable insight.

As the cast took their bows, everyone applauded before standing.

Maddie scanned everyone around her again. Her gaze stopped on Tom McLemore. He'd quickly slipped away, but his body language was odd. He glanced around as if to see if anyone was watching. Then he hurried into the shadows, almost as if he were on a mission.

Strange.

Maddie continued surveying the crowd. Darla stood on the grassy lawn chatting with Nico and his wife. Josh started toward them but stopped before reaching them, almost as if second-guessing himself.

Except Josh never second-guessed himself. Overconfidence seemed to be both his superpower and his super weakness.

A gasp and low murmurings cut through the happy sounds of the luau.

Maddie jerked her head toward the commotion.

One of the lanterns lining the luau area had fallen over, and flames spread across the grass.

But it was more than that, Maddie realized.

The lantern had hit someone on its way down.

Now Darla was flailing her arms as she tried to put the flames out.

BY THE TIME they left the luau, Josh was fuming.

Maddie couldn't really blame him. Between Jared, the UTV incident, and Darla being burned, the retreat had basically been a disaster so far.

She trailed him back to his suite so they could talk privately.

Now she watched as he paced the living area, his hands flying in the air.

"It's like someone is purposefully trying to ruin this event." He practically spit the words out. "Why would anyone do that? Why would anybody hate us that much?"

Maddie licked her lips, trying to be sensitive in her response. But this was the perfect opportunity to find out some information on the people Josh had been investigating. She just needed the right approach.

She kept her voice gentle as she asked, "Didn't you

say that there could be a corporate spy here? That you had someone looking into that? Has your guy found any leads?"

Josh stopped pacing and looked at her before slowly nodding. "You're right. Someone could be trying to sabotage this event to make the company look bad. Who wants to make *me* look bad."

Maddie swallowed before carefully asking, "Did your guy narrow this potential spy down to anyone?"

"Between you and me, yes. They believe a man named Robert Shields might be the one behind this."

Her eyes widened. "Why Robert? Who is he even?"

"He's the new boyfriend of creative director Greta Ericson. Before they dated, he had a brief stint with Apple. He abruptly left the company three years ago. He checks a lot of boxes."

Maddie lowered herself onto the couch as she thought about that news. "What are you going to do about it?"

"The board members and I are still trying to figure this out. If I can find this spy before the board casts their final vote, then I'll look like a hero. But if I accuse someone without evidence, then I look paranoid and unstable. I can't afford that. I really need to think this over." He raked a hand through his hair.

"I guess you do."

He looked up at her, something changing in his gaze. "And speaking of how I look . . . you need to stop hanging around this new group of people."

Maddie's mouth gaped open. "Excuse me?"

"I know your new friends are probably nice, but they're . . . well, for lack of a better word, they're underlings. It doesn't look good for the fiancée of the future CEO of Benchmark to be hanging around people in their position."

Her mouth fell open wider. "I can't believe you just said that."

Josh reached for her arm, but Maddie pulled away before he could touch her.

He dropped his hand and muttered, "I don't mean it that way."

"Then how do you mean it?"

"I just mean that this retreat is important to me. To my career."

She resisted an eye roll. "You've mentioned that before."

"Madison . . ." He tilted his head.

"I need to be going."

Not waiting for a response, Maddie turned on her heel ready to leave.

Before Maddie reached the door, Josh grabbed her arm and yanked her to a stop.

"I didn't mean it like that." His voice was raised but controlled.

She paused, trying to compose herself before

responding. Then she slowly turned. "Then what did you mean? Because what I heard is that the group of people who saved my life isn't good enough for the one and only super important Josh Harding."

"When you say it that way . . ." He sighed and rolled his neck as if trying to crack the tension.

"When I say it that way, you sound like a horrible person."

He lowered his gaze back to meet hers, his voice more mellow now. "I'm sorry, Madison. I'm so tightly wound. There's so much on the line—everything I've worked for. I'm afraid I'll do something wrong and blow it."

Her shoulders softened a little. "That's not an excuse for treating people badly."

He tugged her closer. "I know. And I'm sorry. Your new friends are perfectly nice. Hang out with them as much as you want."

Even though he said the words, she wasn't sure he meant them. Either way, she hadn't planned on changing.

"I know we're still trying to work things out between us," he continued. "And I really do want to make this work. I've been a terrible fiancé lately."

Maddie didn't disagree with him. He had been.

"I'm going to do better," he continued. "I just need to get through this week. It's been so much pressure . . ."

"I imagine it has been." The words were truthful. He had so much stress on him right now.

"Can you be patient with me for just a little while longer?" He gave her those puppy dog eyes that Maddie had first fallen for.

She felt herself softening even more. "I suppose."

He pulled her into his arms. "Thank you. I appreciate that. I appreciate *you*."

For a moment, she felt bonded with Josh again. She remembered the good times, the early days when they'd first fallen in love.

That was before she'd seen his other side—a side she wasn't sure she could live with.

Was his crankiness just a phase? Or were the hard times showing his true character?

Maddie wasn't sure.

"You could stay here with me tonight . . ." Josh's voice sounded as smooth as velvet as he ducked his head closer to her, his voice intimate.

Maddie tensed before pulling back, all her nice feelings disappearing. "You and I have talked about this . . ."

Josh tugged her closer. "I know. I just miss you. I love you."

"And if you love me, you'll wait. You know how I feel about this now."

She waited for him to call her a prude again. Was it truly the stress of his father's death and this new position? Or was this a matter of character?

Maddie thought she knew the answer.

"I could just really use some quality time with you now . . ." He pleaded with her.

She knew what quality time equated to. She'd already told him how she felt about that.

She turned back to the door. "I've got to go."

Before he could say anything else, she left.

CECILIA STOOD in her bedroom and stared at herself in the cracked mirror leaning against her bedroom wall.

She'd found a champagne-colored dress that hugged her curves in all the right places.

One of her friends at Balderston's had helped her pick it out. Cecilia had been eyeing the dress for a while but had known she could never afford it.

Until now. Until Garrick had offered to pay.

Still, when Cecilia thought about the price tag, she'd nearly choked. Her friend and coworker had insisted she should get it, that an amount of money like that was nothing for people like Garrick.

Cecilia had halfway expected when she went to purchase the dress to be told there had been a mistake. That she'd misunderstood what Garrick had said and he wasn't buying this for her.

But there was no misunderstanding. The dress had been added to Garrick's tab as if doing so were a natural, everyday act.

She'd been able to leave work fifteen minutes early, which had given her just enough time to get home to her apartment to get changed. She had to shower and fix her hair. She took an especially long time with her makeup.

That had led her to this moment.

Staring into the mirror and wondering if she'd done enough.

With a nod of approval, she let out a breath.

Yes, she thought she had.

She looked good, even if she had to say so herself. Her blonde hair was pulled back into an elegant French twist. Fake diamond earrings graced her ears. Her makeup—though cheap—was flawless.

Right on time, a knock sounded at her door.

She didn't live in a fancy building with a doorman or any type of security. Anyone could come and go.

She was still embarrassed for Garrick to see her apartment, to see just how little she had. But maybe it was better if he saw this now rather than later. If he was interested in pursuing her, he needed to go in with his eyes wide open. Doing so would spare a lot of heartache later.

Cecilia pulled the door open and did a double take when she saw Garrick standing there wearing the suit she'd helped him pick out—with the blue tie she'd suggested.

He looked as if he had stepped off the pages of a magazine with his coifed hair, chiseled features, and perfect grin.

She still couldn't believe this man had asked her out. She wanted to pinch herself to ensure this wasn't just a fairy tale.

This was her real life.

But she still needed to be careful not to get her hopes up. She had no idea where this was going.

Garrick let out a low whistle. "You look gorgeous."

Her cheeks warmed. "Thank you. What do you think of the dress?"

She slowly twirled before doing a curtsy.

"I think it's perfect." His beaming eyes said everything. He approved—he more than approved. Then he offered his arm. "Are you ready to go?"

"I am."

She ignored the quell of nerves that suddenly rose in her. She grabbed the clutch she'd found tucked in her closet, one she'd picked up at a secondhand store. Then she stepped out and locked the door to her apartment.

So far, so good. But she still had to get through this event with Garrick. She wasn't sure what to expect. Wasn't sure what his friends might be like.

She was more of a blue-collar kind of girl, one who'd grown up going to rodeos and backyard cookouts. Fancy events had meant going to weddings—usually in a church—with a reception following featuring cake, mints, and peanuts.

"I think tonight's going to be a lot of fun," Garrick started, almost as if reading her mind.

They strolled down the hallway toward the apartment's exterior door and the busy street beyond.

"Is that right?" Cecilia glanced up, curious about where he was going with that statement. "What is it going to be like?"

"It's a charity event for the art gallery."

"I'm afraid I don't know a lot about art—except that I know when I like something and when it evokes a feeling in me. But none of those abstract pieces do it for me. They only confuse me."

He chuckled. "Me too, even though sometimes I fake my admiration just to make my friends happy."

His words made her feel a little better.

"Just relax and be yourself." He patted her hand, which was resting through his looped arm. "I know everyone will love you."

Cecilia wished she felt that confident. "Will you have friends and colleagues there?"

"I guess you could say that. There will be a variety of people. Many of them I rub elbows with at these kinds of events. It's always nice to have someone with me so I don't have to navigate these waters alone."

Something about his words caused some of her excitement to dim.

That almost sounded as if he made a habit of bringing different women to these events.

Was Cecilia just one in a long line?

She knew the answer was most likely yes. Garrick definitely had his pick of women. So why had he chosen her?

She didn't ask. Maybe she didn't want to know the truth. She wanted to believe she was special.

As they climbed onto the empty elevator, Garrick turned to her. Using his index finger, he directed her chin to face him. Their gazes locked.

"I know you're about to be plunged into a situation where you may not feel comfortable. But I'll be there right beside you the whole time. You're going to be wonderful."

"And if I'm not?" Her voice quivered, showing the insecurity she tried desperately to conceal.

"I don't even see how that is possible."

She licked her lips as a shiver of delight shimmied up her spine.

She hoped his words were true and that he wasn't just sweet-talking her.

As she stared up at him, she thought she saw sincerity in his gaze.

The connection between them felt undeniable.

Like their souls were somehow linked.

She'd never met a man like him before. She so desperately wanted this to be real, for this fairy tale to never end.

His gaze moved from her eyes, down to her lips, down to her chest, and then back up to her lips again.

Her pulse quickened.

Cecilia thought he might kiss her.

Her eyes began to shut.

Instead of a kiss, Garrick gently smoothed his finger down her cheek, her chin, her neck. "You're a lovely woman, Cecilia. A lovely, lovely woman."

Her throat tightened.

Those were the words she wanted to hear.

The elevator dinged, and they stepped out.

Being with Garrick right now made her realize she could fall in love. However, she'd vowed when she came to the city that wouldn't happen.

There were too many complications.

Mainly, her past.

Garrick *thought* he liked her now.

But what would happen when he learned the truth about her? A woman like Cecilia would never fit into his world.

Yet the heart wanted what the heart wanted.

What her heart wanted right now was Garrick . . . a man whose last name she didn't even know.

THE NEXT DAY, Maddie had been tasked with hosting a spa event for the members and/or spouses of upper management.

She'd initially declined the proposal but had eventually realized acting in this role was important to Josh. She'd acquiesced. But she wasn't looking forward to it.

The good news, however, was that she'd get a massage and a facial, two things she very much looked forward to.

She plastered on a smile as she greeted everyone outside the spa. Twelve guests would be here today, and Maddie's job was to make them all feel welcome.

Her gaze scanned the crowd, and she recognized a couple of people, including Nico's wife, Ashley.

She called everyone together to welcome them. Then she talked about the benefits of relaxation and how they all deserved the very best. Josh had helped her prepare what to say.

The two of them had briefly talked this morning, and he'd given her an update on Darla and the retreat. Things were cordial between them, but she was still bothered by the fact that he'd abandoned her on the UTV and then blamed her. That wasn't okay.

When she finished, she motioned for everyone to follow her beyond a thick white curtain into the treatment area. Massage therapists and estheticians waited to pamper them.

Maddie couldn't wait for her turn.

Not only did she need to relax, but this would be a great opportunity to keep an eye on some of these Benchmark employees.

"Maddie, is that you?" someone whispered from behind.

She turned and saw Adrienne peeking her head around the edge of the curtain.

Maddie paused before stepping closer. "Adrienne . . . what are you doing here?"

"There wasn't room on any of the excursions for me. They were all packed. Mr. Harding—Josh—said I should come here and see if there were any openings."

That sounded awfully thoughtful of Josh. Maddie shouldn't be surprised, but part of her was. Was he trying to make up after their argument last night?

Her shoulders relaxed as she smiled. "That's a great idea. As a matter of fact, there's one more spot for a massage available. Sue Martin canceled because her stomach felt unsettled after eating sushi at a restaurant down the street."

"Do you think I could get in?" A hopeful look filled her gaze.

"Absolutely. Let me just talk to the manager."

A few minutes later, everything was approved. The only caveat was that Maddie and Adrienne would need to be in a couples' massage room, which Maddie was fine with.

Moments later, they were stretched out on their tables with a sheet over them and two therapists kneaded their shoulders. The scent of spearmint and lavender filled the room, and soft instrumental music played in the background.

Adrienne turned her head toward Maddie. "So, I'm surprised you didn't do a helicopter ride today."

Maddie nearly snorted. "With the run of luck I've been having, I thought that would be a very bad idea."

Adrienne let out a quick laugh. "I get that. I'd probably do the same if I were in your shoes."

"That was scary what happened last night at the luau, wasn't it?"

Adrienne's smile dimmed. "It really was. Have you heard any updates on Darla?"

"Josh said she's doing better. She was released with minor burns on her arm and shoulder. The incident scared her more than anything."

Adrienne shook her head in disbelief. "Poor woman.

I was talking to a member of the staff, and they said things like that *never* happen."

"How did it happen? I mean, all the people they have go in and out of this place on a daily basis, certainly safety measures are in place."

"And why did it happen now?" Adrienne murmured.

Maddie had thought that many times herself. "Good question. Maybe the retreat is cursed."

She didn't really believe in curses, but if there was ever a time she might start . . . it would be now.

A few moments of blissful silence passed, and Maddie closed her eyes.

"Brody is out playing golf," Adrienne told her. "Josh too?"

"Yes, he loves playing. Personally, the game bores me to tears."

"Me too! One more thing we have in common."

The two shared a smile.

As the therapist dug her elbow into Maddie's back, Maddie glanced at Adrienne. "So how did you and Brody meet? Have you been dating for long?"

Her eyes opened and then closed again. "Me and Brody? Oh, we've been on again, off again for probably two years. But no matter what happens, we seem to come back to each other. Relationships are like that, aren't they? Except probably not you and Josh. You two seem like you were made for each other."

"You really think?" Maddie contemplated how much to say.

Part of her wanted to pour everything out to someone. But she questioned how wise that would be. Trusting the wrong person could have dire effects.

Instead of sharing, she clamped her lips shut.

"For sure," Adrienne said. "You seem like the ideal couple. You complement each other so well."

All the relaxation Maddie's muscles had undergone moments ago deteriorated, and they tightened again. "I don't know if the ideal couple really exists."

Adrienne raised her eyebrows. "So, to be clear, you two are *not* perfect together?"

"Not by any means." Maddie touched the diamond ring on her finger. "We're far from it, actually."

"Uh oh. Sounds like trouble in paradise."

Again, Maddie wanted to share but chose not to. "It's . . . complicated, you know?"

"I know all about complicated." Adrienne rolled her eyes.

"So you never said how you and Brody met," Maddie prodded, desperate for a subject change.

"Oh, it's such a fun story," Adrienne started. "I hadn't been in the city very long, and I was supposed to meet some friends from work for dinner. But I got totally lost and was wandering around Greenwich Village close to a panic. Then Brody saw me."

"Sounds like this is going to get good."

"He took pity on me," she continued. "He gave me

directions, but I still must have looked confused because he insisted on walking with me to make sure I got to the restaurant safely. When I got there, I asked him to stay and eat—my treat. At first, he refused, but I finally convinced him. The rest, as they say, is history."

"It sounds like he's always been a hero."

Adrienne grinned. "Yes, he really is, isn't he? When I saw him jump into your UTV yesterday . . ." She fanned her face. "I knew he was the man I wanted to marry."

Maddie wished she felt that way about Josh.

Instead, he was the man who'd abandoned her and almost got her killed as he looked out for himself instead.

———

The massage had been wonderful as well as the facial afterward.

Maddie felt markedly more relaxed when her session was over, and she'd enjoyed getting to know Adrienne more.

When they finished, they both changed back into their clothes. Maddie waited for the rest of the group to finish so she, as hostess, could tell everyone goodbye and make sure they'd enjoyed their treatments.

Adrienne volunteered to stay with Maddie as she lingered in the spa lobby.

Adrienne seemed like good friendship material, like the kind of person Maddie would like to hang out with back in New York. She'd had a hard time finding good friends in the city. Then when she started dating Josh, that didn't seem to matter as much.

She wished she hadn't allowed that to happen. Friendships were important.

In the future, she wouldn't make the same mistake.

Hanging out with Adrienne and Bree had helped her to remember how important it was to have women you could confide in—not that she'd confided anything.

She turned to ask Adrienne a question and saw her friend's face had gone pale.

"Adrienne?"

She swallowed hard and pulled her gaze back to Maddie's. "There's one part of my past I haven't told you about—at least not in detail. The part that includes Danny . . . my ex-husband. I keep thinking I see him here, that he's come after me."

Maddie followed Adrienne's gaze from the spa to the doorway of a restaurant across the hall. A hostess stood outside but no one else.

"You think you just saw him now?" Maddie asked.

Adrienne nodded and sank into a nearby chair, almost as if trying to hide. "I'm pretty sure I just saw him go into the restaurant across the lobby. The last thing he said to me was that he wanted to kill me . . . now I'm afraid that he might."

MADDIE'S MIND RACED. Someone might kill Adrienne? Had she even heard correctly?

But she knew she had.

"What does Danny look like?" Maddie asked. "Do you have a picture?"

With trembling hands, Adrienne found one on her phone.

Maddie studied the man. He was stocky with a square face and a thick beard that was pointy on the end. His meaty arms and multiple tattoos showed he wasn't someone to be messed with.

She knew she still had duties to attend to as hostess. But helping out her friend was more important.

"I'm going to go look for him in the restaurant. That way you can know for sure." Maddie took a step toward the Sea Glass Café.

Adrienne grabbed her arm before she left. "Wait. You can't let him know I know you."

"If he's been watching you, then he probably just saw us together," Maddie gently reminded her.

Panic still raced through Adrienne's gaze. "Then you can't let him see you. I don't want him to approach you. He's a bad man."

"Okay, I won't. I'll be stealthy." Maddie tried to take another step, but Adrienne still gripped her arm.

"Really. I mean it, Maddie. He's scary."

The fear in Adrienne's voice set Maddie on edge. But she wasn't going to give up. "I promise to be careful."

Adrienne stared at her another moment, terror in her eyes, until she finally nodded and released her grip on Maddie.

Maddie shook off her nerves and hurried toward the café. She bypassed the hostess, murmuring something in passing about meeting a friend. The hostess didn't question her.

Maddie scanned the dining area. Groups of people were gathered at tables, eating sushi and poke while drinking colorful cocktails. A guitarist strummed in the corner, creating a relaxing atmosphere that didn't fit the intensity she felt now.

She studied the faces, but she didn't see Adrienne's ex anywhere.

Had Adrienne been imagining things?

Maddie needed to be sure.

She began strolling the dining area, searching each face as she did.

She walked the entire perimeter, but she didn't see anyone that looked like Danny.

Had Adrienne been seeing things? Or had Danny ducked away, hoping not to be spotted?

Maddie had no idea.

When she was sure Danny wasn't there, she returned to the spa.

Adrienne still appeared pale and shaky as Maddie approached.

"He's not in there," she told her friend.

Adrienne's shoulders slumped with relief before instantly tightening again. "If he's not at the restaurant, then where did he go?"

Maddie studied her friend's face. "Are you sure you saw him?"

"I'm positive."

Maddie pressed her lips together, unsure what to say. Finally, she settled with, "Then let's keep our eyes open. You should let Brody know so he can be on the lookout as well. You could even talk to the resort's security."

"No! I don't want to draw any unnecessary attention." Adrienne let out a feeble laugh, almost as if she'd heard the paranoia in her own words. She blew out a long breath. "I want to do a good job with this event. I've heard about Josh's reputation for firing people on a whim. I *need* this job."

Maddie had heard about that also, from more than one source.

"I understand." Maddie frowned. "And I'm sorry Josh is impulsive like that."

She'd seen the trait in him before, and she didn't like it. But Josh didn't listen to her. He said that was the way things worked in the business world. A person had to be decisive.

Maybe he was right.

But that still didn't mean Maddie liked it.

"I think I'm going to go lie down for a few minutes." Adrienne stood and fanned her face. "Then I need to get ready for the concert tonight."

"Of course. Do you want me to walk you to your room?"

Adrienne waved her off. "No, I'll be fine. But thank you."

Maddie hesitated a moment before nodding. "Let me know if you need to talk later."

Adrienne paused before pulling Maddie into a quick hug. "Thank you so much for being a friend. I really appreciate it."

Maddie hugged her back, glad she could be there for Adrienne.

The two pulled away, and Maddie watched Adrienne retreat. Then she turned, trying to figure out what to do next.

Her gaze stopped on Detective Kalani.

Just like yesterday, he headed straight toward her.

Dread pooled in her stomach.

What now?

———

"Ms. Waters." Detective Kalani paused in front of her, his voice monotone.

"People are going to see us talking so much that they're going to think we came here together." Maddie crossed her arms casually as she tried to maintain her cool.

He let out a grunt that she thought for a moment might be a chuckle. She couldn't be sure.

"Maybe," he said. "Unfortunately, we keep needing to talk."

"Yes, unfortunately." Maddie drew in a deep breath. "What is it now?"

"I finally heard back from the resort about who might have used their keycard around the time of Jared's murder."

Her blood went cold. "You're officially calling his death a murder now?"

"As a matter of fact, yes, I am. I'm officially investigating Jared's death as a homicide." His expression remained stoic.

Maddie resisted a shiver. "I'm sorry to hear that. Did you discover something? I know it was nothing having to do with my keycard. I was in my room all night."

"Yes, you were—according to your keycard." His

gaze narrowed as if that fact disappointed him. "However, someone you know just happened to leave their room around three and return at four."

"Who would that be?" Maddie held her breath as she waited for his response.

"Your fiancé."

"Josh?" The word squawked out before Maddie could stop it.

A gleam of satisfaction shot through the detective's eyes as quickly as a shooting star that quickly disappeared—so fast that she had to question if she'd seen it even.

"The one and only," Kalani murmured. "Any chance he was paying you a late-night visit?"

She swallowed hard. "He was not."

Detective Kalani nodded slowly, the gears clearly turning in his brain. "I see. So you have no idea where Mr. Harding went for about an hour at that time of night?"

"I have no idea."

But one thing was sure: Maddie planned on finding out.

Would Josh have a reason to kill Jared? Was that why he was awake and came down to the beach so early?

What if Jared had been the spy, and Josh had found out and silenced him permanently? What if Jared had wanted to meet with Maddie and plead for her help? Was that too much of a stretch?

She wasn't sure.

Maddie didn't like these thoughts. But she couldn't ignore the questions either.

TWENTY-SEVEN

MADDIE WAITED in the lobby for Josh to return.

It was the best way to meet up with him. If she waited in her suite, she might not hear him enter his room next door.

Besides, she was restless. She couldn't go back to her room and just stare at the walls.

As she sat on a leather couch, she played with ideas on how to bring up the subject with Josh about his late-night outing on the night Jared died. There didn't seem to be a way to do it naturally. Every scenario she brainstormed sounded accusatory.

She needed to think of something, however. She needed answers.

Finally, a group of golfers returned from their day on the greens.

Maddie searched the faces as they filed back into the resort.

Josh wasn't with them.

Maddie pressed her lips into a grim line. Where was he?

Her shoulders loosened when she saw Brody step inside instead. He spotted her and smiled.

She had to admit that he didn't look like himself in his khaki shorts and pale green polo shirt. He seemed more like a T-shirt and flip-flops kind of guy. More the high adventure sport type than the type to enjoy a slow, leisurely game of golf.

She remembered the conversation they'd started yesterday. She still wanted to finish what she'd been telling him. But privacy was everything, and she hadn't had the right opportunity.

Brody strode toward her and paused. "If you're looking for Josh, he stayed back talking to a couple of the guys who golfed with us."

"I understand. Did you have fun?"

He shrugged. "I've never been much of a golfer, but it wasn't bad. The course was beautiful."

"Everything around here is beautiful." Maddie's gaze drifted behind him, and her breath caught.

Robert Shields stepped inside. One of the people on her list. One of the men on Josh's list.

"What are we watching?" Brody whispered beside her.

She raised her finger, indicating he should wait a minute.

Robert paused and scanned the lobby before his gaze stopped on William Wright, the head of technology.

He headed toward the man, but William didn't appear to see him. He glanced at his watch before turning and walking away.

Robert trailed him.

"Still no explanation?" Brody followed her gaze.

"I'm going to sound crazy." Maddie's voice cracked as if to emphasize her statement.

"I'm used to crazy. What's going on?" His voice sounded sincere, like he meant the words and wasn't judging her.

"I suspect that man might be a corporate spy." She nodded at Robert.

Brody's eyes widened. "What? I was just golfing with him. Seems like a pretty happy-go-lucky guy."

"I told you it was going to sound crazy. But I've been trying to figure out what's going on. I still think the detective thinks I killed Jared—"

"You started saying that the other day. But we didn't have the chance to finish that conversation. Why would the detective think that?"

She kept her gaze on Robert still, not wanting to lose him. "Because I talked to Jared for five seconds at the airport. Because he was seen arguing with someone on the beach before he died. Because the person he was arguing with returned to the same wing where I'm staying."

Brody pursed his lips skeptically. "That evidence is flimsy at best."

"I agree. But I still think Detective Kalani has his sights set on me. He's talked to me several times since Jared died."

"I'm sorry to hear that." Brody watched Robert as he disappeared down the hallway. "You really think Robert could be responsible for Jared's death? All because he could be a corporate spy?"

"This new product Benchmark is about to launch is high-value and the information on it is highly classified. Josh is worried that someone—a corporate spy—may work at Benchmark or might be the plus one of someone here."

Brody tilted his head in surprise. "That's serious."

Maddie twisted her lips together, hoping she didn't regret sharing as much as she did. After all, what if *Brody* was the spy?

She had a hard time seeing it. But any spy worth his or her weight would be able to disguise who they really were.

"So what are you thinking about doing?" Brody studied her face, something brewing in his mind—maybe concern. Maybe curiosity. Maybe the impulse that he should run away from her and her crazy ideas.

She expected a reprimand or scolding from him. His reaction was a pleasant surprise.

"I'm going to follow him," Maddie announced.

Brody's eyebrows climbed higher. "Doing some investigating of your own?"

"I am."

"I know you told me some of that stuff yesterday about what's going on. But investigating could be dangerous, Maddie." His voice held an underlying warning.

"I know. But so is going to prison for a crime I didn't commit."

"I can't argue with that." He paused. "You mind if I come along?"

Maddie's initial thought was to say no. But Brody could be an asset. He knew what he was doing, and a second set of eyes could only benefit her.

"As long as you can be subtle," she told him.

Amusement danced in his eyes. "Subtle is my middle name."

"Then yes, come with me. Let's see where this guy is heading."

———

Maddie and Brody trailed Robert as Robert trailed William.

They tried to look casual, like two people talking and enjoying the resort. But Maddie never took her eyes off Robert. The man was clearly on a mission.

"Who exactly is this guy?" Brody whispered.

"He's dating creative director Greta Ericson."

"And . . ."

"And given his past work history, we believe he might have a motive for trying to steal information from the company." They bypassed a family headed toward the pool area with innertubes and towels.

"Why Robert?"

"He had a brief stint with Apple, but then he abruptly left the company three years ago. His girlfriend before Greta also worked for a tech company—one that went under last year. He checks a lot of boxes."

"I guess he does."

As William stopped to talk to someone outside the fitness center, Robert paused also. He stared at William as if gathering his courage.

Maddie and Brody paused near a corner to see what was going to happen.

The next moment, Robert sucked in a deep breath before striding toward William. Robert glanced around as he got closer, almost as if double-checking to make sure no one else was around.

What exactly was about to go down?

"Excuse me!" Robert called. "Can I have a moment of your time?"

William's eyes widened. "What's this about?"

"It's about an offer I think you'll find hard to turn down."

Maddie exchanged a glance with Brody.

Maybe this was the lead she'd been searching for.

CHAPTER
TWENTY-EIGHT

MADDIE REMAINED AROUND THE CORNER, holding her breath as she listened for whatever Robert would say next.

"I've noticed you've been looking a little sluggish," Robert said. "I used to feel that way also. Then I discovered NutriHealth."

Her brow wrinkled. NutriHealth?

Maddie and Brody exchanged a look. A wrinkle of confusion formed across Brody's brow also.

Robert continued, "These shakes have changed my life by giving me the energy and nutrition I need on a daily basis."

Realization washed through her.

Robert was trying to get William involved in an MLM scheme, wasn't he?

She pressed her lips together and held her breath as she tried to contain her laughter.

She and Brody exchanged another look before creeping away. As soon as they were out of earshot, Maddie laughed so hard that her stomach hurt.

She'd had that totally wrong.

Robert wasn't a corporate spy. He was a salesman trying to hustle anyone he encountered who looked tired or worn down.

She bent forward, grateful for a moment of levity amongst the stress she'd been under.

Brody gave in and laughed along with her as he ran a hand through his hair. "I guess you can rule Robert out."

"I guess so. And I can make a note to avoid him if I'm ever tired."

"What are you guys doing?" A voice cut into their conversation.

Maddie looked over to see Josh standing a few feet away, accusation in his gaze.

Maddie quickly straightened as her giggles instantly faded. "Nothing."

How could she explain that she'd been following Robert and that he wasn't guilty?

"It doesn't look like nothing." Josh's gaze slid back and forth from Maddie to Brody.

Josh had assumed she and Brody were flirting, hadn't he?

"It's not what you think," she started.

His cheeks reddened. "Then what is it?"

"Let's talk." Maddie stepped toward him, trying to stop him from making a scene. "But not here."

He turned on his heel and began to walk at a fast clip back toward the west wing.

Maddie muttered an apology to Brody before following Josh.

Talking to him right now was the last thing she wanted.

But she would try to mend fences . . . for now.

———

"So you're hanging out with that Brody guy now?" Josh stared at her, something flashing in his eyes.

He didn't speak to her until they were in his suite with the door closed.

Typical Josh. Maddie was surprised he'd made a scene in the lobby at all.

"Brody was helping me with something," Maddie insisted. "Do you have a problem with that?"

Josh tossed his navy-blue Titleist hat on the dresser. "I'm just saying the two of you looked pretty cozy laughing while you were tucked in the corner."

"Cozy?" She nearly gaped. "We weren't *cozy*. And we weren't tucked in anywhere. We were *talking*."

"It looks bad for my fiancée to be hanging out with another man." He threw her a pointed look.

"I'm sorry I might have made you look bad." However, there was no sincerity in Maddie's words, only anger. All Josh cared about was how people perceived him.

He shot daggers at her with his gaze. "Look, you know it's a big responsibility to be my fiancée."

"You've said that many times." She turned before he could see her exaggerated eyeroll.

"Are you sure you're up to the task?"

"As we've talked about before, no, I'm not sure at all. I'm not sure at all that we should be together. But you already knew that."

Silence rippled between them.

Maddie licked her lips, hesitating just a moment before asking, "Where did you go on the morning Jared was murdered? I know you left your suite during the night."

Surprise flickered in his gaze. "I went to the gym to work out. Police can check the record if they want since I needed my keycard to get into the workout room."

Maddie said nothing.

"Wait . . . you don't think I had something to do with that, do you?" Irritation saturated his gaze. "I didn't kill him if that's what you're implying."

"I'm just asking questions."

He let out a long breath as if trying to remain in control. Then he opened the patio door. "Okay. We both need to cool off. Maybe some fresh air would be good for us."

Fresh air sounded like a great idea.

She stepped onto the balcony.

Then she heard Josh behind her and turned toward him.

He stepped closer and grasped her hand. "I thought we were giving this another chance. Giving *us* another chance."

"You asked me to wait until after the retreat to make any decisions. But I feel like the decision is being made for me."

"Madison . . ." His voice turned whiny soft.

She pulled her hand away from his touch. "Don't *Madison* me. I don't appreciate your insinuations."

His whininess disappeared as his gaze darkened and he stepped closer. "I wish you would just be cooperative!"

"I think I've been plenty cooperative!" She took a step back, trying to put space between them.

As Maddie went to lean against the railing, she felt it give.

The next instant, she felt nothing but air beneath her.

TWENTY-NINE

MADDIE'S ARMS FLAILED, and she screamed as she felt herself falling.

In an instant, it became clear to her what would happen if she hit the ground below.

Pain. So much pain.

Above her, someone yelled. Then someone else shouted.

Her hand hit something.

Caught it.

Or it caught her.

Josh. He'd caught her.

Somehow, he had managed to lunge forward, land on his stomach, and grab her hand before she fell too far.

But she now dangled four stories in the air.

She made the mistake of glancing down.

Her head spun when she saw the manicured grass below her.

It was too far below for her comfort.

"Maddie?" someone screeched nearby.

She glanced over. Adrienne and Brody stood on the balcony next door.

They gawked at her.

The next instant, Brody climbed onto the railing of his balcony. He carefully skirted around the ledge before landing on the patio beside Josh.

Wasting no time, he dropped to a prone position and reached for her.

He grabbed her other hand.

On the count of three, Brody and Josh pulled her onto the balcony.

She sprawled on the tile there, her cheek pressed into the dirty floor. She was safe.

It would take a few minutes for her body to catch on to that fact.

Her heart raced out of control as she tried to catch her breath.

That could have been really, really ugly.

She was so thankful Josh had been able to grab her. That Brody had been close. That together they'd been able to lift her to safety.

Brody squatted on one side of her and Josh on the other.

"Are you okay?" Josh asked.

"Now I am." She sounded breathless as she said the words. "Thank you. Thank you both."

Brody looked up at Josh. "What happened?"

Maddie rolled onto her back and kept her eyes open, watching the interaction, wanting to know the answers to those questions herself.

"I don't know." Josh rocked back, resting on his palms as he took in shallow breaths. "She leaned against the railing, and the next thing I knew she was falling."

Brody stood. Hands on his hips, he paced the balcony.

Maddie watched him from her position on the floor.

Brody paused from his pacing and peered at the wall where the railing had been bolted to it. "I don't see any signs of damage."

"Is it rusty or something?" Josh asked.

Brody continued to examine the wall, his gaze darkening. "It doesn't look like it."

"I need to call the manager," Josh muttered. "He needs to know what happened."

"I'd say so, especially if this might be a risk for other people as well," Brody agreed.

Maddie listened to the two men talk. But deep inside, she knew this wasn't a maintenance problem.

Someone had done this on purpose.

For the sole purpose of hurting someone . . . either her or Josh.

———

Five minutes later, the hotel manager was in the room, along with the head of maintenance and Adrienne, who'd run from her room and had been let inside Josh's suite. She hadn't tried to scale the wall between their balconies like Brody had.

Josh put a blanket around Maddie's shoulders as she sat on the bed. Even though Maddie wasn't cold, she couldn't stop shaking.

Adrienne sat beside her with an arm around Maddie's shoulders.

Maddie watched as the manager—a balding, fifty-something Kauai native named Harris Toler—examined the balcony along with the head of maintenance. Josh stood close by observing everything, as did Brody.

"I can't believe this happened," Maddie quietly told Adrienne. She wanted to keep her voice low in case someone on the balcony said something she needed to hear.

"Me either." Adrienne shook her head. "How horrific."

"I'm glad you guys were close," Maddie whispered. "I'm not sure if Josh could have pulled me up on his own."

"I had no idea we were neighbors. I guess we've been coming and going from our rooms at different times."

Maddie nodded, exhaustion overtaking her as her adrenaline faded. "I guess so."

"It looks like the bolts have been loosened," the head of maintenance said.

She pulled herself upright.

The bolts had been loosened? Then Maddie's theory was probably right. Someone *had* done this on purpose.

Except this wasn't her room. So had someone done this in hopes of hurting Josh?

"I was out on the balcony earlier, and the railing seemed fine," Josh muttered. "I didn't lean against it or anything, but it seems like I would have noticed if it was loose."

Maddie hardly heard him.

Instead, her thoughts churned. Maybe Josh was the target all along—except she wasn't sure how much sense that made. In fact, maybe she was reading entirely too much into this. Maybe these were all accidents, crazy coincidences.

Deep inside, she knew that wasn't true, however.

Detective Kalani had said that Josh left his room on the night of Jared's murder.

Josh claimed he'd gone to the gym. But had he?

The last thing she wanted to do was bring up the subject of the detective. She feared Josh would ask too many questions and realize she was a suspect.

But she *was* curious.

Either way, how were all these events connected?

Maddie couldn't put the pieces together yet.

"I knew we shouldn't have picked this hotel." Josh's voice filled the air, louder than it needed to be.

"I assure you that we're a fine establishment and things like this don't normally happen." Harris raised his head, his nose slightly upturned.

Then Josh turned to Adrienne. "Weren't you the one who chose this location?"

Adrienne dropped her arm from around Maddie and froze. "I was. I mean, yes, my team and I picked this specific resort."

"Well, you did a terrible job." Josh practically spit out the words as he shook his head with disgust.

"I don't think that's fair." Adrienne drew back, clearly offended.

"It's completely fair!" Josh's nostrils flared. "Did I not emphasize enough to you just how important this event was?"

"Josh . . ." Soft warning filled Maddie's voice.

"What?" Josh's eyes flashed with anger. "You don't think it's clear that someone is starting to sabotage me? Is it you?" His gaze burned into Adrienne.

"Why would I do that? How would I benefit from doing so?"

"You need to lay off, man." Brody stepped closer, anger edging his voice.

But Josh seemed to hardly hear him. He still faced Adrienne, accusation in his gaze. "Is it you? Have you been behind these incidents the whole time?"

"I . . . I don't know what you're talking about." Her voice shook. "I thought this was the perfect location."

"Excuse me." Harris's voice cut into the conversation. "I assure you that we're going to get to the bottom of this and make things right. We're so thankful that nothing worse happened."

"You *should* be thankful," Josh muttered, his eyes narrowed. "Because if my fiancée had been killed because of this . . ."

Silence hung in the air. Maddie could fill in the blanks.

Josh would have sued the resort for all they were worth.

Because money always made things better. She frowned at the thought, knowing it was far from the truth.

"I've already put in a call to my head of security. They are checking the room key log to see who else has come into your room today." Harris paused as his phone buzzed. "It appears they're calling me back now."

He put his phone to his ear. A few minutes later, he ended the call and turned to them again.

"We have record of the maid coming just before lunch," Harris explained. "Then at eleven-thirty, maintenance came to fix the toilet, which apparently wouldn't stop running. Also, Mr. Harding left this morning around eight, then returned at twelve-thirty, but only stayed ten minutes. Then returned again closer to four."

Maddie's gaze shot to Josh. "Weren't you playing golf at twelve-thirty?"

His face went still. "Yes, I was."

"Who else has a key to your room?" Harris turned to Maddie. "Did you come up perhaps?"

Familiar dread gripped Maddie. "No, I'm not staying in here."

The familiar look of confusion crossed his face.

Maddie waited for it to pass.

Finally, the manager looked back at Josh. "Anyone else?"

Josh shook his head. "No."

"Then we'll pull up security footage. I assure you, I will get to the bottom of this if it is the last thing that I do."

With his words still echoing in the room, Maddie's phone buzzed.

It's a good thing someone heard you SCREAM.

A knot lodged in her throat as she read the words from the same unknown number.

Why was someone intent on torturing her like this?

MADDIE PUT her phone away before anyone could see the message.

Who had sent her that text?

She knew the answer—the person who'd sent the text was the same one who'd hoped she would be hurt on the balcony.

She'd briefly considered Josh. It was his idea to go out there. He was the one who'd stepped toward her causing her to take a step back.

Would he really take things that far?

She wanted the answer to be a resounding no, but she couldn't say it was.

Right now, he paced, almost as if he were nervous.

Harris was still in the room with them, along with Brody and Adrienne. Maddie had a feeling that Josh wanted them to leave, but Maddie wanted them there. If

Josh tried to make her friends give them some privacy, she vowed to raise a fuss.

"Unfortunately, the resort is at capacity right now, and we don't have any other rooms to offer," Harris said. "Is there someone else you could stay with until the balcony is fixed?"

Josh looked at her, but she shook her head.

His nostrils flared, but he kept his expression even otherwise. "If you could do a temporary fix on the balcony, I think I'll be fine."

"Very well." Harris turned to the head of maintenance and asked him to get some supplies.

As he left, a woman in a navy-blue skirt and white blouse stepped inside and introduced herself as the head of IT.

"I have the security footage." The woman went to the table, opened her laptop, and without missing a beat began typing something.

She clearly meant business.

"Here's the person who entered your room at twelve-thirty." She hit Play before looking back at Josh. "Do you recognize her?"

Her?

Maddie rose and stepped closer for a better look at this person.

Her eyes narrowed as she watched someone pause outside Josh's room, glance around, and then swipe a card and step inside.

Maddie couldn't see the woman's face since her back

was to the camera, but something about her seemed awfully familiar.

They continued to wait, the woman at the computer fast-forwarding to the part where the intruder left. Then she paused the footage.

Maddie leaned closer for a better look.

Her mouth gaped open when she realized who it was.

Logan.

Logan had been in Josh's room at twelve-thirty.

Why did that woman have a key to get into his room? And had she messed with the balcony? Even worse—what if Logan and Josh had schemed this together, all in hope of seeing Maddie harmed?

———

Maddie's gaze turned to Josh, and she didn't bother to hide the accusation in her eyes. "Why in the world does Logan have a key to your room?"

Josh raised his hands, his voice terse as he said, "I can explain."

Maddie crossed her arms over her chest, not caring if they had an audience. She knew Josh hated looking bad in front of others. But right now, Josh's opinion didn't matter.

"I gave Logan a key and asked if she could come up to my room and grab a revised schedule for me."

"Why would you need her to do that for you? Are

you saying you don't have access to this revised schedule via your phone?" Maddie wasn't going to be taken for a fool. This sounded like a lame excuse he'd made up to ensure he didn't look bad.

"We should go." Adrienne stood and pointed to the door.

Brody took a step but hesitated, almost as if he didn't feel comfortable leaving Maddie with Josh. Or maybe she was imagining things.

She wasn't sure.

She nodded to reassure him she'd be okay.

With one last glance from Brody, he and Adrienne slipped from the suite.

"The hotel requested a printed copy of the schedule, so I asked Logan to come to my room and print one," Josh explained when they were gone. "She *is* on the event committee, so it made sense for her to take care of that detail."

"She didn't have a copy of the revised schedule in her own belongings?" Maddie asked.

Josh's gaze flickered with irritation. "She had one on her computer, but she didn't have a printer. I needed a hard copy."

His words stopped Maddie.

Josh had brought a printer. The kind of printer that might have been used to send that note to her?

The question echoed in her head.

She shouldn't be surprised that Josh had a printer.

He *had* brought two large suitcases with him on the trip. She'd only brought one medium-sized one.

Josh probably wanted to print out his acceptance speech for when he was named CEO. Or print information on this new product launch. She supposed there were multiple reasons.

Even though his excuse—whatever it was—might be viable, Maddie still didn't like what she'd seen.

"Can we talk about this later?" Josh lowered his voice and cut his gaze toward the other people in the room.

Maddie shook her head. "You know what? I'm suddenly not feeling well. I'm going to skip out on the concert tonight and go lie down."

"Madison—" Josh started.

"I just need some time by myself."

Before anyone could stop her, Maddie stormed from Josh's room. At this point, she didn't care if she ever saw or spoke to the man again.

THIRTY-ONE

THINGS ARE GOING SWIMMINGLY.

I love that word. It sounds so fancy.

And it seems so perfect for this situation.

People turning on each other. Bad things happening. Paranoia rearing its gloriously suspicious head.

It's all so beautiful, really.

To be honest, everything has been easier than I'd thought it would be.

With any luck, I'll get my way, and no one will be the wiser.

I stand near a column as the concert is about to begin.

To my knowledge, no one knows what's really going on—no one except me.

There have been murmurings. People have been getting nervous because there have been so many incidents. And Darla? Well, her accident had been truly that.

Just think . . . without me here, that might have been the only accident that happened on this retreat. What fun would that be?

I only hope Maddie doesn't make this any more difficult.

I mean, I could have just killed her outright.

But my plan is much better because it involves suffering.

My smile slips.

People really should mind their own business.

I'm not done yet.

Lessons still need to be learned.

And I can't wait to see everything play out.

With that, I begin to sing along with the performer on stage as he belts out "Livin' La Vida Loca."

How appropriate. How very, very appropriate.

My voice gets louder as I fully embrace the lyrics.

MADDIE IGNORED THE PHONE CALLS. Ignored the knocks on her door.

She didn't want to talk to anyone.

She'd had some time to mull things over. She supposed in one way Logan entering Josh's room could have been more suspicious. At least Josh hadn't been inside at the time.

But he *had* given the woman a key. She'd left the golf course and gone into his suite.

Had she given his key back? Or had she saved it to use later?

The questions swirled in Maddie's head.

Truthfully, she didn't even care if Josh wanted to be with Logan instead of her. But Maddie deserved the respect of him telling her first at least.

After staring into space for entirely too long, Maddie decided to take a shower. Her body ached from the fall.

When Josh had grabbed her, her arm had jerked pretty hard, and now her shoulder was sore.

If only the shower could wash away her worries and concerns.

But the warm, pounding water did no such thing.

She took her time getting dried off and dressed. Then she stepped onto her balcony—careful not to go too close to the edge, mostly out of paranoia—and she saw the concert/dance party had started.

A cover band played, and disco lights shone.

Everyone from Benchmark should be there. Certainly Josh would be present and putting on his best game face.

Maddie knew going to the party would be fun. But with everybody occupied with the concert, this would be a good time to look for more answers.

She left her room and began to wander the lobby and outside patio. Random people mingled in the area, but no one she recognized.

Until she spotted a lounge chair tucked to the side of an outdoor area.

Darla sat there, the white bandage around her bicep a reminder of the tiki torch incident. The seat was secluded with plants and rocks surrounding it on three sides.

Maddie ducked back around a column to see what Darla was doing.

She had a laptop on her legs and was typing something.

The same laptop that Jared had sent those emails to? Had Darla ever told Detective Kalani about those? What if they were significant?

Even more so, how could Maddie find out?

She nibbled on her bottom lip as she considered her options.

She needed to find answers. But sometimes that required ruffling some feathers—something that wouldn't make Josh very happy.

What should she do?

When Darla got a phone call and stepped away, leaving her computer and bag on the chair, Maddie had her answer.

———

Maddie glanced around, making sure nobody else was watching.

There was no one.

She glanced to the side and saw that Darla had gone into the lobby.

Maddie couldn't believe the woman had left her computer out here. Maybe she thought it was okay because the resort felt safe. Because her chair was so isolated. Because she hadn't known Maddie was watching.

If Maddie was going to act, she didn't have much time.

She crept closer to the computer, still glancing around yet trying to remain casual.

If she was caught doing this . . .

She couldn't complete that thought. It would be ugly.

But this opportunity had practically been handed to her.

She went toward the lounger and sat next to the computer.

The laptop was still on.

It seemed irresponsible for Darla to leave it like this, Maddie mused. Especially since there were so many company secrets that management was protective about.

But Maddie wasn't complaining. This was her chance to snoop.

She quickly glanced at the screen and found the emails app. She clicked on the icon.

The screen changed as emails filled it.

Maddie quickly scanned them, looking for anything from Jared.

She spotted his name.

Her heart beat harder.

Maddie glanced around one more time, just to be certain.

Still no Darla. But she didn't know how much time she had until the woman returned.

Maddie scanned the messages from Jared and frowned.

These had nothing to do with his death, at least not

as far as she could tell. They were all about Jared wanting to go to a Mexican restaurant to celebrate his birthday with his coworkers. He mentioned something about wearing a sombrero and having everyone sing to him.

Had he been drunk when he typed some of this? That was how it sounded.

No wonder Darla had said the messages were strange—strange but not threatening or suspicious, however.

Disappointment pressed on her.

Maybe there were others . . .

She glanced around one more time, but Darla was nowhere in sight.

Quickly, she scanned the rest of the woman's emails. Maddie's gaze stopped on one from Nico.

Out of curiosity, she clicked on it.

Her eyes widened as she read Nico's words.

I'm glad to hear I have your support. I assure you if I'm promoted to CEO that you will benefit. I truly believe you deserve to be one of Benchmark's vice presidents. Your talent has gone unnoticed for too long. But not by me.

Maddie's heart pounded in her ears as she comprehended those words.

Darla was rooting against Josh becoming CEO?

Maybe Maddie shouldn't be shocked, but she was.

How many other people were nice to Josh's face while secretly plotting his career demise?

Would someone want him to fail enough that they might even try to kill him? Or sideline him by injuring Maddie?

Maddie still wasn't sure who was the target. She or Josh. But either way, someone was playing a deadly game.

A woman's voice sounded nearby.

Darla, she realized.

Maddie had to get out of here.

Now.

CHAPTER
THIRTY-THREE

QUICKLY, Maddie closed the email program and stood.

But she was trapped. There was only the one exit—the one Darla was headed toward.

She had nowhere to go.

She could cut through the plants, but slick rocks lay on the other side and a cascading manmade waterfall beyond that.

Maddie pictured herself tumbling down it and *really* making a scene.

She couldn't risk it.

But she couldn't just stand here either.

Darla's voice got closer and closer.

If Maddie suddenly darted away, Darla would see her. Would know she'd been up to something.

"Darla?" a new voice called.

Darla paused.

Why was that other voice so familiar?

Then Maddie realized it was Adrienne. What was Adrienne doing here talking to Darla?

Maddie peered around the corner and saw the two women talking. They paced away from the area.

Perfect.

This just might be Maddie's only opportunity to get away.

Remaining close to a wall, she slunk away from the lounge chair.

Darla's back remained toward Maddie as she slipped back into the lobby.

But Adrienne's gaze grazed her.

Adrienne had known Maddie was there, hadn't she? She'd called Darla as a distraction.

Relief filled Maddie. She was more thankful than ever for her new friend. Adrienne had really gone out on a limb for her.

Maddie paced back to the lobby, lingering near the atrium as she waited to see if Adrienne would come back this way.

A few minutes later, her friend appeared.

Maddie could have hugged her. "How did you know?"

"I was looking for a place to sit when I saw you. Then I saw Darla headed that way, and everything made sense. I knew I had to do something."

"You're a true lifesaver. Thank you."

"Of course." Adrienne frowned as she studied Maddie's face. "Is everything okay?"

Maddie nibbled on her bottom lip. How much should she say?

She wasn't exactly sure.

She finally settled on, "The less you know, the better."

"I get that." She nodded slowly.

That was when Maddie noticed that Adrienne's eyes looked red, absent of the sparkle usually dancing in her gaze.

"What are you doing out here?" Maddie asked. "I figured you'd be helping with the concert."

"My part is mostly done. So now I'm just enjoying the event. However, I decided I needed a little breather."

Maddie nodded, her thoughts churning back to what had happened earlier. "Look, I want to apologize for Josh—"

"You don't have to apologize for him." Adrienne frowned, but her gaze remained serious. "You're not his keeper."

"I know, but what he said to you wasn't fair. It wasn't right." Maddie was still bothered by that conversation.

"It wasn't. He can be a hothead at times. Then again, I guess most guys can be." She offered a half shrug.

Something about the way Adrienne said the words caught Maddie's attention. "Is everything okay?"

Adrienne waved her hand in the air, moisture filling her eyes. "Brody and I had a fight right before the concert. I think . . . I think I get on his nerves sometimes."

Maddie reminded herself that not everything was about her. She'd been focusing so much on herself and her problems that she hadn't even realized Adrienne's turmoil.

"I'm sorry to hear that," she murmured.

"I think I always pick the wrong type of guy. I, apparently, have a type." She looked toward the sky, moisture still flooding her gaze.

It took Maddie a moment to comprehend what Adrienne had implied. "Are you saying Brody and Danny are alike?"

From what Adrienne had told her, Brody and Danny sounded *nothing* alike. Danny was a controlling stalker whereas Brody was laid-back and easygoing.

Maddie just couldn't see it. Maybe she'd misunderstood Adrienne.

Or maybe she wasn't ready for Brody to be knocked off the pedestal she'd placed him on.

"The two of them are more alike than I'd care to admit." Adrienne shook her head. "I feel like I just keep kissing frogs trying to find my handsome prince."

Maddie squeezed her arm. "He's out there. You just have to be patient. And if he's not out there, then you're still a queen."

"I like that." Adrienne nodded slowly and pointed

her finger at Maddie. "Being queen sounds pretty rad. I guess it's just been one of those days, you know?"

Maddie let out an almost bitter chuckle. "Unfortunately, yes. I do know."

Adrienne gave her a look. "I'm sorry. I shouldn't be complaining after what happened to you."

"I certainly don't have exclusivity to hard times."

"They're just a part of life, unfortunately." Adrienne threw her a look full of both gratitude and compassion. Then something shifted in her gaze. "I can't believe those bolts on Josh's balcony might have been loosened on purpose."

A knot lodged in her throat. "I know. I can't either. It blows my mind."

"Was someone targeting Josh?" Adrienne tilted her head in curiosity. "I mean, it just doesn't make sense."

Maddie pressed her lips together as she considered what to say. She'd been playing with the idea of telling someone about the notes and texts she'd received. But she'd always stopped herself, figuring it was better to keep those things private.

Maybe getting the truth out there would feel good. Maybe she needed to hear someone else's opinion on what was going on.

But if Maddie said the words, would she later regret speaking so honestly?

She glanced at Adrienne's curious expression.

She wasn't sure what she should do.

CHAPTER
THIRTY-FOUR

"IF I TELL YOU SOMETHING, do you promise to keep it between the two of us?" Maddie paused as she and Adrienne stepped outside near a garden area.

Concern filled Adrienne's gaze. "Yes, of course. What's going on?"

Maddie took Adrienne's arm and pulled her farther away from the path, toward a stone bench perched amongst some hibiscus plants.

Maddie shifted toward Adrienne. "I think someone is plotting against Josh."

"What?" A knot formed on Adrienne's brow. "What do you mean?"

"I mean, I think there are people in this company who don't want to see Josh named CEO. They're banding against him and trying to convince the board to choose Nico instead."

Her eyes widened. "Wow . . . I hadn't heard. I guess

I'm not in a position of power, so no one has bothered to mention it to little old me."

"There's more . . ." Now that Maddie had started, she might as well finish. "I wonder if someone is so desperate to keep Josh from becoming CEO that they're taking it a step further. I'm wondering if someone wants to get him out of the way—permanently."

"You mean by trying to kill him?" Her words came out quickly and in a hushed whisper.

Maddie hesitated a minute before nodding. "Yes, by trying to kill him. Maybe the balcony incident was meant for him, not me. And the slashed tire on the side-by-side? Maybe that wasn't a coincidence either."

Adrienne blinked in surprise. "Wow. I never considered that maybe someone had more sinister motives. But that's extreme, right?"

"It is. But when you're talking about a company with this much power and money, the stakes are high."

"I can't argue with that." She tilted her head as she observed Maddie. "What are you going to do?"

"I'm trying to figure out what's going on. I just might be a target also, by default."

Adrienne's eyes widened. "That's terrible. Should you even stay?"

"I'm a suspect in Jared's death. The detective pretty much said I needed to stay in Kauai. But I feel like I'm caught in a dangerous game I never signed up to be part of."

"I'd say." Adrienne softly gripped Maddie's arm. "What can I do to help?"

"You don't need to do anything. But I need to find some answers before anyone else gets hurt."

"Where do you even start?" She dropped her hand and leaned back, but her gaze remained intense.

"I start by making a list of who might hate me—or Josh. And why."

"That sounds like a tall order." Hesitation marred her voice. "Most people aren't going to admit to anything."

"I know. Believe me, I know."

"I could talk to some people who work at Benchmark," Adrienne offered. "Get the office gossip, so to speak."

"I could never ask you to do that."

"It's going to be easier for me. I talk to people at the company all the time. As an assistant, most of the employees don't even notice me."

She had a point but . . . "I can't pull you into this."

"I *want* to help. I can see what I can find out."

Maddie studied Adrienne's face, still hesitant to accept the offer. "Are you sure?"

"I'm positive. I'm going to keep my eyes peeled and my ears open."

"Whatever you do, don't put yourself in danger. Promise me." Maddie stared her friend dead in the eye to drive home her point.

Adrienne nodded. "I promise."

———

Before the concert ended, Maddie started back to her room. As she headed through the lobby toward the corridor leading to the west wing, movement ahead caught her eye.

Someone had quickly darted out of sight.

She was pretty sure it was a woman in a red dress.

Maddie quickened her steps to get a better look. This person couldn't have gotten very far away. Maddie should be able to catch up.

She paused at the corner and peered around it as she searched for the mystery woman.

Her breath caught as she spotted her.

It was just as she'd thought.

Logan.

The woman had left the concert, and now she was headed to the west wing of the resort.

Was that because her room was this direction? Or was she headed this way for another purpose? Maybe to see Josh? To wait for him in his room?

Maddie slowed her steps, curious about what the woman was doing.

But she kept a steady pace behind her, making sure her steps were quiet. Every time Logan glanced behind her, Maddie ducked out of the way.

She followed the woman up the stairs.

To the fourth floor.

As Logan turned another corner, Maddie crept closer. Her heart pounded in her ears with anticipation.

She paused at the next hallway, knowing a long stretch was ahead with no place to hide. She couldn't show her hand now. Instead, she peered around the corner.

Just as Maddie thought, it looked like Logan was headed . . . to Josh's room.

A door to another room opened behind her, and Maddie ducked back behind the wall. She plastered on a casual smile at the man who emerged and started in the opposite direction.

The door slammed behind him.

When Maddie glanced back at Logan, the woman was hurrying down the hallway, away from Josh's suite.

Was that because she'd been spooked? Or had she never planned on stopping at Josh's room at all?

It was impossible to know, and Maddie vowed not to jump to conclusions. But it was hard not to given the circumstances.

CHAPTER
THIRTY-FIVE

AS MADDIE HURRIED toward her suite, her thoughts continued to churn.

It had felt good to tell Adrienne about her fears. The woman seemed trustworthy. But Maddie was still surprised by Adrienne's statement concerning Brody.

Were Brody and Danny really alike?

Maddie just couldn't see it. But everyone could put on their best face for a short time. As you got to know people, their true colors usually emerged.

Maybe Brody wasn't an exception to that.

However, Maddie thought she'd seen something real and sincere in him. Part of her hoped her assessment was true. It was nice to believe good people were still out there.

That belief had died sometime over the past couple of years.

Since her Poppy died.

Since she'd moved to New York.

New York had been a mistake.

Maddie had told herself city life wouldn't change her. But since she'd begun dating Josh, she'd found herself morphing into someone she didn't even recognize. She'd turned into a person who liked nice clothes. Who rubbed elbows with self-important people. Who preferred to eat at certain kinds of restaurants.

How had that even happened?

Then there was her accident. It had reminded her of what was important.

Only Josh wasn't on the same wavelength. He didn't like the changes Maddie had begun to put in place for herself. That had caused a rift between them.

Still, it was better if these differences happened now than if they happened later.

People were multifaceted, and change was a part of life. But if Maddie ever got married, it needed to be to someone who would accept her, no matter what phase she was in.

She reached the door and used her bracelet to enter the room. But as soon as she stepped inside, she spotted another folded piece of paper on the floor.

Her stomach dropped.

It looked an awful lot like the other notes that had been left for her.

She closed the door behind her, her arms beginning to tremble.

Dreading what she would find, she picked up the note and slowly opened it.

Inside, there was a picture.

Of her.

Twelve years ago.

Only it wasn't just any picture. It was the mugshot from when she'd been arrested.

Underneath the photo were the printed words, **Stop acting DAZED AND CONFUSED.**

CECILIA WAS IN LOVE. She had no doubt about it.

She twirled in the middle of her living room floor, overjoyed at this new development in her life.

Garrick would be here at any minute to pick her up for another date tonight. They hadn't seen each other in a few days, and she missed him. She couldn't wait to catch up. To feel his arms around her. To smell his expensive cologne.

She and Garrick had been seeing each other for a month now.

Ever since the fundraiser, they'd been inseparable. Well, inseparable other than when they had to work, which was often, especially for Garrick.

The fundraiser had gone well except for one slight snafu.

One of Garrick's colleagues had mentioned getting a

tennis bracelet for his wife. And Cecilia had muttered, "Oh, does she enjoy playing tennis?"

Everyone around her had laughed.

Her cheeks had reddened when she realized she must have said something stupid.

When she asked Garrick about it later, he explained the term and assured her that she shouldn't be embarrassed. In fact, the term came about from a tennis player.

Cecilia hadn't grown up in a well-to-do family, but she should have known what a tennis bracelet was.

She'd feared what Garrick's friends must think about her.

But just last week, Garrick had told her he loved her, so he must not be too embarrassed.

Another grin tugged at her lips.

Her life was going to change. She could feel it in her bones.

If things between the two of them continued to progress, then there would be no more living in the slums for her. No more surviving from paycheck to paycheck. No more worries about paying rent or having enough money for food.

She'd met her real-life prince charming.

Squealing, she turned in another circle.

She could pinch herself she was so happy.

She let out another sigh and glanced at the time.

Garrick was supposed to be here, but he was three

minutes late. Which was unusual. He was always so punctual.

Cecilia walked to her window and looked outside, hoping to catch a glimpse of him as he walked up to her apartment.

She'd dressed in a red sweater and some tight blue jeans. She'd specifically picked this outfit because Garrick had told her that red was his favorite color. She wanted to see his eyes light up when he saw her. She wanted him not to be able to keep his hands off her.

For a while, she'd wondered if coming to the city had been a mistake. But now she knew it wasn't.

In fact, it was the best decision she'd ever made. No other man had made her feel as special as Garrick.

She watched out the window several more minutes before frowning and glancing at her watch again.

Garrick was now ten minutes late.

Was he okay? Had something happened to him? This was just so unlike him.

She tried to keep her worries at bay.

She could call him. But Garrick preferred not to get phone calls, especially when he was working. He was often in meetings. Even if Cecilia tried to call, there was a good chance his phone would be on silent. That was what he'd told her.

It made sense. When you had an important job, that happened. Cecilia couldn't fault him for that.

After twenty more minutes passed, she gave up

watching out the window. Gave up twirling in the middle of her living room.

Instead, she plopped down on her faded navy-blue couch and glanced at her phone.

Should she call Garrick anyway? Just to make sure that nothing had happened?

Then, as if right on cue, her phone rang.

Her heart lifted. It was him. Garrick.

She pressed Talk and put the phone to her ear, her voice a mix of worry and excitement. "Hey, everything okay? I was getting worried."

"I'm sorry I'm late, sweetie. But something popped up, and I couldn't get away."

"That's all right. Just come on over whenever you're ready."

"Unfortunately," his voice dropped, "I'm going to have to cancel on you."

Her heart panged with disappointment at his unexpected words. "Oh? What's going on?"

"It's a work thing that can't wait. I've had to cancel all my foreseeable plans until I get this issue taken care of."

"Oh." Her voice sagged. "I'm sorry to hear that."

"But I'll make it up to you," he told her. "I promise."

He had told her he might take her to his house in the Hamptons one day. Cecilia had dreamed about the moment when that actually took place. She'd love nothing more than a whole weekend with the man she loved.

As if reading her mind, he said, "Next weekend, I want to take you away. To my summer home on the water. How does that sound?"

She reminded herself not to sound too excited, to keep her cool. "I think I can make that work."

"Great." His voice warmed. "See if you can get off work, and I'll take you for the best weekend of your life."

"I'll see what I can do."

"Perfect. And again, I'm sorry about tonight."

"I forgive you."

She would have to save this red sweater for another date.

Now she had the whole evening to do something else. She wasn't sure what. Maybe she would watch some movies and eat popcorn.

It wouldn't be the same as going out with Garrick.

But at least she had next weekend to look forward to.

A grin spread across her face as she thought about it, and she let out a squeal.

CHAPTER
THIRTY-SEVEN

BENCHMARK SUNNY DAYS
RETREAT, DAY 5

TODAY'S EXCURSION was a kayaking trip down the river, followed by a hike through the jungle, ending at a waterfall with a swimming hole beneath it.

Maddie and Josh had already signed up to participate in the excursion before all the near-death experiences started happening. Maddie decided to go anyway, to not cower in fear. However, she would need to be careful.

Especially after someone had sent her that mugshot.

Seeing it had freaked her out. What if someone else saw it?

In order to ensure that didn't happen, she'd torn it into hundreds of small pieces. Then she'd flushed it down the toilet. She couldn't risk anyone seeing it in her room.

Josh had met her outside this morning and had

agreed they could both be civil enough to stick to their plans. Josh had tried to talk about more, but Maddie had shushed him. Now, a cool tension rippled between them.

At the river, they'd met their guide, Nightmarcher—but they could call him Nighty. The man, in his late thirties, was muscular but stout and stoically serious.

The trip up the river in the kayak had been quiet. Other people had been around them in their own kayaks, and Maddie made sure to stay close so Josh wouldn't force her into a tense conversation.

Her shoulder still hurt from her fall off the balcony. Paddling a kayak had been uncomfortable, to say the least.

Memories of her mugshot distracted her from her pain, however.

How had someone found out about her past? She'd done everything in her power to hide what had happened. She'd been desperate to conceal it.

That one event had changed everything about her life.

If people knew that aspect about her past, no one would ever want to hire her. To be associated with her. At least not people of reputable character.

Those reasons were why Maddie had worked so hard to become a different person.

Now everything was threatened.

Not even Josh knew her secret, and Maddie never intended on sharing it with him.

But it might be too late. Now someone here at this retreat knew the truth. They could tell Josh.

Maddie knew she should tell him before someone else did. But she couldn't bring herself to do it. She was too upset with him and the way he was treating her—as well as others—lately.

After kayaking, they hiked through jungle grasses and over large river rocks as they headed toward an unnamed "secret" waterfall. There were so many waterfalls on Kauai that she had to wonder if most of them had names or not.

The good news was that Adrienne and Brody as well as Bree and Fowler were on this trip. Their presence made the whole thing so much more bearable. None of them made her feel like she was being scrutinized or under a microscope. The instant bond she felt with them was refreshing, something she hadn't experienced in a long time.

Darla, Tom, and Nico were also on the excursion. Another group from the company had been scheduled to leave an hour later, so they'd most likely run into that crowd at some point also.

Maddie vowed to keep her distance from Brody from here forward. She was attracted to the man and had to put some space between them. Brody was with Adrienne. Maddie was officially with Josh.

Her feelings were inappropriate, yet every time she was around the man, her attraction seemed to grow. She'd always dreamed about marrying someone strong and protective yet laid-back. She'd given up thinking that person existed. And Josh had seemed like the total package at first. She'd been swept away. But now she realized he wasn't the person for her.

She glanced in front of her now at Adrienne and Brody as they hiked. She still remembered Adrienne's statement about Brody. About how he was like Danny.

Maddie wasn't sure why the thought bothered her so much. But it still did.

The two images didn't merge in her mind. Because of that, she didn't know exactly what to think.

She supposed whatever was happening between Adrienne and Brody wasn't any of her business. Every relationship had problems. The two people involved eventually had to figure out whether or not working through those problems and staying together was worth the effort—preferably before they tied the knot.

As far as Maddie and Josh . . . the two of them shouldn't be together. She'd known that for a while. But confirmations kept coming, validating her feelings on the matter.

Even though she'd promised Josh to wait until after the retreat to broach the subject of their future again, Maddie didn't know if that was possible. The tension between them kept growing at an alarming speed.

Maddie focused on the uneven path as their guide led them up to a seven-foot ledge. They used roots and rocks as leverage to climb up. Then they walked over more slippery rocks, through two more creeks, and finally reached a waterfall that plunged from a hundred twenty feet above.

She stood in awe as she watched the power of the cascading water.

Beside her, Adrienne squealed and pulled off her tank top, revealing a bikini beneath. "Who's ready to go for a swim?"

Before anyone could answer, Adrienne threw her shirt onto one of the large boulders and dove into the water, still wearing her jean shorts. Most of the rest of the group followed.

"Maddie, can we talk?"

She turned to see Josh beside her.

He wanted to talk? Now?

She swung her head back and forth before muttering, "I'm not ready."

Before Josh could try to change her mind, she hopped to another rock.

She looked up in time to see Brody climb from the water, his gaze on them. No doubt he'd noticed her cool interaction with Josh.

Maddie averted her gaze, determined not to care what Brody thought, determined not to become hyper-aware of the handsome man. The one who was off-limits. The one who was unlike anyone else she'd ever met.

Instead, she scanned everything around her, looking

for any signs of danger. She couldn't afford to let down her guard.

Nothing is going to happen here, Maddie reminded herself.

This was a waterfall swim. It was fairly safe, as long as people followed the rules. That was what Nighty had said.

Maddie prayed that was true as she stripped to her bathing suit and waded into the cool, refreshing water.

But based on everything that had happened so far on this retreat, trouble was following them. Why should it end now?

———

As the gang continued to hang out at the waterfall, some of the tension faded from Maddie. She sat on an oversized rock trying to dry off before the hike back.

Josh wasn't acting as stuck-up as usual. Maybe he actually felt bad about everything that had happened. Maybe he regretted letting Logan go into his room— though he still claimed the reason was legitimate.

Maddie had thought about it. If Josh wasn't in the room when Logan was there, then she supposed it was no harm, no foul. Yet she still felt irritated.

It was like the two of them were a little too comfortable with each other.

Really, however, it boiled down to the fact she didn't trust him.

At least the woman wasn't on the outing with them this time. Maddie was surprised she hadn't somehow arranged to be here also.

Maddie had tried to relax and let down her guard. Something about the waterfall pounding on her shoulders and head relaxed her.

After they'd enjoyed the swimming hole for about an hour, Nighty clapped to get the group's attention. "Five minutes until we head back! Start grabbing your things. If you need to go to the restroom, now is the time. Climb this ridge. If you can't see us, we most likely can't see you. Note I used the words *most likely*."

Everyone chuckled.

As they all dried off and put their clothes on, Fowler and Josh disappeared up the boulders to the "restrooms."

Adrienne stepped closer, still towel drying her hair. She lowered her voice as she asked, "You doing okay today?"

"I'm fine," Maddie insisted. "Thank you for asking."

The two of them hadn't had much time to talk one-on-one.

"It seems like this retreat might be the test of a lot of our relationships, huh?" Adrienne continued.

"Does that mean things aren't any better between you and Brody?" Maddie had noticed that the two of them hadn't been affectionate today. But they never were. Not really.

In fact, Adrienne and Brody really acted more like

friends than lovers. The couple of times Adrienne had touched Brody, he'd almost seemed to flinch.

The reaction seemed strange. But it wasn't any of Maddie's business, she reminded herself.

She glanced up at the rocks and saw Josh descending them, heading back toward the group.

Her stomach clenched at the sight of him. The two of them needed to have a serious talk tonight. This time, Josh wasn't going to change her mind.

"Okay, everybody!" Nighty clapped his hands as he stood on a boulder near the trail. "It's time to start back. Do we have everyone in our group?"

He began counting.

"Fowler's still not back!" Bree called from a few rocks away where she pulled on her shorts.

Maddie glanced up the side of the hill, toward the boulders where Fowler had disappeared five minutes ago. "Josh, did you see where he went?"

"No, I lost sight of him at the top." He shook his head as he scanned the ridge. "Figured we both wanted privacy."

"I'll go check on him," Brody offered before climbing the slick boulders and appearing as if he did this type of thing every day.

Maddie, on the other hand, had to watch her every step for fear of twisting her ankle. She'd never been much of an athlete, and this hike was proving that.

Brody, however, was one of those naturally agile types who made everything look easy.

They waited for Brody to return with Fowler. But a few seconds later, Brody popped out from behind a rock at the top of the incline.

Alone.

He cupped his hands over his mouth as he shouted to be heard over the waterfall. "I don't know where he went."

Bree's face went pale. "What do you mean?"

"He's not behind these boulders and trees. I even climbed a little higher to see if he'd found a more suitable place to do his business. He wasn't there either."

"That's weird." Bree squinted with confusion. "Where could he have gone?"

Maddie glanced at Nighty and saw his face tighten. Their guide clearly didn't like this update, and Maddie could see why. He was in charge of getting this whole group to and from their destinations safely.

"These mountains aren't anything to be messed with." Nighty sounded even more serious than earlier. "That's why I always tell people to stay on the trail."

No, he *definitely* didn't sound happy.

Brody climbed back down to the group, and after everyone started calling Fowler's name with no response, things got serious.

"Everybody stay here." Nighty sounded stern as he glanced at each of them. "I'm going to see if I can find him. Nobody else gets lost. Got it?"

They all murmured their acknowledgement.

Maddie exchanged a look with Adrienne and then Bree and then Brody.

They were all on the same wavelength.

Fowler didn't seem the type who'd simply go off on his own and not respond to their calls.

What if something had happened to him?

CHAPTER
THIRTY-EIGHT

I LOVE BEING in the thick of things.

Seeing my plans play out while everyone is clueless about the tragedies awaiting.

The trick to these things is being the smartest one in the room.

Or, in this case, the forest.

People underestimate me, but I'm really quite brilliant. I'm meant for great things. Soon, people will see. I won't be overlooked.

Worry grips everyone around me. I feel it in the air, and it's glorious.

What happened to Fowler? That's what they murmur to those around them.

And then there's the even bigger question . . . will they be next?

Even people who aren't involved in all of this are getting nervous.

I know I shouldn't, but a smile tries to curl my lips. I must keep the reaction under control. If someone saw me . . .

I sober. No one can know it's me.

If they find out, my plan will be ruined.

That won't be okay.

I've worked entirely too hard to get to this point only to fail.

No, in just a couple more days the fruit of my labor will pay off.

I actually *love* what I'm doing. I'm good at it. Part of me will be sad when it's over.

Wait—what? I catch myself.

Why would I think that?

I won't be sad.

Life will be even better when this is over.

For so many reasons. I glance at the waterfall and fight another smile. For so many reasons.

THIRTY-NINE

AN HOUR HAD PASSED.

An hour with no sign of Fowler.

Nighty tried to remain calm, but Maddie could see the distress in his gaze.

He'd already hiked to the top of another ridge to make an emergency call. Meanwhile, he left a different guide with them to ensure he didn't lose anyone else.

A nervous whisper traveled through the group. Even Josh appeared apprehensive as his eyes darted around and he ran his hands through his hair.

Where could Fowler have gone? It didn't make any sense to Maddie. The guy was level-headed and cautious. He was one of the only people in the group who'd brought a walking stick with him on the hike, and Bree had said he liked to always be prepared.

He wasn't a risk-taker.

"It's not like him to just leave." Bree sounded frail,

on the verge of panic as she stared up at the area where she'd last seen him. "He has no reason to do that. He loves his job. He loves *me*."

"You're right." Brody's jaw tightened. "It doesn't make any sense, but maybe there's a logical explanation. Let's just give it some time."

"If he got into an accident of some sort, you would have seen him, right?" Maddie studied Brody, temporarily forgetting her vow not to talk to him. Finding Fowler was more important.

Brody nodded slowly as if thinking through her question. "I would think so. It's not like there's a steep cliff on the other side where he could have fallen. I would have seen him."

"So what could have happened?" Adrienne's voice lilted higher with confusion, and she wrapped her striped, teal towel around her shoulders, pulling it tight. "This doesn't make any sense."

"Let's wait to hear what Nighty says," Brody told them. "He knows this landscape much better than I do."

Brody was right. They shouldn't jump to any conclusions. The best thing was to be patient.

Maybe if Fowler had wandered off, he would find his way back soon.

Ten minutes later, Nighty appeared on top of the ridge, a pensive look still on his face.

That probably meant he didn't have good news. Her throat tightened with apprehension.

She squeezed Bree's hand, sensing her friend's anxiety.

Nighty came closer before announcing, "I'm sorry, but I didn't see him."

A cry of despair escaped from Bree.

Maddie and Adrienne wrapped their arms around her.

"I know that's not what anyone wants to hear—including me," Nighty continued, appearing like the antithesis of his name. "But we have a great search and rescue team here on the island. They'll find him. They're already on their way."

"What do we do now?" Josh asked. He'd been strangely quiet.

Had he had time to do something to Fowler when they both were up there?

Her heart thudded into her chest at the thought.

She didn't think so, but she couldn't totally rule out the possibility either.

"I need everyone to head back to the dock," Nighty said. "The best thing we can do is to get you all somewhere safe and out of the way. It's supposed to rain soon, and sometimes that can make the creek crossings more treacherous. We need to go now."

"But what about my boyfriend?" Tears rolled down Bree's cheeks. "We can't just leave him out here."

"We're going to do everything we can to find him," Nighty assured her. "Search and rescue is sending up a helicopter to have a better view of the area."

"Where could he be?" Josh stepped closer. "He couldn't have just disappeared. There aren't any roads out here. Only mountains, right?"

Based on the tension stretched across their guide's face, Nighty had at least one idea of what could have gone wrong.

"This probably isn't what happened," Nighty said. "But if your friend wandered another twelve feet up that rocky path, there *is* a sinkhole. If he accidentally fell through it, the cavern would have spit him out down at the base of the mountain, near another waterfall. But . . ."

"But what?" Bree's voice cracked with tension.

"It's extremely treacherous." Nighty rubbed his jaw as if he were carefully considering what to say. "We can't send people down there unless we know for sure that's where he is. It's too risky."

"I'll go check then. I need to see if he's there." Bree started to rush forward, but Maddie and Adrienne grabbed her arms to hold her back.

The woman was stronger than Maddie assumed, and she had to lock her legs to keep Bree from doing anything stupid.

"I know you want to do everything you can to help him." Nighty held a hand up to stop Bree from going farther. "But the best thing we can do is to leave this to the professionals."

"Then I'll wait here in case he comes back." Bree's voice quivered.

"Then what if something happens to you?" Nighty sounded dead serious. "We don't want another mishap to slow us down and hinder our efforts to find Fowler. Understand?"

Bree slowly nodded as his words seemed to settle on her. If she did something stupid, then it would take even more time to locate Fowler.

The grim reality seemed to set in with the entire group.

"Good. Everyone start back to the kayaks." Nighty pointed to the trail. "Please, be careful and stay together. No more surprises, okay?"

Maddie's own thoughts echoed his.

The trip of a lifetime had turned out to be a total nightmare . . . for more than one person. And it was a nightmare she'd yet to wake up from . . . which could mean there was more to come.

Everyone was notably more somber as they headed back toward the dock.

Especially Bree.

Brody had let her and Adrienne ride in his kayak. He'd towed Bree's now-empty kayak behind them.

Maddie couldn't stop thinking about what Bree must be going through. She wished she could do something to help. But there was nothing she could do but pray, which was definitely important. She kept reminding herself of that fact.

Josh was quiet as they paddled, other than yelling out paddling instructions to Maddie on occasion.

When everyone got back to the dock, they pulled the kayaks ashore and stashed their lifejackets and dry bags.

Two police officers waited for Bree, along with the owner of the tour company.

Bree insisted she could talk to them by herself.

Maddie waited for a signal as to what to do next. She thought Josh might try to talk to her again as they stood there. Instead, he talked to one of his colleagues near the water.

She did a double take as she glanced over at him.

The conversation appeared serious—Josh's eyes were dark and his motions tense.

Based on the dirty look Josh threw Maddie over his shoulder, their talk wasn't about Fowler. Was the conversation about *her*?

A few minutes later, Josh walked away from the group. His gaze still looked dark—almost angry.

He didn't join her. Instead, he took another phone call.

"I feel so bad for Bree." Adrienne appeared beside her, pulling Maddie from her thoughts.

"Me too." She glanced at Bree again. She was still talking to the police.

"What a nightmare, right?"

"It almost seems like an understatement at this point."

"You can say that again."

Their bus pulled up, and they all boarded. She sat beside Josh out of obligation.

Neither of them spoke. She wanted to talk, to ask him what was wrong.

But the bus didn't seem like the right place.

Maddie couldn't stop thinking about Fowler. Couldn't stop imagining what might have happened to him. He didn't seem like the type to just go off exploring on his own.

Which meant something had happened.

But was it something accidental? Or had someone done something to Fowler in an effort to sabotage this retreat?

Unease jostled in her gut.

If Maddie could jump on a plane right now and head home, she would.

It seemed like bad luck lurked around every corner here, simply waiting to pounce.

One of these times, she might not be lucky enough to survive.

BACK AT THE RESORT, Maddie paused in the lobby. Adrienne and Brody remained beside her.

Josh had stayed outside, talking to more retreat members.

It felt so anticlimactic to go back to her room. How was Bree? Had search and rescue found Fowler? It was probably too soon.

But Maddie definitely felt on edge.

As someone walked in, her gaze swerved toward the door. Was it Bree?

Her breath caught when she saw that it was Josh . . . with Logan. The two of them laughed together, almost as if nothing had happened. In fact, they looked awfully happy to be together.

Maybe too happy.

"I'm sorry," Adrienne said quietly.

Maddie turned to her friend and squinted in confusion. "Sorry about what?"

"About Josh."

Caution rippled through her chest. "What about him?"

Adrienne's eyes widened with alarm, almost as if she'd said something she hadn't intended. "Oh, it's nothing . . ."

Maddie wasn't going to let that comment drop. "Adrienne . . . what are you talking about? Don't say nothing."

She frowned and glanced at Josh again as he leaned close to talk to Logan. "It's just that . . ."

"Just say it. I'm a big girl. I can handle it."

Adrienne pressed her lips together before whispering, "Josh has a wandering eye. He . . . he likes beautiful women. The more variety, the better."

"What?" Maddie's voice rose, and she reminded herself to stay calm.

"I'm sorry." Adrienne looked away and ran a hand over her face. "I shouldn't have said anything. Yet another part of me thought you should know . . . I even wondered if you *did* know and maybe you were okay with it. But then I just saw the look in your eyes . . ."

"I need to know. Tell me more." Her voice hardened.

"It's just . . ." Adrienne's gaze drifted to Josh again, and she frowned again. "It's pretty well known around the office that he likes women—a lot. Since you're not at the Benchmark building, I guess you haven't seen the women parading in and out of his office."

"No, I haven't." Part of her wasn't surprised. And another part had hoped for the best, had hoped that he was a man of character. Maybe deep inside, she'd known for a while that he wasn't. She'd just been in denial. "So Josh and Logan? It hasn't just been my imagination?"

Adrienne didn't say anything. She only shook her head.

Maddie's throat tightened.

Josh must think that she was a fool. Maybe she was.

But not anymore.

The two of them were going to have a long talk.

Bree arrived back at the resort. Paramedics had given her some medication to keep her calm. It worked, but apparently, it also made her drowsy.

Adrienne offered to go back to Bree's room and sit with her, stating she shouldn't be alone right now.

Maddie agreed.

Part of Maddie wished she could go with Bree also. But she needed to talk to Josh, who'd disappeared several minutes ago without so much as a word.

She didn't need to talk to Josh *only* about Logan and his unfaithful escapades. He'd been acting strange ever since that conversation he'd had with his colleagues on the dock after kayaking.

She wanted to know why. No more tiptoeing around the truth or assuming the best or making excuses. Those things had been going on for entirely too long.

The two of them needed to get everything out in the open.

Maddie walked down the hallway to her suite. Despite the anger simmering through her, caution continued to nudge her. She couldn't afford to let her distress distract her from the danger haunting her. Letting down her guard could be a death wish.

What if one of the women Josh had messed around with was behind these dangerous incidents that had been happening? It made sense.

Who else was there besides Logan and Darla?

There were plenty of beautiful women working for Benchmark—and plenty who'd want to be with Josh because of his position at the company, because of his money, because of his looks.

Just as Maddie had once thought, other women would also think he was the total package.

He wasn't.

Maddie glanced around as she walked, but she didn't see anyone lurking in the shadows or watching her. She continued to scan her surroundings as she hurried down the hall.

Several minutes later, she paused outside Josh's

suite. She drew in a deep breath and lifted a prayer before knocking.

Not even two seconds later, he pulled the door open. His eyes were still hard and angry as he stared at her.

He was angry? Why did he have a reason to be upset with her?

Keep control of your emotions. Stay level-headed.

She licked her lips before asking, "Can we talk?"

Josh only opened the door wider and walked away, leaving her to interpret his body language.

After a moment of hesitation, Maddie drew in a deep breath and stepped inside. She quietly closed the door behind her and followed Josh into the living room. But she didn't bother to sit down once she got there. Instead, she crossed her arms and turned to face him.

She was about to confront him when he started.

"You're a suspect in Jared's death?" It wasn't as much of a question as it was an accusation.

The blood drained from her face. Maddie had considered telling him before he found out another way. But she'd decided not to.

Was it a mistake? Maddie still wasn't sure.

"I haven't been officially charged with anything." But now that Maddie mentioned it, she hadn't seen Kalani today.

That was a new record since the detective had been stopping by nearly every day. She fully expected him to announce her guilt on any one of those visits.

"Why didn't you tell me?" Accusation shot like fire from Josh's gaze.

Like he had any right to be upset with her after what he'd done.

But she would let this play out another moment before she confronted him.

She wanted to hear what he had to say.

Then Maddie would give Josh an earful of her own.

MADDIE'S VOICE was calm and even as she said, "I didn't say anything because it didn't seem important and because you seemed to have other things on your mind. I didn't want to add more stress."

"You should have told me, Madison." Josh's nostrils flared. "Do you have any idea how embarrassing it was for me to find out from my subordinates?"

"I didn't realize anyone else even knew." The words were true. To her knowledge, the only other people who knew were Adrienne and Brody. Bree and Fowler had already left that night when Kalani spoke with Maddie for the first time.

"You had to know news like this would spread like wildfire!" His voice rose with every word.

"I didn't do anything to Jared. You know that."

"It doesn't matter what *I* know." Josh narrowed his eyes. "What matters is what *other people think*." He jammed his index finger into the air to emphasize his last three words.

Maddie had been trying to remain calm. But all that resolve seemed to disappear like a rainbow as storm clouds rolled in. "I thought the most important thing for you would be me, not your reputation and how this would make you look. I was only trying to watch out for you when I didn't tell you."

"I've told you everything that's involved here!" He stared at her, his eyes burning holes through her. "It's almost like you *want* to ruin this retreat."

Her mouth dropped open. "*I* want to ruin your retreat? Why would I want to do that? I didn't even want to be here, but *you* talked me into coming. All so it would look good for you and increase your prospects for becoming CEO."

"When you tried to break things off with me, I explained I was going through a rough patch. I thought you understood and cared about me enough to give us another chance. I guess I was wrong."

"And I thought you cared about me enough to remain faithful. But I guess I was wrong."

Josh froze. Then, at once, the dam broke.

"What?" His hands flew in the air. "What does that even mean?"

He wasn't going to change her mind that easily. Maddie could spot gaslighting a mile away.

"It means I know about all your extra little rendezvous," she told him. "I'm not stupid!"

Josh went still and stared at her, unblinking. "I don't know what you're talking about."

"Stop lying. Let me start with you and Logan."

His eyes turned colder. "What about her?"

Maddie crossed her arms. "Don't play stupid. Everyone knows about the two of you, and you aren't even keeping your feelings a secret. I thought you were smarter than that. Or did you think I wouldn't notice?"

"What did you expect me to do?" He hurled the words at her. "You became so cold and distant. Don't you realize how important sex is to a man?"

Anger coursed through her veins. "Don't you realize how important it is to a woman that you respect her boundaries? That you remain faithful?"

They stared at each other several minutes, reams of unspoken conversations pulling taut between them.

Finally, Maddie shook her head and took a step back. "You know what? I'm done. I've *been* done. I'm tired of pretending we're going to be something we're not. The two of us started off strong, and I thought we had a lot of potential. But as we've tried to navigate life together it's become clear we're too different. We want different things in life. I'm so thankful I realized this before we tied the knot and made it official."

Josh closed his eyes, and his head dipped forward as if he'd suddenly sobered. "Madison . . . you don't mean that. We can make this right."

"It's too late to make things right." Her voice didn't leave any room for argument. "Goodbye, Josh."

Before he could stop her, Maddie stormed toward the door and slammed it shut as she left.

———

Maddie thought when she got back to her room that she might feel bad. Burdened. Sad.

Instead, she felt lighter than she had in months.

She should have stuck to her guns and called things off with Josh when she initially realized they weren't meant to be a couple. Staying together simply because he'd asked had been a major mistake.

Maddie had known it. She couldn't deny she had.

But at least she'd done the right thing now.

She dropped onto the edge of her bed and looked at the beautiful two carat diamond ring on her hand. She'd been so excited the day Josh had proposed in Central Park in a horse-drawn carriage. She hadn't had a single doubt in her mind when she said yes.

Thankfully, the two of them hadn't rushed to the altar. That would have been a huge mistake. Because so much had changed since then. Or perhaps more accurately, so much had *been revealed* since then.

Maddie took the ring off and set it on her nightstand.

If she'd been thinking things through clearly, she would have given the ring back while she was in Josh's room. However, she had no desire to go back there now and face him. She'd give him the ring later, after they'd both calmed down.

As she sat there, a door closed next door.

Josh's door. Was he leaving?

She held her breath, praying he didn't come to her room to try to talk again.

Preemptively, she rushed to her door and pressed her face into the peep hole.

Instead of coming to her room, Josh stomped down the hall, probably heading out to get a drink.

She squinted in surprise.

Maybe he wasn't as broken up over their split as she thought.

That was good. The realization didn't bother her. It was simply unexpected. But he should move on.

At least he wasn't trying to have another conversation with her.

As she took a step back, her gaze skimmed the floor and she gasped.

A folded piece of paper waited there.

She blinked. How had she missed that when she'd walked in earlier? She supposed she'd been too distracted by her breakup. And the paper was close to the wall, so when she'd stepped inside, the note most likely was obscured by the door.

Maddie's hands shook as she reached down to pick it up.

She opened it. It was another picture.

But this time, it wasn't a photo of Maddie from many years ago.

No, it was a photo of Josh. With Logan. Based on the surroundings, it had been taken here at the retreat.

The two were caught up in a lip-lock.

Want to know 10 THINGS I HATE ABOUT JOSH? Here's one of many.

Someone wanted her to know about Josh's affairs. Someone didn't know she already knew and wanted to make sure the truth got out there.

Just what was the sender of these notes trying to accomplish? Mental distress? Emotional?

Or was this person's ultimate goal total destruction?

THE WEEKEND at Garrick's house in the Hamptons had been even better than Cecilia had imagined.

His home was fantastic. The place was sprawling, with cedar siding and dormers. It was located on the Long Island Sound and had a sparkling pool and inviting hot tub nestled between intricately landscaped shrubs and trees.

This summer house was the very picture of the kind of luxury Cecilia had only dreamed about.

Garrick had been such a gentleman the entire time they were together. He'd even given her a gold necklace with a ruby pendant to make up for canceling on her last week.

The jewelry was gorgeous and something she'd always treasure.

Plus, the necklace would remind her of this weekend.

Cecilia didn't make it a habit to go home with guys. But she was so glad she'd gone home with Garrick. The whole weekend had been absolutely perfect.

So when one thing had led to another, she hadn't resisted the way their relationship had progressed.

Cecilia knew deep in her heart that she and Garrick would be together forever.

That was why she'd said yes when Garrick had invited her into his bedroom. She wished she could say that part of the night was everything she'd dreamed about.

But it wasn't. It was . . . rushed, she supposed.

Still, they had time to figure everything out. She envisioned many more opportunities.

But right now, she was back at work straightening racks of clothing and dealing with persnickety customers at Balderston's.

She glanced up as one of them walked her way.

Her breath caught as she recognized the man.

It was one of Garrick's friends, one she'd met at the fundraiser. What was his name again? John, she thought. But she didn't feel confident.

He barely looked at her as he approached. "I need a new suit for a dinner I'm going to. Can you help?"

"Of course." She ran a hand down her dress, hoping she looked presentable. Certainly as soon as the man looked up, he would recognize her and say hello.

But even as she grabbed several things for him to try on, he didn't seem to remember her.

The realization caused a lump to form in her throat.

Was she that forgettable? Or was it the fact that maybe he hadn't expected a woman who was dating Garrick to work a job in retail?

An hour later, he'd found his new suit, and she rang him up.

Cecilia wondered if she should bring up the fact they'd met before. What could it hurt?

She swallowed hard as she scanned another tag. "I met you at the fundraiser a while back."

He studied her, still nothing in his gaze. "Is that right?"

"I was there with Garrick."

Something flashed in his eyes, and then a tight smile stretched across his face. "That's right. I thought you looked familiar. I didn't realize you worked here."

"I've been here a couple of years now."

He observed her another moment, a strange look in his gaze. "I guess this is your side hustle?"

"My side hustle?" What did he mean by that?

Surprise fluttered through his gaze, and he shook his head. "Never mind."

"No, I want to know."

He stared at her again, an unreadable look in his gaze. "What's the total?"

He was going to totally blow off her question?

Her jaw tightened. She wanted to demand that he answer.

But that would only cause a scene. And a scene might get her fired.

He wasn't going to answer that question.

Cecilia rattled off the amount he owed, trying to remain professional.

After he paid, he looked at her another moment.

Then he winked.

Winked?

What was that about?

Their whole interaction left her feeling unsettled . . . and as if she was in the dark about something.

FORTY-THREE
NOW

MADDIE WAS TOO restless to stay in her room.

Though she didn't want to run into Josh, she needed to get some fresh air.

There was no better place to do that than the beach. She knew Josh would most likely be hanging out in the bar. He'd never been much of a beachgoer.

She kept her eyes open as she walked, trying to avoid anyone who might ask questions. To her surprise, she successfully reached the beach without interruption.

As her feet hit the sand, she noted that the sun was already beginning to sink in the sky. What a long day. A long, horrific day.

Yet, in some ways, it had been a wonderful day.

Her life would look different without Josh in it. But it would look different in a better way. She felt confident about that fact.

Maybe she would resign from the nonprofit. Though

she was doing good work there, she preferred to be hands-on. Maybe she could get her old job with the government back. In fact, maybe she would call her old boss tomorrow. She didn't want to be impulsive, but she suddenly felt invigorated.

She pulled her flip-flops off, linking her finger through the toe straps as she began to walk down the shore, watching the waves crash.

Memories of seeing Jared here filled her thoughts.

It had been a horrible start to a horrible week.

Maddie still wasn't even sure what had happened to the man or if someone had truly murdered him.

Were all the incidents that had happened during the retreat connected? Was someone trying to kill Josh so he wouldn't become CEO? Would one of his colleagues take it that far?

Or did someone have other motives for wanting to silence either her or Josh? Maddie wasn't sure what those motives might be, but certainly there had to be a reason all this was happening.

"I wasn't expecting to see you out here," a deep voice said beside her.

She paused, the wind whipping through her hair as she turned.

Brody strode toward her.

Handsome, alluring Brody with his Matthew McConaughey vibes.

Against her wishes, her pulse quickened. She needed

to put a kibosh on her feelings. But as much as she willed her heart to calm down, it didn't.

She swallowed the lump in her throat before saying, "I just needed some fresh air."

"You and me both." He fell into step beside her, his hands casually tucked into the pockets of his shorts. "Do you mind if I join you? Or did you want some time alone?"

She had wanted some time alone . . . until she ran into Brody.

"I'd love some company," she murmured.

Unfortunately, she liked the idea of Brody walking with her more than she should. The realization brought another surge of guilt.

She had no right to feel that way.

She'd vowed to stay away from him. Yet here she was, ignoring her resolve—just like she'd ignored her resolve to initially break up with Josh. Look where that had gotten her—into mounds of trouble and heartache.

She couldn't repeat those mistakes. So how was Maddie going to protect herself now?

"This has been quite the retreat, hasn't it?" Brody asked.

The conversation seemed safe enough. She'd started to tell him about the threats against her earlier, but they'd been cut off. Maybe that was a good thing— though part of her would love his perspective and advice.

Instead of talking about that, she let out a wary breath. "You can say that again."

"Any updates on Fowler?"

Brody was probably assuming Josh would have heard something and told her.

She shook her head. "Not yet. I'm sure Adrienne told you that Bree is still resting."

"She mentioned that. I hope he's okay."

"You and me both."

Maddie and Brody walked several minutes in silence. But it was nice silence. Comfortable silence.

Then Brody blurted, "You're not wearing your ring."

———

Maddie's eyes widened as she glanced at her hand. She hadn't thought anyone would notice. But she shouldn't be surprised.

She started to skirt around the truth about the situation but changed her mind. Covering up what had happened would only lead to more headaches, more lies. She was so tired of the pretention.

"We broke up," she announced. "The two of us weren't well suited for each other, and I tried to break things off with him about a month ago. But Josh asked me to reconsider and think about it a while longer—specifically until this retreat was over. He seems to think having a fiancée makes him look more stable, which gives people more confidence in him as the future CEO."

Brody made a face, making it clear he didn't approve of that line of reasoning.

"I'm sorry," he finally muttered.

"Don't be. I feel lighter than I have in a long time. Josh isn't the person I fell in love with. In fact, the person I fell in love with may not have been real at all."

They walked a few more steps in silence.

"You never said how the two of you met," Brody finally said.

Memories of those days flooded back to her. "It was actually back when I was investigating elder abuse. Josh's father had filed a claim against the assisted living home where his mother—Josh's grandmother—was living. I was called to investigate."

"That sounds unfortunate."

"It was. One of the aides at the facility was being rough with the patients. Honestly, it broke my heart when I saw it. And, of course, as you well know, investigations are rarely fast. So as I was working on securing all the evidence I needed, Josh came to make a statement about what he'd witnessed. We started talking, and that was that."

"I see," Brody muttered. "Well, it's like you said. I suppose it's better that you discover this now rather than later."

"Yes, it is."

"Are you going to stick around now that the two of you have broken up?" he asked.

"That's a good question, one I'm still trying to figure out." She didn't mention what the detective had told her, how he'd warned her to stay.

As they walked a few more steps in silence, Maddie's thoughts drifted to Brody and Adrienne. She remembered what Adrienne had told her yesterday about how Brody wasn't who he seemed to be.

Maddie couldn't get that thought out of her head, mostly because it bothered her. That information, the two different sides of him, didn't gel in her head—and she usually considered herself a good judge of character.

She wanted to know more—and she needed to find out information that would only drive home the fact that Brody was a taken man.

"So, how long have you and Adrienne been together?" she finally asked.

Brody's eyes widened as if the question surprised him. "Me and Adrienne? Oh, we're not together."

Maddie halted and stared at him in confusion. "What do you mean?"

Had they just broken up also?

Brody twisted his neck as if confused as he observed her. "You mean, Adrienne didn't tell you?"

"Tell me what?"

"The two of us broke up . . . over a year ago."

FORTY-FOUR

MADDIE BLINKED, certain she hadn't heard Brody correctly. "I'm *so* confused. What do you mean you and Adrienne broke up a year ago? You mean, you broke up but got back together before this retreat?"

Brody shook his head, a wrinkle of confusion between his eyes. "No, we're not together. I thought Adrienne told you about that."

Maddie searched her thoughts, replaying her past conversations with Adrienne. But she didn't recall her friend saying anything of that sort.

"Maybe she was too embarrassed," Brody finally said, uncertainty in his voice. "I'm not really sure."

"If you're not together then why are you here at the retreat with her?" Maddie tried to put together the pieces until they made sense. But his words had been the last thing she expected.

Brody let out a breath and stared out over the water.

"Adrienne's ex has been stalking her. She's been terri-fied—terrified enough that she thought he might follow her here to Kauai."

"She did tell me she thought she'd seen him a few times."

"She told me that too," Brody said. "And I don't doubt what she's telling us, though I haven't seen Danny myself. She's terrified of the man, afraid he might retaliate."

Maddie blinked, her head still spinning. "So let me get this straight. You came here with Adrienne so her ex would think that you were together and leave her alone?"

"No, I came here because Adrienne asked me to be her bodyguard. But she didn't want it to be obvious because that might make her seem weak. For that reason, we weren't going around telling people any details."

"Aren't you staying in the same room?"

"In two separate beds, of course." He shrugged as if it weren't a big deal.

Maddie tried to reconcile what he was telling her with the assumptions she'd made. They weren't a couple? This whole time she'd thought they were. But that would explain why they weren't particularly affec-tionate with each other, she supposed.

"I can't believe you guys aren't together."

"It's like I said, I thought you knew," Brody said. "I wasn't going to go around advertising our status. It isn't ideal coming on a trip like this with your ex. But she needed me. Besides, I owed her one."

"You owed her one?" Maddie knew she probably shouldn't ask the question, but she was curious. There was so much more to this story than she'd ever guessed.

He stared out over the water again, appearing as if his mind drifted back in time. "She was there for me after a really hard time in my life. I figured coming here to help her out was the least I could do—plus, I love Hawaii. She promised there were no strings attached."

For some reason, that update brought Maddie a small measure of delight.

It shouldn't.

Because Adrienne clearly still had feelings for Brody, and Adrienne was Maddie's friend.

That meant that even though Brody was single, he was off-limits. Besides, Maddie wasn't looking to jump into another relationship.

This conversation still didn't explain why Adrienne had said Brody and Danny were a lot alike. Maybe it was because Adrienne and Brody had some tough talks about not dating or being together maybe. Maddie couldn't be sure.

But she certainly hadn't been expecting that news . . . nor was she sure what to do with it.

———

Maddie felt like she could stay out here all night with Brody. She wanted nothing more than to watch the sunset or look for sea turtles resting on the shore.

But doing those things together wasn't appropriate.

Even if Adrienne and Brody weren't dating . . . and if Maddie and Josh had broken up . . . the thought of admitting or acting on her feelings to Brody still had the ick factor.

Maddie paused as she and Brody approached a jetty going into the water. They'd reached the end of the beach and had gone as far as they could walk.

This was where they had to turn around and go back. But part of her didn't want this to ever end. Talking to Brody had been a nice break from the headache of everything else that had happened. It had been refreshing.

But good things had to come to an end. She had to use her head right now instead of her heart.

She offered a soft smile as she glanced up at Brody. "I've enjoyed talking with you."

He smiled down at her also. "You too. I'm glad we had the chance to talk one-on-one."

They stared at each other a moment, something unspoken passing between them.

Brody felt the same way Maddie did, didn't he? Yet he also seemed to share the sentiment that they needed to keep their distance—like any reputable man might.

Maddie quickly broke eye contact, realizing she needed to get this man out of her mind and stop toying with the idea of exploring a relationship with him.

She started to say they should probably head back when a familiar figure on the beach caught her eye.

Logan.

The woman walked down the shore alone. By all appearances, she hadn't realized Maddie was in front of her.

When Logan looked up and the two locked gazes, surprise washed over the woman's face.

She froze, almost looking as if she wanted to turn and run.

But Maddie wasn't going to let her do that.

"Excuse me a moment," she muttered to Brody.

She called Logan's name and jogged closer. She hadn't planned to confront the woman. Maddie mostly blamed what had happened on Josh. But she wasn't going to tuck her tail between her legs and act like a victim either.

Logan's gaze turned cool as Maddie got closer. "I didn't expect to see you out here."

"I'm sure you didn't." Maddie paused in front of her, her hands going on her hips. "I know about you and Josh."

"It took you long enough to realize." Her eyebrows flickered with smugness.

The woman's absolute lack of remorse felt like a slap in the face. How could she be so heartless and calloused —not to mention have such a lack of a moral compass?

"It doesn't matter anymore," Maddie told her. "He's all yours now."

Logan's eyes widened. She clearly hadn't heard that Josh and Maddie had broken up. Had *really* broken up. It was anyone's guess what Josh had told Logan about the status of their relationship.

Logan's surprise disappeared and the smugness returned. "I knew the two of you were never right for each other. You can't give him what he wants."

Maddie's lips parted as anger burned through her veins. She didn't even care that Brody had caught up and was listening to everything. She couldn't cower to this woman's words.

"You know what?" Maddie said. "As far as I'm concerned, Josh can be your problem now."

Logan shrugged. "He always made it abundantly clear that he was much happier with me anyway."

Maddie tried not to show any surprise. Not necessarily because of what Logan said. But because of the woman's vindictive attitude.

"I'll let you continue your walk." Maddie kept her voice cool and controlled. "I just wanted to clear the air."

As Maddie took a step away, Brody joining her, Logan threw out one last barb. "I know it was you on the beach that morning, that you were the one arguing with Jared."

The words stopped her cold, and Maddie slowly

turned back toward the woman. "You're the witness that Detective Kalani mentioned?"

Logan smirked. "That's right. I saw it all, and I wasn't afraid to let the detective know it was you."

"That's impossible," Maddie told her. "You didn't see me out there with him. I wasn't the one arguing with him on the beach. The first time I saw him was in the water."

"That's not what I saw." Logan shrugged as if her mind was made up.

Maddie shook her head. "That's conjecture."

Logan smirked again, making it clear she didn't give any credence to Maddie's words.

The woman didn't care about the truth.

She only cared about getting what she wanted.

Brody put his hand on Maddie's elbow and pulled her away from Logan right in the nick of time—right before she said something she might regret.

"Let's get back," he murmured.

Maddie threw one last dirty look at Logan before walking away.

"DON'T LET her get to you," Brody said as he continued to lead Maddie down the beach, away from Logan.

"I can't believe she said that," Maddie muttered, resisting the urge to steal a glance behind her shoulder at Logan again—and to gawk at her audacity. "I wasn't out there with Jared. But if Logan told the detective that . . ."

"A shark is a shark. She's the kind of woman who will do whatever it takes to get what she wants. I would just ignore her."

Maddie wished it was that easy. "But it's my word against hers."

"The truth will win," Brody assured her. "It has to."

Maddie wanted to believe him. But she was having a hard time doing that. She'd seen plenty of people lose entirely too much because of lies.

She remembered the mugshot someone had sent her.

Could Logan be behind that too?

It was hard to say.

But someone knew about her past. If this person chose to release that information . . . it would look bad for Maddie.

Individuals like those at this retreat didn't accept people with a criminal history—unless maybe they'd been found guilty of a white-collar offense.

But Maddie . . . she'd gone to prison for a horrible crime.

She'd paid her time.

Then she'd worked hard to prove she was a good person.

It was just one more reason why she'd continued to try to turn her life around after the car accident.

For the longest time, she hadn't been able to forgive herself for her past. But the thought that maybe God could forgive her . . . that had changed the way she looked at life. She'd felt hope for the first time in years.

But had God really forgiven her?

Because after she had been found guilty of murder, her whole life had been turned upside down.

———

As soon as they reached the resort, Maddie's phone buzzed and pulled her from her thoughts.

It was Detective Kalani.

She excused herself and took a few steps away from Brody. "Hello?"

"Ms. Waters . . . aloha. I'm here at the hotel, and I was wondering if we could speak."

A lump formed in her throat. "Of course."

"I'm in Bree's room. Would you mind coming here to meet?"

"Not at all. I'll head there now."

"Mahalo."

As Maddie ended the call, she tried to maintain her composure. She couldn't panic.

Did Kalani think Maddie had done something to Fowler also? She hadn't been anywhere near the top of that ridge when he'd disappeared. She had witnesses to prove it this time.

Her paranoia was starting to get the best of her, she realized.

Maybe Logan's words had affected her more than she'd thought.

Maddie had to stay in control. She knew she was innocent. Feeling guilty over things she hadn't done would only make her look guilty.

Brody touched her elbow as he stared down at her. "Everything okay?"

"It was the detective." She slid the phone back into her pocket. "He's talking to Bree and asked if I could join them."

His eyebrows knit together. "Why would he want you to join him in regard to Fowler?"

"I don't have any idea." Maddie held back a frown. "I guess I'm going to find out."

"I'll walk back with you."

Part of Maddie felt like she should refuse. But she didn't. She couldn't.

Her legs felt like Jello, and she wasn't sure she'd be able to make it up to Bree's room by herself.

She cut through the pool area, keeping her eyes on the paved pathway. She didn't want to know if anyone was watching. Didn't want anyone to look her in the eye and see how unnerved she was.

All she could think about was Kalani and whatever this upcoming conversation would hold.

Finally, they reached Bree's room. As they did, Brody took a step back as if about to leave.

It *would* look funny if the two of them walked in together.

But before he could say goodbye, the door opened.

Adrienne stood there. Her gaze flickered from Maddie to Brody. Questions pooled there, but in a blink they disappeared.

"I wasn't expecting to see both of you," she muttered. "Come in. Brody . . . I'm not sure if the detective will want you in here or not. But I'm fine with you staying if everyone else is."

Brody exchanged a quick look with Maddie, then the two of them slipped inside the room—one considerably smaller than Maddie's suite. Two queen-size beds, two conversation chairs against the wall, and a table in the corner stared back at her.

The detective stood near the patio doors observing everyone, and Bree sat in a chair near one of the beds.

The woman's eyes were red and bloodshot, and her hands trembled. Maybe some of the medication she'd been given was wearing off.

Or maybe she'd gotten bad news.

Maddie didn't want to think that might be true, but it was a possibility.

"You wanted to see me?" Maddie's gaze stopped on the detective.

"That's right." He nodded, his voice absent of any emotion. "Why don't you have a seat?"

"What's going on?" She still felt confused about why she was called here. She slowly lowered herself onto the edge of the bed.

Adrienne and Brody remained in the background, but the detective didn't ask them to leave.

"Is this about Fowler?" Maddie rubbed her hands against her jean shorts when she realized they were sweaty.

"We still haven't found him." Kalani sounded professional and stiff—and all business, as usual.

Maddie reached toward Bree and squeezed her hand. "I'm so sorry, honey."

"Maddie . . . the police don't think something bad happened to him." Bree's voice trembled. "They think he walked away . . . on purpose."

"What?" Maddie's head spun with the thought.

Why in the world would Fowler leave on purpose? And why had Kalani asked Maddie to come here? What did any of this have to do with her?

The questions swirled in her head as a pounding began at her temples.

MADDIE LOOKED from Bree to Detective Kalani to Adrienne then Brody.

Then she glanced back at Kalani. He was the only one who could answer her questions. "What are you talking about? People think Fowler walked off on his own? Why would he do that?"

Silence stretched through the air. Not just any silence.

Awkward silence.

"I wanted to talk to you before I talked to your fiancé," Detective Kalani started.

Maddie touched her empty ring finger, but this didn't seem like the right time to bring up the fact they'd broken up.

"I'm still unclear why you want to talk to me," she said instead. "Or Josh."

"Because a couple of hours ago, we examined Fowler's laptop."

"Because you think he left on his own and that there could be evidence in his files?" Maddie clarified, still not sure she was following.

"Perhaps," Kalani said. "But we found something far different."

Maddie didn't like where this was going. Didn't like the fact she'd been pulled into it either. "Okay . . ."

"We found hidden emails." Kalani shifted in front of the patio doors, his perceptive gaze still on her. "Emails that indicated Fowler was trying to sell company secrets to the highest bidder."

Maddie's lips parted.

Fowler? He was the corporate spy?

No . . .

Her gaze snapped back to the detective. "I know the company suspected someone might be trying to sell plans involving their technology."

"And now we have evidence that it may have been Fowler," Kalani finished.

"So you think Fowler saw our hiking trip as an opportunity to disappear before anyone found out what he did?" Maddie clarified. "That he just walked away? Still, he couldn't just disappear. He's out there somewhere."

"If one of his new colleagues was in on this with him, then Fowler could have had someone meet him in the woods and help him disappear."

"The thought is just ridiculous." Bree adamantly shook her head. "He would never do something like this."

"Then how do you explain the emails?" Kalani stared at her.

"I don't know, okay? I've tried not to ask him about his work too much. But he's not the type to do something like this. I know him." Bree's chin trembled.

"He does, however, have quite a bit of gambling debt." Kalani said the words slowly, carefully. "That might be a good reason for him to want a nice-sized payout."

"He would never want Blue to succeed!" Bree practically shouted.

The detective paused, tilting his head as he observed Bree. "I never said anything about Blue . . ."

———

Tension clutched Maddie's chest.

Everything was unraveling.

Everything.

Fowler could have been the corporate spy? He could have sold Benchmark out for a paycheck?

And Bree may have been in on it?

A million thoughts rushed through Maddie's head at the same time as she tried to figure everything out.

"I only said Blue because that's the company that makes the most sense." Bree's voice wavered defensively, and a burst of life ignited in her gaze. "They're Benchmark's top competitor. That doesn't mean I had anything to do with this—not that I think that there is a *this*." She did air quotes around the word.

"That's what we're still looking into," Kalani continued. "But if you know anything else, now is the time to share. Corporate spying is a criminal offense."

"I don't know anything because there's nothing to know!" Bree's hand sliced through the air. "Fowler wouldn't have done this. Now that you think he's a traitor, does this mean that you're going to stop looking for him? What if he didn't disappear by his own volition?"

"We still have crews out looking for him in the helicopters. But it's getting dark, so we'll have to resume the search in the morning."

"But what if he's hurt?" Bree's voice cracked. She was clearly distraught—as anyone in her shoes would be.

"I assure you that we're doing everything we can." Then Detective Kalani looked at Maddie again.

Why had he called her? She didn't have anything to do with this conversation.

But he'd wanted her here for a reason.

"We're going to need to talk to your fiancé," Kalani explained. "We haven't been able to locate him. I was hoping you'd know where to find him."

Maddie swallowed hard and held up her empty ring finger. "We actually just broke up a few hours ago. I don't know where he went. I'm sorry I can't be of more help."

The detective observed her another moment, long enough to make Maddie cringe.

What was he thinking right now? Probably about something that made her look bad.

"May I ask why you two split?" Kalani finally asked.

"Because we weren't right for each other." That was all the detective needed to know. He didn't need to know that Josh had cheated on her. That he was a jerk. That all he cared about was his career and how people perceived him.

Those things had nothing to do with this investigation.

"I heard there was an incident with his balcony last night," Kalani finally said.

Maddie swallowed hard. "That's right. Thankfully, Josh and Brody were able to keep me from falling. It could have been really ugly."

The detective let out a thoughtful grunt—almost as if he didn't buy that explanation—before nodding.

"I'm going to go see if I can track Josh down." He glanced at Bree again. "I'll be in touch with any updates. Aloha."

EVERYONE SAT in silence after the detective left.

What a mess.

Nothing was as it seemed, was it? Maddie mused.

Josh had been cheating on her.

Adrienne and Brody weren't really together.

Fowler might be a spy, and Bree might be in on it.

Maddie was a murderer.

She swallowed hard at that last one.

There was more to her story. Maybe there was more to everyone else's stories as well. She shouldn't jump to conclusions. Yet she should remain cautious considering what was at stake here.

What was at stake might possibly be her life.

Could Fowler really be a spy? Was Bree in on this with him?

If so, she was a great actress. She truly seemed heartbroken over his disappearance.

Maddie scanned the room as everyone remained silent.

She'd been so excited to find these new vacation friends as she'd gleefully called them when they'd first met. It turned out her new friends weren't as perfect as she thought. Nowhere close, for that matter.

She could lump herself in that same category, however. Imperfect.

Finally, Maddie stood. "I'm going back to my suite. It's been a long day . . . for all of us. I, for one, could use some rest to clear my head."

"Fowler's not a corporate spy." Bree's words came out fast. "And neither am I. I don't know anything about those emails the detective found. What if they were planted?"

Maddie supposed that was a possibility. But she was too exhausted to form any opinions at the moment.

Besides, if these two were corporate spies . . . then she needed to distance herself from them. Not for the sake of Benchmark. But because those weren't the kind of people she wanted in her life.

"I hope they find him soon," Maddie finally said.

She stepped toward the door, not in the mood to talk anymore. As she walked by, she stole a glance at Brody. There was no need to add her growing feelings for the man to her list of complications.

Just as she stepped out, Adrienne called to her.

Maddie turned to see that her friend had followed her into the hallway and shut the door behind her.

"That was something in there, wasn't it?" Adrienne started, a frown tugging at her lips.

"You can say that again." Maddie ran a hand through her hair, her headache persisting.

Adrienne rubbed a hand across her cheek and then her neck before saying, "I'm sorry to hear about you and Josh breaking up. Is it because of what I told you earlier?"

Maddie shrugged as she considered how to respond. "It was a long time coming."

Adrienne nodded stiffly. "I see."

Maddie's thoughts wandered to what Brody had told her about his relationship with Adrienne. She wasn't sure if she should bring up the subject or not. But since everything was already on the line . . . could things get any more awkward?

She swallowed hard before saying, "I ran into Brody at the beach. He told me the two of you aren't dating."

Adrienne's eyes widened. "What? He told you that?"

"He did."

She let out a long breath. "We have a complicated history. But we love each other. And he certainly led me to believe we were back together when he kissed me."

"He kissed you?" The words slipped out before Maddie could stop them.

"Yeah, you could say that. More than once." Adrienne looked into the distance and quickly shook her head. "I don't know why he told you that . . . unless he likes you or something. When he told you, did he know you and Josh had broken up?"

Maddie's throat squeezed. She shouldn't have brought this up. She was only causing more drama. But it was too late to take her words back.

She nodded instead. "He did."

Adrienne's nostrils flared. "I see the way he looks at you. Ever since that first morning at the beach, I've suspected he's attracted to you. But I never thought he'd be the type to cheat."

"He didn't cheat," Maddie quickly told her. "He didn't do anything, and there's nothing between us. I'm sorry I brought this up. I was just confused."

Adrienne let out a long breath before shaking her head. She rubbed her lips together as if contemplating her next words.

Finally, she said, "The truth is, his sister died in a domestic violence incident a year or so ago. Her death changed him. I gave him some time to get himself together before we reunited. But something about Brody has been different ever since then, almost like he has two personalities or something."

Maddie's throat tightened. She didn't like the sound of that.

Out of everyone she'd met here, Brody had seemed the most trustworthy. But maybe she'd been wrong. Maybe she'd been wrong about so much. Maybe her gut instincts couldn't be trusted after all.

This whole trip had been one big fat mistake.

She composed herself as she realized Adrienne was still in front of her, still waiting for a response. "I hope you and Brody can work things out."

Then, before she felt the need to say anything else, Maddie waved goodbye and hurried down the hall.

————

Maddie walked briskly back to her room, praying she didn't run into anyone.

She couldn't handle any more hard conversations today. She'd already had enough.

She especially didn't want to run into Josh.

She'd had enough of that man to last for a lifetime.

Reaching her room, she unlocked the door before slipping inside.

Her mission to walk back without running into anyone had been successful.

But her sense of victory only lasted a minute.

Something felt strange in the room, but she wasn't sure what. She couldn't put her finger on it right away. Maddie only knew her lungs tightened.

She reached behind her and gripped the door handle again, ready to flee.

Or was she just being paranoid?

No, she wasn't.

Her TV was on, she realized, though the volume was off. The light from the screen flickered in the room, though she couldn't see the screen itself.

Take a deep breath, Maddie. This might not mean anything.

She knew sometimes TVs in places like this came on with advertisements for the resort and things to do around the area. Maybe that was what had happened— something logical instead of sinister.

For all Maddie knew, she could have left the TV on when she was here last. She'd been so distracted that maybe she hadn't noticed. Watching television hadn't seemed that important after her conversation with Josh.

Her thoughts felt scattered, and she couldn't make sense of them.

Maddie resisted the urge to run. She'd already had too much attention on herself, and she didn't want any more.

She could do this. She'd keep her eyes wide open. At the first sign of trouble she would call for help.

As a precaution, she pulled out her phone and dialed 911. She didn't hit Send. Instead, her thumb lingered over the button. If anything frightened her, she'd make the call.

Slowly, she stepped forward and peered into the bathroom. Into the shower. Behind the door.

No one.

She continued beyond the front entry of the suite and into the living room.

She scanned the couch and the chairs and the tables. There were very few places a person could hide in here if they wanted.

There was no one.

She wanted to let down her guard, to relax some. But she couldn't.

Not yet.

Instead, she walked into her bedroom. Stood in the doorway. Scanned the space.

Again, nothing looked amiss.

No one could be beneath the bed because it was an enclosed wooden box.

That only left the closet.

Her hands shook as she walked toward it. She drew in a deep breath as she reached for the door.

Everything in her wanted to run.

What if someone was hiding inside? What if when she opened the door, this person jumped out?

He might easily knock her down. Maddie might drop the phone before she could call for help.

He could also have a knife or a gun. Some kind of weapon.

She needed to think each of these scenarios through.

Or this could all be nothing.

That was what it most likely was. *Nothing*.

She closed her eyes and lifted a prayer. Then she grabbed the door handle and jerked it open.

An empty closet stared back—empty other than a few hangers, a complimentary robe, and a safe.

Maddie let out her breath, chiding herself for such a foolish reaction.

No one was in her hotel room.

She was simply being paranoid.

She clicked off her phone screen before she accidentally called 911, and she shoved her cell back into her pocket.

Then she walked into the living area to turn off the TV.

But when she reached it, she finally glanced at the screen.

She hadn't thought that whatever was on it would be significant—advertising, most likely.

But there on the screen was a man with an elongated white mask on and a knife in his hands.

Her pulse quickened.

It was the villain from *Scream*.

The horror movie played on the screen.

Maddie didn't care what anyone told her.

She knew this movie wasn't playing in her room by coincidence.

MADDIE TURNED off the TV and sat on the edge of the couch. Whoever had turned this on was gone. They'd been trying to scare her.

It had worked.

She knew her room was clear. She'd checked every possible space. But now it would be nearly impossible to relax. She had too much on her mind.

She still needed to give the engagement ring back to Josh. In fact, she really should have put the jewelry in the safe before she'd left earlier. But she hadn't. She hadn't been thinking clearly at the time.

Maddie forced herself to stand. She should just do this now while she was thinking about it.

She walked to the nightstand. But when she reached the table, the top was empty.

The ring wasn't there.

Panic raced through her.

Had the person who'd turned on the TV seen the ring and taken it?

She quickly searched her belongings. Nothing else seemed to be missing.

Maybe in the stress of the situation, she was misre-membering where she'd left it.

She searched the rest of the room, determined to find that ring. It was worth a lot of money. She should have never left it out.

She searched under the bedspread and tables and in drawers and under pillows. There was still no ring.

Maddie scanned the room again, wondering where else she could check. There weren't that many other places it could be.

It couldn't have somehow fallen into one of the vents. They were all high on the wall.

At the thought, she looked up at the vents.

Her eyes stopped at one. Something on the cover appeared out of place.

She squinted, unsure if she was seeing things correctly.

Grabbing a wooden chair from the table, she walked toward the grate. She stood, found her balance, and then used her fingernails to pry the clasp up.

The metal grate opened.

Her blood grew cold at what she saw inside.

A small camera had been mounted to the edge.

Someone had placed a *camera* in her room?

Someone had been watching her.

Maybe even recording her.

Before Maddie could stop it, nausea rose in her.

She leaned over and threw up on the carpeted floor.

FORTY-NINE
THEN

ANOTHER MONTH HAD PASSED. Another month with more broken promises.

Cecilia hated it.

Yet another part of her understood.

Garrick's job was demanding. She couldn't fault him for that. He didn't get to the position he was in in life by being lazy.

He did what was demanded of him. He'd told Cecilia that was why he hadn't gotten married yet—because most women didn't understand the sacrifices his job required.

Cecilia wanted to be different. She wanted to be one of the women who *did* understand. Who supported him. Who gave him a soft place to fall.

Every giant needed someone to care and nurture them behind the scenes.

She thought about that concept a lot, about how she wanted to be that person.

But she had to admit that all the cancellations were getting old.

She felt as if her entire social life depended on whether or not Garrick carried through with his plans with her.

As she leaned back onto the ratty couch in her living room, she touched the necklace at her throat. At least she had this. Garrick always looked out for her.

She jerked forward as an idea hit her.

Garrick was working late tonight. Maybe she could bring him his favorite chocolate chip cookies from the bakery down the street.

She'd never been into his office before. But he'd never told her not to come.

Maybe if he saw her, it would be the pick-me-up he needed. He'd sounded so stressed lately.

Cecilia thought about the idea for several more minutes before a grin spread across her lips.

Yes, that was what she would do. If Garrick couldn't come to her, then she would go to him.

She was already dressed and looked presentable. But, just in case, she quickly glanced at her hair and makeup in the mirror. She looked a little tired but otherwise acceptable . . . except that she wore some old jeans and a T-shirt.

Should she change? Would Garrick care?

Certainly, he wouldn't. He loved her however she

looked. She hoped that just seeing her would cheer him up. That was how love worked, right?

Feeling more and more excited about her surprise, she headed down the street, purchased three cookies from the bakery, and then started toward Garrick's office building.

The business district seemed like a different world from the one she lived in. She couldn't imagine what it might be like to come here every day to work. Everything just felt expensive and fast-paced and highbrow.

As she walked into his building, she noticed the marble floor beneath her. The stone columns. The richly wallpapered walls

Everything smelled like polish, like only royalty graced this area.

Suddenly, her jeans and T-shirt didn't seem like enough. She *definitely* should have changed. Everyone else wore suits and shiny shoes.

But she was already here. It would take too long to walk back to her place and switch her outfit.

She could do this. Even though this wasn't her world, that didn't mean it couldn't be one day. She could learn. She would get used to this kind of splendor.

She strode to the front desk, unsure which floor Garrick's office was located on.

The receptionist, a pretty blonde who looked straight out of modeling school, eyed her warily as she approached. "Can I help you?"

She told the woman who she was here to see.

The receptionist pressed her lips together. "I'm sorry, but he's not in."

Cecilia faltered. "He told me he's working tonight."

The receptionist checked something else on her computer. "No. I'm sorry. He's not here."

She gripped the cookies in her hand tighter. "Are you sure?"

The woman offered a tight smile. "Yes, I double-checked."

"But . . ."

What was Cecilia supposed to say? That Garrick had told her he'd be here? Besides, just because he had a meeting didn't mean that it would be here at the office. Certainly he had meetings over cocktails or dinner or maybe even while playing golf—though it was too late to play golf now.

Cecilia forced a smile at the receptionist. "I understand. Could you give this to him when he comes in?" She handed the woman the box of cookies. "Tell him that Cecilia was here?"

"Of course."

Cecilia noticed how the woman turned up her nose ever so slightly as she took the box. She acted like she might disinfect her hands after being so close to Cecilia.

Or was Cecilia reading too much into things? She didn't have money, but she knew she was pretty.

Either way, it didn't matter.

Cecilia turned to leave, an unsettled feeling in her chest.

That hadn't gone as she planned.

But there would be more opportunities to take care of Garrick in the future. She just had to plan her surprises a little better.

MADDIE WOKE UP EARLY, still feeling troubled. Brody had tried to call her a couple of times last night, but she hadn't answered. Josh had tried to call also, but she'd ignored him.

She'd just wanted to be alone.

She wanted to be alone today also.

Part of her felt as if she should call Bree and check on her. But knowing that Fowler might be a corporate spy, and that Bree might have been helping him made her want to stay away.

She was supposed to go to a hula class and then a lei-making class, but she'd decided to cancel. She ordered room service instead—fresh fruit and toast.

She needed to figure out her plan. She wasn't supposed to leave until Friday evening, and today was Thursday.

Feeling cagey, she cracked open the door to her balcony to let in the fresh breeze.

A noise outside caught her ear.

It wasn't the normal joyful sounds of people playing in the pools, laughing, and having a good time.

Something about this sound was ominous and urgent.

She stepped onto the patio, careful not to get too close to the railing.

As she peered outside at the ocean, her eyes narrowed.

A group of people had gathered on the seashore.

What was happening out there now?

Maddie instinctually knew that whatever it was, it wasn't good.

Her throat tightened as memories of Jared's death filled her mind.

No. Not again . . .

What if it was someone she knew this time?

Everyone was too far away for Maddie to make out any details. Whatever the crowd gawked at, their bodies blocked her sight of it.

Part of her didn't want to know. But some kind of internal urgency pressed on her. She had to find out what was happening.

She stepped away from the balcony.

Despite her reservations, Maddie needed to get down to the beach so she could see for herself what the newest tragedy surrounding this trip might be.

———

Maddie flew down the steps and outside.

She'd pulled her hair into a ponytail and thrown on a blue romper, one that Josh hated because it made her figure look shapeless—his words, not hers.

She'd brought it with her for hanging out in her suite, never intending on leaving the room wearing it. Not with Josh.

Now that didn't matter. She no longer cared.

She cut through the bushes to the beach.

Paramedics had arrived on the scene, and the crowd had grown larger.

Maddie's gaze darted around as she looked for anyone she knew.

She didn't see any familiar faces. Not yet.

She cut through the onlookers murmuring "excuse me" until she reached the front.

Her stomach dropped at the sight of what everyone was staring at. She blinked, certain she wasn't seeing things correctly.

But she was.

It was Logan.

The woman lay on the sand, just at the water's edge. Occasionally, a wave lapped her, making her long hair fan out all around her. She wore a red evening gown, one like she might have put on for a fancy dinner the night before.

Maddie knew without a doubt by looking at her that the woman was dead.

Her heart pounded in her ears.

Another fatality on this trip.

How had this happened?

And when would it end?

CHAPTER
FIFTY-ONE

MADDIE STARTED TO BACK AWAY. She'd come here to see what was happening. Now she knew.

Logan was dead.

The paramedics had surrounded the woman. Checked her pulse.

Even they knew there was nothing left to do.

Her throat tightened until a soft cry escaped.

Logan . . . she didn't like the woman, but she didn't want to see her dead.

Who had done this?

Then Josh's image filled her mind.

No . . .

There was no reason for Maddie to stay out here any longer. She knew everything she had come to find out.

As she turned to leave, she practically collided with someone.

She drew in a shaky breath as she looked up.

Detective Kalani.

Dread pooled in her stomach.

"Ms. Waters," he murmured, his gaze glimmering with curiosity. "The two of us just keep running into each other."

The words could have sounded warm. But not coming from Kalani. They only sounded detached and calculated.

She tried to control the tremble going through her, but it felt nearly impossible.

Jared dead. Fowler missing. Logan now dead also.

It was all too much . . .

"I saw the people gathering from my balcony, and I came down to see what was happening. I had no idea it was going to be—" Her voice caught, and she couldn't finish her statement.

Kalani stared at her, not saying anything. Finally, he murmured, "You need to stick around."

Stick around? What did that mean? Was he going to try to frame her for this also? Then she realized she had no alibi, no alibi other than her room key.

Even more dread filled her stomach. How was this happening?

Who had done this to Logan?

What about Fowler? Were there any updates on him?

Her head pounded as she tried to figure out exactly what she should do.

For now, she crossed her arms over her chest and

paced away. She would wait here. Just like the detective told her.

But she wouldn't like it.

————

An hour later, Detective Kalani made his way back toward her.

Maddie had found a lounge chair on the beach, and she sat staring at the waves as she waited.

No one had bothered her—a fact for which she was thankful. Talking to people was the last thing she wanted.

But now it was time to talk to Kalani, who sat on a lounge chair beside her, also facing the water. He didn't say anything a moment.

"What happened to Logan?" Maddie quietly asked.

"The medical examiner will tell us for sure."

"Foul play?" Part of her didn't want to know, to hear the confirmation, even if she already knew the truth.

"It's hard to say without the proper examination. But if I had to guess, I would say yes."

Maddie turned toward the detective, wanting to see his eyes as she asked the next question. "Do you think I did something to her?"

"*Did* you do something to her?" He remained stone-faced as he asked the question, his expression showing no hints as to what he was thinking, what his pre-drawn conclusions were.

"No. I was in my room all night. Alone."

His face remained placid. "It seems as if this retreat has been rough for the company."

"You can say that again." She almost wanted to chuckle, but she didn't. "You might be able to claim that one incident was just bad luck. But things are piling up so much that it's clear this company and the people in it are being targeted."

"You have no idea why that might be?"

Maddie shook her head, hating how heavy and burdened her actions felt. "No, I don't."

She briefly considered telling him about everything that had happened to her. All the things she'd tried to keep quiet, mostly in an effort to stay out of the spotlight.

She still wasn't sure it was a good idea to share too much. She needed to be careful what she said and consider each of her words.

She swallowed hard. "Maybe I don't have a right to ask this, but are there any updates on Fowler? I can't stop thinking about what might have happened to him."

"Search and rescue is actively looking for him."

Maddie had thought about everything all night, considering possibilities and theories. "This might be a strange question, but could someone have set him up with those emails and made it look as if he was a corporate spy?"

Kalani clicked his tongue. "I suppose it could be a possibility, but it would take someone with a lot of computer expertise to do that. Of course, one of the tech companies that's on the forefront of cutting-edge products is having a retreat here this weekend."

Maddie swallowed hard, unable to deny his words. If that was the criteria, then the suspects were practically limitless.

Bree's image came to mind also. The woman worked in cybersecurity. Had she set up her own boyfriend?

It seemed like a stretch. But with stakes so high, no theory should be eliminated.

Maddie cleared her throat, suddenly desperate to get back to her room. "Is there anything else you need from me?"

Kalani shook his head. "Not unless you have something else to tell me."

"I don't." She paused before adding, "I know Logan was the witness who said she saw two people on the beach when Jared died."

"She was." The detective paused. "And I heard you had an argument with her last night. Heard she was having an affair with your fiancé."

So he *did* know about that. Maddie had wondered.

Was that the reason he wanted to talk to her?

More anxiety churned inside her.

"That's all true," Maddie told him. "But that doesn't mean I'd kill her. She can have Josh. Or, she could have had him . . ." Her voice trailed as she realized her mistake.

Kalani stared at her, his expression unreadable.

Then the corner of his lip tugged up. "I never thought he was good enough for you."

Maddie's eyes widened. Had she just heard him correctly?

"I thought you hated me." Truly, she had. She'd been certain the detective wanted someone to blame and had his sights set on her.

"I don't hate you." He shrugged. "I'm just doing my job."

Her thoughts raced. Was this some type of ploy so the man could gain her trust? So she would confess to something?

It was hard to know. She'd trusted the wrong people before. She didn't want to do it again.

But maybe she should throw out something instead of hiding everything that had happened to her.

She licked her lips before saying, "I left my engagement ring in my room after Josh and I broke up yesterday. I wasn't thinking. I was too upset. But when I came back, it was gone."

Something flickered in his gaze—maybe curiosity. Maybe assumptions.

She wasn't sure.

"Do you think Josh took it?" he asked.

"He didn't have a key to my place. And . . ." Maddie hesitated, unsure if she should share the rest and open up Pandora's Box.

"Go on."

She let out a shaky breath before saying, "And

someone left a hidden camera in one of the AC vents in my room."

Kalani's eyebrows shot up. "What?"

She nodded, still in disbelief herself. The discovery had felt so violating. She didn't want to think about what someone had done with any images they'd captured.

"I found it when I was looking for the ring," she told him.

His eyebrows remained suspended. "And you didn't report this?"

How *did* she explain that? "I'm trying not to draw any unnecessary attention to myself."

He frowned. "I'm going to send one of my guys to pick that up. That's not okay, Maddie."

"I know."

"Anything else?" he asked one last time as he studied her face.

She considered telling him about the threats she'd received. But then he might dig deep enough to find out about her mugshot also. That was her ultimate fear.

She needed to keep her past in the past.

She'd told him enough, she decided.

For that matter, Maddie prayed she hadn't told him too much.

TONIGHT IS THE NIGHT.

Only no one knows except me.

I smile at the thought, at my gloriously deadly secret.

Soon, people will know.

Justice will be served.

People will get what they deserve.

Including me.

This morning, I'd stood in the distance and watched everything as it played out.

The scene at the beach brought me great delight.

Killing Logan hadn't originally been a part of my plan. I'd caught her watching me, and I'd seen the look in her eyes. She was suspicious. I couldn't take the chance that she might talk.

So, using someone else's name, I'd asked her to meet. She'd said yes, which wasn't surprising considering the name I'd used.

People aren't going to treat me like I'm a nobody, like I'm unworthy.

I worked for so long on my plan for today. Everything has to be in place.

And I think it is.

The events of this evening will be one of my greatest accomplishments.

I take a bite of my pineapple as I stand outside the resort.

Then I see Maddie.

She's heading closer.

Dear, sweet Maddie. Wearing a frumpy outfit with her hair pulled back in a ponytail.

She doesn't belong in this world.

But I do.

Soon, how she looks won't matter.

Only survival will.

When I see the look on her face, when she realizes what's really happening, all of this will be worth it.

I can't wait.

FIFTY-THREE

JUST AS MADDIE stepped inside the west wing, she looked up and saw . . . Josh walking right toward her.

He wore a bathing suit and had a towel draped over his shoulders.

Her stomach filled with dread. He was the last person she wanted to see.

Josh paused and raised his chin stiffly. "I was hoping to run into you sometime."

"Really? Funny, I was feeling the exact opposite."

A frown flickered across his face. Then he glanced around before lowering his voice. "Listen. Could we talk?"

"I'm not ready."

More annoyance filled his gaze. "The gala is tonight."

"I know. Have you told people we broke up?"

Because that was what this boiled down to, wasn't it? How their breakup would look for his career.

Josh shook his head. "I prefer to keep my personal life personal."

"Everyone is going to find out," Maddie told him.

"How are people going to find out?" He narrowed his eyes. "Have you told them?"

"Only a couple of people—"

"You mean your new little friends?" Derision dripped from his words.

"It doesn't matter who. I have the right to tell people what I'm going through if I want to."

His gaze darkened, and he looked away shaking his head again. "The timing of this couldn't be worse."

Maddie pressed her eyes closed. That was Josh for you. Always thinking of himself and his career and advancement.

The charming person she'd first met had only been an act.

What did relationship experts call it? Love bombing?

Yes, that was what it was.

None of it had been real.

He glanced around again before his gaze stopped at her hand. "I'll need the ring back if you're not going to wear it."

"That might be a little difficult." Maddie's throat tightened.

How was she going to tell him what happened?

Would he even believe her given the tension between them?

"Someone stole it," she finally said.

"What?" His voice rose. "What do you mean?"

"I mean exactly what I said. Someone took it. I left the ring in my room, and when I came back, it was gone."

His nostrils flared, but he kept his voice low this time. "You sure you just didn't pawn it? I always knew you only liked me for my money."

Fire ignited inside her at his accusation. "You know that's not true. I have never asked for one dime from you."

"No, you were just waiting until the big day, weren't you? It's probably the only reason you agreed to stay together for as long as you did."

"That statement does not even deserve a response." Irritation simmered in her voice. "Just call your insurance company. They'll get it sorted out."

The startled look on his face said it all.

She shook her head. "You didn't take out insurance on a two-carat diamond ring?"

His gaze darkened again. "Why would I? I never expected you to take it off your finger."

Josh was unbelievable. Again, this was going to be her fault in his eyes.

"I need to go." She brushed past him.

He started to call for her, but Maddie raised her hand to cut him off.

He didn't appear to know about Logan yet. But he'd find out soon.

Would he cry for his lost lover?

Maddie didn't know. She didn't know what parts of him were real.

Given everything that had happened, would he be named the new CEO tonight? Would he get everything he wanted despite his bad behavior? Would they delay the ceremony in light of everything that had happened?

She didn't know. Truthfully, she didn't care. She just wanted to go home.

———

Maddie went back to her room, more cautious now when she stepped inside, than she had been earlier.

But there were no notes under her door.

No scary movies on the TV.

And nothing appeared to be missing.

She should feel relieved, but she didn't.

There was more to come. She was sure of it.

Her phone buzzed, and she glanced at the screen.

It was Brody. Again.

Just as before, she didn't answer.

If Brody had been lying to her about his relationship with Adrienne, then Maddie didn't want anything to do with the man. Besides, she had too many other things on her mind right now to worry about him and how quickly he'd fallen off his pedestal.

Besides, a relationship between them would have never worked. Cutting him off was the best choice.

Instead of talking to him, she called her attorney in New York and talked to him for several minutes.

When Maddie hung up, she jumped on the computer to search flights.

Though Detective Kalani had warned her that she needed to stay in town, he had no legal grounds to keep her unless she was officially charged as a suspect.

For that reason, Maddie was going to buy the earliest plane ticket she could find to get out of here.

She was done with this island. With this retreat. With all these people.

She wanted to get back to New York and start over.

In fact, maybe she wanted to start over somewhere far away from New York. She didn't know. All she knew was that she wanted to get out of this place.

She would let Josh dig his way out of his own mess. She'd let others figure out if Fowler and Bree were corporate spies. She'd let Kalani figure out who might have killed Logan or if Jared's death had anything to do with the company.

But Maddie was done.

Totally and completely done.

CECILIA DIDN'T MENTION to Garrick that she'd stopped by the office. And he'd never mentioned to her that he'd gotten the cookies she left.

Was that because the receptionist hadn't given them to him? Or was it because he didn't appreciate her kind gesture?

She wasn't sure. That had been two days ago. The two of them were supposed to go back to the summer house in the Hamptons this weekend. Knowing that they'd be there and she'd have quality time with Garrick made everything more bearable. But she still needed to decide if she was going to bring up those cookies.

The best idea would probably be to stay silent.

But how could she? Something was nagging at the back of her mind, something she'd rather ignore.

She wanted to believe things were perfect between her and Garrick. But that didn't seem wise. Her gut told her that Garrick, though he seemed perfect, had his own secrets.

Maybe even his own demons.

Those thoughts played over and over again in her head as they drove toward the house. Garrick was mainly quiet, chatting a little about work. But he'd reached over and gripped her hand.

She liked it when he did that. It made her feel like they were a team.

At a lull in the conversation, she licked her lips and then said, "By the way, someone you work with came into the store the other day."

Though it had happened a while ago, Cecilia hadn't brought it up yet. The encounter, though strange, hadn't seemed important.

But if she were honest with herself, she'd admit that the exchange bugged her. However, she wasn't sure why.

"Oh, yeah?" Garrick asked. "Who was that?"

"I don't recall his name. John something or other. But he was at the fundraiser."

"Did he recognize you?"

She shook her head. "He didn't seem to until I mentioned it. But he *did* say something weird."

Garrick's fingers twitched around hers. But when Cecilia glanced at his face, his expression was still calm.

"Oh, yeah?" he asked. "What was that?"

"He asked if I was working that job as a side hustle. I'm still not sure what he meant by that."

His cheek twitched. "It's probably nothing. It's best not to read too much into these kinds of things."

Cecilia nodded. "I agree with that. I . . . I was just curious."

She didn't mention the wink he'd given her.

It still gave her the creeps.

"Maybe he thinks I take care of you all the time so you don't need to work. Would you like that? Would you like it if I took care of you all the time?"

Something about the way Garrick said those words made her heart stutter.

She hated to admit it, but she loved that idea. It had been so long since she'd had someone to look out for her. And doing life on her own, though satisfying, was also exhausting.

"I don't even know what to say."

He glanced at her and grinned. "Don't say anything right now. Just think about it. Think about our future and what you might like for it to look like."

Cecilia would very much enjoy doing that.

His phone buzzed just then, and he glanced at the screen and frowned.

Instead of answering like he sometimes did, he put the phone away.

"Is everything okay?" she asked.

"It's fine. Just a work thing I don't really want to deal with at this very second."

She could understand that.

In fact, nothing would make her happier than having him not think about work for this entire weekend.

Cecilia would do her best to ensure that happened.

———

That night, Cecilia rolled over in bed and noticed that Garrick was no longer there.

She ran her hand across the empty sheets. Then she noticed the bathroom door was closed and a light on beneath it.

She glanced at the time.

It was only nine p.m. They had turned in early for the evening.

She smiled as she remembered their time together.

Things between them in bed still weren't amazing. But she could live with it, knowing there would be a learning curve.

Especially now that she knew he might want to take care of her in the future.

That was his way of saying that he wanted to get married, right?

She wanted to squeal at the thought.

Wrapping a sheet around her, she crept out of bed toward the bathroom door. But before she opened it, Garrick's voice rang out on the other side.

Who was he talking to? He must be on the phone, she realized. That was the only thing that made sense.

He'd promised to try to stay away from work. But it appeared he hadn't been able to resist. Go figure.

She started to head back to the bed and not interrupt him. It didn't seem nearly as romantic to surprise him in the bathroom now that she knew he was talking to one of his colleagues.

But before she stepped away, part of the conversation drifted to her.

"I know," Garrick said. "I'm sorry about all these work trips. I promise, it won't be like this forever."

Wait. Was that something that he would say to a colleague?

The thought left a bad feeling in her belly.

Then he said, "I love you too."

Cecilia's heart beat faster. No . . .

Before she could get back to the bed, the door opened, and Garrick stepped out. His eyes widened when he saw her.

"I'm sorry," she stuttered, taking a step back. "I was going to surprise you, and I didn't realize that you were on the phone."

His gaze looked heavier than usual. "I was trying not to wake you."

What should she say? Should she confront him?

How could she not? Especially after what she'd heard.

He'd told somebody he loved them.

There was no need to pretend that she hadn't heard.

"Are you cheating on me?" The words sounded raw as they left Cecilia's lips.

"Cheating on you?" His voice hardened. "What are you talking about?"

"I heard part of your conversation. Don't try to deny it."

He gripped her arms, harder than she'd expected. "You shouldn't eavesdrop, Cecilia."

"Like I said, I didn't mean to. It was just that—"

"I was talking to my mom," he told her.

All the tension seemed to leave her body in a whoosh.

Her cheeks reddened.

His mom?

Of course. It made perfect sense. She should have known. But she'd jumped to conclusions . . .

She was so foolish.

"I'm sorry," she whispered.

"You should be. I thought you thought more highly of me than that."

"I did. I do," she quickly corrected. "I just got all panicky and jumped to conclusions."

"We're going to need to set some ground rules about that. I don't like being accused of things that I'm not guilty of."

"I understand." She pushed a hair behind her ear and looked down, suddenly ashamed of herself.

Then Garrick released his grip on her arms and,

using his index finger, nudged her chin up until her gaze met his. "I forgive you."

Her lungs loosened. She was glad he'd seen it in his heart to let this go. Accusing him of cheating was a horrible thing to do. She should have kept herself in check more. Shouldn't have eavesdropped.

The next moment, he reached for her, and his lips covered hers. But this kiss was different than the others.

There was almost a possessiveness about it.

He pulled away and his lips trailed down her jawline all the way to her ear. Then he whispered, "I love you."

Delight flooded through her.

She realized she loved him too.

MADDIE'S PHONE buzzed as she packed her suitcase.

Go to the pool. Now. You'll see why. Don't get CABIN FEVER.

She paused as she considered the words.

Should Maddie even play with the idea of agreeing to this?

Her first instinct was no. But what harm could it be going out to the pool? Was someone planning on pushing her in? There were too many people around for that.

She paused from packing and stepped onto her patio. Her gaze drifted to the pool area.

Nothing seemed suspicious—except for the fact that Josh had been headed that way. When Maddie ran into him earlier, he'd been wearing a bathing suit. Did this have something to do with him?

She stared at the pool another moment, trying to figure out what to do.

In five hours, she needed to be at the airport. That was the earliest flight she could book.

Then she'd be done with all this.

She thought about her choices another moment before deciding to throw caution to the wind. She would see what this text was about. She would play this little game that someone unknown to her had set up.

She headed from her room toward the pool area.

Where was she supposed to go when she got out there? It was a large area—five acres.

Maddie decided to wander around. Someone had wanted her out here for a reason. Now she needed to figure out why.

She plastered on her best smile as she passed several people. Thankfully, no one stopped to talk. But she didn't see anything suspicious either.

She paused near a bridge over the lazy river and glanced at her phone. No new messages waited for her.

Why had this person lured her outside? It didn't make any sense.

Maybe she should go back to her room and forget about that text.

She straightened as she spotted Nico. He appeared to be headed toward a large hot tub nestled on the edge of the outdoor area. She could see it from where she was; it was currently empty.

As she glanced farther down the walkway, she saw

Josh headed in that same direction with a fruity cocktail in hand.

Was this what someone wanted her to see? If so, why?

She remained where she was and watched.

Was this some type of unofficial meeting between Josh and Nico? Were the two of them discussing the future of the company? Or maybe Josh would try to convince Nico not to take the position, even if it was offered.

Nico dropped his towel and stepped into the hot tub.

Right as he did, a pop of electricity sounded.

A faint scent of smoke filled the air.

Nico froze, his body suddenly vibrating as he stood there.

Maddie's breath caught.

Was he being . . . electrocuted?

———

Maddie only stared at the scene for a split second.

Nico would die unless someone did something.

She rushed toward Nico and glanced around, looking for something she could use to help—something that wouldn't conduct electricity.

Her gaze stopped on his towel. It appeared to be dry.

Quickly, she grabbed it and slung it around his waist like a rope. She couldn't touch him, or she would be electrocuted also.

Using all her energy, she jerked him back, hoping to break the flow of electricity.

He fell back, taking her with him as he tumbled into the bushes surrounding the hot tub.

Maddie gasped in deep breaths as she tried to figure out if her rescue plan had worked.

Crawling onto her knees, she peered over him.

He wasn't breathing.

Had she been too late?

AS A HOTEL EMPLOYEE ran over and began CPR on Nico, Maddie scooted back to give him space.

She still couldn't get a deep breath. Her nerves felt as if they were on fire, and her heart raced.

"Maddie?" Josh peered at her.

She ignored him. Instead, she pulled herself up on shaky legs. As other guests wandered over, she warned them to stay away from the electrified hot tub.

The employee doing CPR shouted for someone to call 911.

Nico still wasn't moving.

Maddie lifted a prayer.

Would he be okay? How had this even happened?

Even more . . . who had been the target? Nico or Josh?

Then the biggest question of all hit her.

Had Josh planned this to get rid of the competition?

For that matter, had he killed Logan before she could come forward with any of his secrets?

If that was the case, what would he do to Maddie?

Instinctively, she took a few steps back from Josh.

Maybe her suspicions were right. Maybe he *had* been behind those mysterious incidents before the trip, those opportunities where she could have died. Maybe Josh wanted to gain sympathy among the board members.

The thought had sounded outlandish before.

But maybe it wasn't.

"He's alive!" the hotel employee yelled. "I've got a pulse."

Maddie's lungs finally loosened enough for her to catch her breath.

She glanced at Josh in time to see a frown flicker across his face before quickly disappearing.

Cement filled her lungs again.

Maybe—just maybe—her suspicions were correct and she wasn't paranoid after all.

What if her former fiancé was a killer?

———

Kalani showed up on the scene fifteen minutes later, and Maddie wasn't surprised. At this point, the man might as well get a room here at the resort.

Just as before, he indicated she should wait as he talked to several people near the hot tub.

Paramedics had arrived several minutes ago. They'd

checked Maddie's heart rate and breathing before declaring her "fine."

Nico, on the other hand, had gone to the hospital to be examined.

As Maddie stood at the edge of the crowd, her limbs still shook. She'd been replaying what happened over and over again in her mind.

Nico could have so easily died.

Maddie could have too. Grabbing him with that towel had been risky. Yet she wouldn't have been able to live with herself if she'd just stood there and watched the man be electrocuted.

While she waited for Kalani, she thought about what she wanted to say to him.

Maybe the detective wasn't such a bad guy after all. Maybe he wasn't looking for a reason to blame her for all that had gone wrong.

But Maddie promised herself at the first sign that he was trying to pull the wool over her eyes, she'd guard her words as if they were gold inside Fort Knox.

Finally, Kalani wandered toward her. He sat in the chair next to her, and the two faced the ocean. They probably looked like two old friends talking—though their body language was stiff.

Kalani glanced at her. "How are you feeling?"

She shrugged. "To be honest, I've been better. I really don't want to be close friends with death."

"It was heroic what you did. Most likely, Mr. Rankin wouldn't be alive right now if you hadn't been close."

"I'm glad I was here when I was." She rubbed her neck as she remembered the text she'd received.

Kalani tilted his head as he examined her. "Exactly why were you here?"

She hesitated, drawing in a deep breath as she considered what to say.

If she didn't tell the truth, then she'd probably only continue to look suspicious. Besides, what could it hurt at this point? She hadn't been fiddling with that hot tub.

She pulled out her phone and found the text. Instead of reading it, she showed it to him.

His eyebrows shot up as he scanned the words.

Then he looked back at her, his head still tilted. "Someone sent that to you . . . ?"

"Yes. It hasn't been the only one."

"May I see these others?"

She pressed her lips together, knowing she had no choice but to show him.

"Scroll up," she murmured.

She peered over his shoulder at the words.

I know something you need to know. Someone is out to get you. I need to explain in person and not through text. Meet me at 5:30 a.m. on the beach. Tell no one—trust no one. Delete this message.

Jeepers Creepers.

Don't be Clueless.

"The words in these messages . . ." He studied the phone with squinty eyes. "I feel like they're references to something."

"They're all titles to movies from the nineties and early two-thousands. Mostly campy thrillers or rom-coms."

He squinted even more. "Any idea why someone would reference these?"

"I used to watch a lot of those movies with my granddad before he died," she admitted. "Those were some of his favorites, especially when he was in a nursing home. He was actually an extra in a few. Later in life, he decided he wanted to be an actor, and he went for it. He was happy just being in the background."

Curiosity glimmered in the detective's eyes. "Sounds like you had a strong bond."

"We did. There were more messages, other than the texts. Someone also slipped a paper under my door that said: *Someone you know has cruel intentions. I'd be careful.* They sent another saying something about *10 things I hate about Josh.* There was a picture of Josh and Logan together."

She decided not to mention the note that read, *I know what you did that summer.* And, of course, she wasn't about to mention her mugshot.

"Who else knows you liked to watch these movies? Josh, I assume."

"Yes, Josh. No one else here—at least, not that I know about."

Kalani nodded slowly. "Did you ever post anything about these movies on social media?"

Maddie nibbled on her bottom lip. "I thought about that, and I don't think so. I did a quick search on my phone, but I didn't find any references on posts I made. I'm not really active on any of the socials. They seem like a waste of time."

He grunted. "I'm going to want those notes. Also, I'll need to see if I can trace this phone number. I assume you don't recognize it?"

"I don't."

"So now my question is: Did someone want you out here so you could watch Nico or Josh die? Or for some other reason?"

Maddie's heart beat harder as he voiced the question out loud—a question she'd also been asking herself.

"And why did Josh take his time getting to the hot tub?" she asked quietly. "He usually walks faster than he did."

"That's a great question."

She glanced down the pathway to where Josh now stood talking to some of his colleagues.

How was he connected to all of this?

Maddie wasn't sure, but she was determined to find out.

CHAPTER
FIFTY-SEVEN

IT WAS hard to believe that four months had gone by since Cecilia and Garrick had begun to see each other. In so many ways it seemed like a dream come true. Yet in other ways, it did not.

Cecilia stared at the white stick in her hand, waiting another moment.

Then two pink lines appeared.

Her heart felt as if it might stop.

That couldn't be right. She couldn't be pregnant.

She'd bought more than one test, so she grabbed another one, ripped the package open, and tried again.

But this pregnancy test showed the same result.

Panic raced through her.

What was she going to do? How was Garrick going to feel? He'd always said he wanted to wait a while before having kids. And he was so busy . . . how would he squeeze a baby into his schedule? It would be one more thing to stress him out.

She had to tell him though. He had to know. It was only right.

Her hands trembled as she looked at herself in the mirror.

She tried to picture how Garrick might react. But she wasn't sure.

She needed to talk to him. She needed to hear his reassurance.

This wasn't about him. It was about her.

He would need to operate on her timing now.

She grabbed her phone and tried to call him. She didn't care if he fussed at her. They had to talk.

But he didn't answer.

He'd mentioned he had a meeting tonight. Maybe it would be over soon. Then they could talk.

Before she stopped herself, she grabbed her purse. She would walk to his building. She had to see him. This couldn't wait until morning.

Twenty minutes later, she arrived at his office.

Just as before, their receptionist claimed he wasn't in.

Cecilia didn't believe her.

She rushed past the desk to an elevator.

The woman called behind her, but Cecilia pretended as if she didn't hear.

She'd asked Garrick in a casual conversation what floor he worked on. He'd said the twentieth.

The elevator came right away, and Cecilia slipped

inside and hit the Door Close button before the receptionist could reach her.

She practically held her breath as the elevator climbed higher and higher.

She hadn't planned out exactly what she would say. But she prayed this went well.

Amazingly, the elevator didn't stop. When it dinged, she was on the twentieth floor.

She was shaking by the time she stepped off. She glanced around but did not see anybody.

How hard could it be to find Garrick's office?

That was what she would do. She would find him here.

She rushed down the hallway, listening for any signs of where someone was. Looking at the nameplates on the doors. Since he was CEO, she could only assume he would have one of the larger offices, maybe even in the back of this space.

She headed that way.

Finally, she spotted a sprawling office ahead. His name stretched across a plaque on the door. *Garrick Harding.*

She rushed toward it and, without knocking, twisted the handle. She practically fell inside.

Garrick sat behind his desk, and a woman stood beside him. The two talked in low tones.

Cecilia stopped cold. Even though Garrick wasn't touching the woman, something about the moment seemed intimate.

"Cecilia?" He straightened. "What are you doing here?"

He didn't exactly sound thrilled to see her.

"There's something I must talk to you about," she told him. "It couldn't wait. I had to tell you now."

He glanced at the woman beside him. "Could you give us a minute?"

The woman nodded before glancing at Cecilia and then slipping from the room.

Cecilia paused in front of Garrick's desk. "Who was that?"

"She works downstairs, and we were discussing some marketing plans."

She supposed that that made sense. Maybe she was reading too much into things.

"What are you doing here?" Garrick asked, his voice unusually stiff.

He was annoyed, wasn't he?

But when Cecilia told him the news, he'd understand.

"I knew you came one other time before," he continued. "But I just assumed that was a once in a lifetime mistake."

His words felt like a slap. A once in a lifetime *mistake*? What did that even mean?

And this whole time he *had* known she'd left him those cookies, and he hadn't said a word? Not even a thank you?

Cecilia wasn't sure what she thought about that.

"This couldn't wait, and you weren't answering your phone," she explained as she remembered her purpose in coming here.

"What's going on, Cecilia? It's a bad time."

She glanced at the floor beyond his desk, and something red caught her eye. Something silky and red.

Garrick seemed to know she'd seen it and used his foot to push it out of the way.

It was a negligee, wasn't it?

No, what sense would that make? It wasn't as if she ever came into the office. And that would just be weird anyway.

Maybe it was a silk pocket square. But why would he push it out of the way if that was all it was?

"You came here to tell me something," he prodded her.

Her hand went to her stomach. "I'm pregnant."

She watched his face carefully, unsure how he'd react. But she hoped it was one of delight.

Instead, his eyes narrowed. "What do you mean?"

"I took two tests. I'm definitely pregnant. I guess that explains why I've been feeling a little nauseous lately."

"Whose baby is it?"

Again, she felt as if she had been slapped. "Yours, of course. Whose do you think it would be? I haven't been with anyone else. You know me better than that."

He pressed his lips together and didn't say anything a moment.

Cecilia gave him some time to process the news. She knew it was a lot to swallow.

"I don't know how that happened," he finally said. "I thought we took precautions."

"I don't know what happened either. I didn't plan on having a baby anytime soon. But I was hoping we might speed up that timeline of you taking care of me."

He narrowed his eyes as he observed her. "What exactly did you think I meant by that?"

Why did he make it sound as if he'd never said something like that? She'd heard his tone when he'd asked that question. It had been intimate and full of promises.

She wasn't losing her mind.

"I thought that meant you wanted to be with me," she said, trying to keep the whine out of her voice.

Garrick stared at her, something hardening in his gaze. "Well, you don't need to worry. I will take care of you. I'll give you money to take care of the pregnancy."

"You mean, money to pay for my doctor's visits?"

His gaze remained cold. "I mean so you can eliminate the pregnancy."

She gasped, both hands protecting her belly now. "Why would I ever do that? A baby's life is precious. This is your child we are talking about. My child."

"Neither of us are in a good place to have a child right now. I think we both know that."

He said the words so matter-of-factly. He sounded so convincing.

But her mind was made up.

"I can't have an abortion," she told him. "I won't."

He stood, his demeanor suddenly changing. No longer was he all hard lines. Instead, his eyes grew soft. Using the back of his hand, he stroked her cheek.

"Sweetie, you really need to think this through," he murmured.

"I have thought it through, and I know I'll never terminate this pregnancy."

He glanced at her belly. For a moment, a shock of fear raced through her. She imagined Garrick taking matters into his own hands and ramming his fist into her gut to eliminate this pregnancy himself.

Then just as quickly as that thought occurred to her, the softness returned to his gaze again. "Then we'll figure it out. Both of us. Okay?"

Relief swept through her.

She'd totally misread his reaction earlier, hadn't she? He would get through this. They would get through this. Together.

That was the way couples went through life.

Maybe it would take him awhile to warm up to the idea, but they were having a child together. They would have a beautiful life as a family of three. She knew it in her gut.

Cecilia would stop working at the department store. Become a stay-at-home mom. Maybe some of the other wives here at the company could mentor her, show her how to become one of them. She would do whatever it took.

Whatever it took.

———

Cecilia hit End and lowered her cell phone.

Garrick wasn't answering.

It had been two days since she'd gone into his office.

Two days since he asked for the abortion but changed his mind.

Two days since he assured her everything would be fine.

Nothing felt fine.

Why wasn't he returning her calls? Sure, they had periods when they didn't see each other. But they usually talked at least once a day.

But not since she told him about the baby.

The silence was driving her crazy.

She didn't consider herself the obsessive type.

But she had to see him. Had to know they were okay.

She didn't think she could be a single mom. Didn't think she could support a baby on what she brought in from Balderston's. And she definitely couldn't afford childcare while she was working a minimum wage job. The bill for that would cost more than she even earned.

All those thoughts had been racing inside her for the past twenty-four hours if not longer.

All Garrick had to do was call her back, and he could reassure her that everything would be okay. That was all she needed. Was she asking too much?

She squeezed her phone harder and leaned against the buckling kitchen counter.

She'd worked this morning, and it had been a particularly rough day, especially with her morning sickness. She'd had to leave the floor a couple of times to throw up. Unfortunately, it had been in the middle of helping clients. Very entitled clients.

They hadn't been happy, and her boss had given her a stern lecture.

Cecilia hadn't wanted to say yet that she was pregnant. She wanted to wait a while longer just to make sure the baby was okay.

But what if she got fired? Then what would she do?

Maybe she could go see Garrick again. She knew the last time she'd gone to his office had been a mistake. But what if this time she simply waited outside the office for him? Then when he left work she could surprise him and maybe they could go to dinner together.

That sounded like a nice idea.

Yes, maybe that was what she would do.

Waiting outside wasn't as intrusive as rushing into his office. He would understand that.

This time, Cecilia fixed herself up before she went. She wanted to make sure she knocked the socks off him when they saw each other.

She dressed in his favorite color again—red.

Then she sprayed on her favorite perfume and put on that ruby necklace Garrick had given her.

She flashed a grin in the mirror. She didn't quite have that pregnancy glow yet. She felt too sick. But she hoped Garrick would find that sexy when it finally happened.

She touched up her red lipstick one last time before hurrying out the door.

By the time she arrived at his building, it was dark outside. Thankfully, this area of town was fairly safe. Especially compared to where she lived.

She dreaded the walk back home afterward.

Maybe one day she could see his apartment here in the city. Maybe even stay there. After all, it had to be a lot nicer than hers. And in a safer area of town too.

It was strange she hadn't seen it yet. Why was that?

Garrick had always told her it was nothing to be excited about. He'd insisted that he was immaculately organized at work but, in return, a messy slob at home. That his place wasn't suitable for a woman for that reason.

He'd insisted it was better if they dined at restaurants or went to his summer house. Once they'd even gotten a hotel room here in the city.

It had been fantastic.

Cecilia reached the doors to his building and paused. She would wait here. Look casual.

She knew now which office was his. She'd counted

the floors to find his. Had seen the light on in his corner office.

But it was too high up to see anything else.

She rubbed her belly again as she often did these days.

She wondered what they might name the baby. If it would be a boy or girl.

She imagined she and Garrick sitting on the couch and talking about ideas. She'd always loved the name Samuel. And if it was a girl, Olivia.

What would Garrick think about those names?

She hoped he liked them also.

Finally, twenty minutes after Cecilia arrived, the light in his office flickered off.

She released a pent-up breath. She was growing weary of waiting, so knowing he would be coming down soon made her feel better. She'd been on her feet all day, and really all she wanted to do was kick back and relax.

Ten minutes later, someone exited the building.

It was Garrick. He was with three other men in suits. Two of the men walked beside him and one behind him.

When Garrick saw her, he glanced away.

Cecilia flinched.

He must not have recognized her. He probably hadn't been expecting to see her here.

Because that was *not* the reaction she'd been expecting.

Nowhere close for that matter.

"Garrick," she called taking a step behind him.

But he kept walking.

What was going on here? Was she losing her mind?

She quickened her steps, trying to catch up with him. Clearly, he hadn't heard her.

"Garrick! It's me. Cecilia."

Again, he kept walking.

The man behind him paused and turned toward her.

The look in his eyes wasn't kind. He raised a hand, and it hit her shoulder, stopping her in her tracks.

"Ma'am, I'm going to have to ask you to stop stalking Mr. Harding."

She blinked, certain she hadn't heard him correctly. "Excuse me?"

"We know about the gifts you've left him. How you ran past security and went to his office. How you've called his receptionist more than once. It needs to end. Mr. Harding is trying to be nice about this, but this is your last warning."

As her eyes widened, she shook her head. "You don't understand. He's my boyfriend."

"He said that you might say that. But we all know who you really are."

"What do you mean who I really am?" What was he talking about?

"Listen, I think I've said enough." He took a step back.

"What do you mean?"

"We all know you're an escort."

Her mouth dropped open. "No, I'm not. I'm his girlfriend."

"Ma'am, he's engaged—and not to you."

Cecilia's head swirled, and everything began to blur around her.

The man in front of her caught her elbows before she collapsed to the ground.

What was happening here? It was almost as if she had been dropped into an alternate reality.

But the man in front of her—was he a bodyguard?—looked dead serious.

And Garrick still hadn't turned around or acknowledged her.

Nothing made sense.

Cecilia had no idea what she would do to make things better.

CHAPTER
FIFTY-EIGHT

NOW

TODAY HADN'T GONE as Maddie planned.

Between finding Logan dead on the beach, talking to Detective Kalani twice, and everything that happened with Nico, her day had flown by like a speeding bullet charging toward an unsuspecting target.

In between all the trauma and drama, she'd packed her suitcase. She would go to the airport early. The sooner she could get away from this place, the better.

Right now, she knew the gala was about to start. She didn't want to attend, but she was curious about the event. It was taking place on the Grand Lawn, the same area where they'd had the luau.

When Maddie knew the dinner had started, she wandered toward the Grand Lawn.

She'd donned some black dress slacks and a beige shirt for traveling along with some comfortable black canvas sneakers. The innocuous outfit shouldn't draw any attention. She didn't want to be seen—only to watch.

She reached the area and found some shrubs where she could stand just out of sight from most of the guests. She tried to look like she belonged there as she occasionally glanced at her phone. Hopefully she wouldn't draw any attention from the waitstaff.

People were seated at tables, wearing their fanciest clothing. She recognized several faces, but no one looked her way. At the front stood a stage with a podium and a large screen behind it.

She'd seen the schedule earlier. She knew the plan was for everyone to eat, and then after dessert the board would name the new CEO.

She scanned the crowd one more time. Her gaze stopped on Nico and his wife. Despite his brush with death, he was here.

He must have gone to the hospital and been cleared in record time.

Had he insisted on leaving early because he hoped to be named CEO?

She searched the crowd again, and her gaze stopped on Brody. He was at a table closer to the back and on the edge of the lawn.

He sat beside Adrienne. Were the two of them really together?

It didn't matter.

Bree wasn't here. She was probably still in her room or still doing everything possible to find Fowler.

Nico and several board members, including Darla and Tom, sat near the front with Josh.

Halfway through the dinner, Detective Kalani appeared, standing on the edge of the seating area opposite her.

He glanced her way and nodded.

Guilt filled her. He'd told her not to leave. But legally, he couldn't make her stay here.

A few minutes later, all the board members took place on stage.

This was it.

Would Josh get what he had always wanted and take over his father's company, or would his dreams disintegrate in front of everyone?

———

Maddie held her breath as she waited for them to make the announcement.

As Tom stepped in front of the lectern, the crowd quieted. "When this company was started thirty years ago, we had a different leader at the helm." An image of Josh's father appeared on the screen. "This man right here was a wonderful entrepreneur and innovator that put Benchmark on the map. His death was a great loss and left big shoes to fill."

Applause sounded.

As it did, Adrienne rose and slipped out.

Why was she leaving before the announcement?

It seemed strange, but she probably had a good reason.

Brody rose a moment later and followed her.

"I'm going to be honest and say that this week has been a tough one," Tom continued. "A lot has happened. We've had great losses. But I know all those we've lost would want us to go on. Everyone who works for Benchmark believes in our mission. But we can't continue forward without reflecting on these lives that were lost."

Pictures of Jared and Logan filled the screen as somber music played.

They had a moment of silence for the lost employees.

When an appropriate amount of time had passed, Tom continued.

"In a moment, after we announce our new CEO, we're going to introduce the new products we're so proud to launch. All of you will be the first to know about this innovative technology we've been working so hard to create. Benchmark is committed to remaining on the cutting-edge of the industry."

More applause.

"What do we do when we face adversity?" Tom continued. "Benchmark has seen its fair share of this in the past, and we'll certainly see it in the future. Just as we do with our projects, we learn from the past as we hope for the future. We mourn, but we move on. We use setbacks as steppingstones."

Using Jared and Logan's death as inspiration to

move on seemed uncouth to Maddie. But no one had asked her.

"With that said, we're proud to announce the newest CEO of Benchmark Technologies. This person is someone who can continue moving us forward and remind us about what is important. Who has a vision for this company. Who has more focus than anyone I've ever met. Our newest CEO is . . ."

Maddie held her breath.

Then Tom McLemore announced, "Garrick Joshua Harding!"

Maddie wasn't sure if a gasp swept through the audience or if it was just her.

After all the plotting and planning on the part of others to dethrone Josh, he'd still gotten the position. The board either didn't know about his escapades or they didn't care.

She'd guess they only cared about the bottom line.

A round of applause swept through the crowd.

Josh's picture appeared on the screen. A picture of him with his perfect hair and winning smile. The picture of fake perfection.

Then Josh strode on stage looking as handsome and put together as ever.

Not that Maddie was surprised. Looking at him now, no one would guess that anything had happened. No one would guess that the woman he'd been sleeping with was killed. That his fiancée had broken up with him. That people who worked for him were dead or missing.

Nope, it was all business with Josh right now. He was the king of compartmentalization.

Before he could say anything, a video started playing that highlighted his accomplishments at Benchmark.

Maddie watched in curiosity before her stomach clenched with disgust.

Josh wasn't a good person. Maybe most people who got these kinds of positions weren't good people. Maybe in order to be powerful, people had to fight and claw their way to the top not caring who they hurt on the way.

Which just proved to Maddie that this wasn't the kind of life she ever wanted for herself.

She'd seen enough.

She turned to leave.

But she'd only taken three steps when the sound of the video changed.

She froze, part of her subconscious realizing what she was listening to. Another part refusing to accept it.

As if on autopilot, she slowly turned.

A video of her and Josh appeared on the screen

A video of them in his hotel room.

Arguing about their relationship. About Logan.

Her room wasn't the only one that had cameras planted in it. So had Josh's.

Their break-up had been recorded and was now airing for everyone to see.

"I didn't do anything to Jared," Maddie said. "You know that."

"It doesn't matter what I know," Josh shot back. "What matters is what other people think."

"I thought the most important thing for you would be me, not your reputation and how this would make you look. I was only trying to watch out for you when I didn't tell you."

"I've told you everything that's involved here!" Josh yelled. "It's almost like you want to ruin this retreat."

"I want to ruin your retreat? Why would I want to do that? I didn't even want to be here, but you talked me into coming. All so it would look good for you and increase your prospects for becoming CEO."

"When you tried to break things off with me, I explained I was going through a rough patch. I thought you understood and cared about me enough to give us another chance. I guess I was wrong."

"And I thought you cared about me enough to remain faithful," Maddie said. "But I guess I was wrong."

"What?" Josh asked. "What does that even mean?"

"It means I know about all your extra little rendezvous. I'm not stupid!"

"I don't know what you're talking about."

"Stop lying," Maddie said. "Let me start with you and Logan."

"What about her?"

"Don't play stupid. Everyone knows about the two of you, and you aren't even keeping your feelings a secret. I thought *you were smarter than that. Or did you think I wouldn't notice?"*

"What did you expect me to do?" Josh asked. *"You became so cold and distant. Don't you realize how important sex is to a man?"*

"Don't you realize how important it is to a woman that you respect her boundaries? That you remain faithful?"

Two board members ran toward the back of the Grand Lawn, waving at the tech guys to stop the video. But the guy behind the computer shook his head and threw his hands in the air as if things were out of his control.

Who had done this?

The video finally stopped, but the silence only emphasized the murmurs running through the crowd.

Maddie took a step back, embarrassed to face anyone.

She glanced at Josh. His cheeks were red, and his nostrils flared.

That barely controlled anger she'd seen so many times before had surfaced.

She needed to get out of here. Staying to watch any of this had been a mistake. She had to catch her flight.

Before she could turn away, a new image filled the screen.

This time it was a picture of her mugshot.

NAUSEA ROSE IN MADDIE.

How could someone do this?

Now everyone here knew about her past.

Including Josh. Brody. Detective Kalani.

This only served to make her look more guilty.

Everyone would now know what she had done . . . just not *why* she had done it. They would make assumptions, however.

She couldn't stay here anymore. Couldn't bear to see anything else someone might want to put on that screen for everyone to watch.

She hurried back toward her room, tears blurring her eyes as she rushed through the pool area toward her wing. She kept her head down, hoping no one would see how upset she was. Praying no one would ask questions.

How could this have happened? She should have

never come. She should have broken up with Josh when she tried to the first time.

She just didn't understand why anyone would do this. Was it to ruin her? To ruin Josh?

Nothing made sense.

She would get her luggage and get out of here. Not look back.

She sprinted all the way back to her room, her arms trembling as she threw her door open.

Wasting no time, she grabbed her suitcase, which she'd left by the door.

Maddie would catch the shuttle to the airport and wait there for as long as necessary before her flight.

She stepped toward the door, ready to go. But then her phone buzzed.

Dread pooled in her stomach when she remembered something.

She'd seen Adrienne leave. Had seen Brody follow.

Could this have happened since then? It had only been probably thirty minutes.

She forced herself to take the phone out of her pocket. To look at the screen.

What she saw there horrified her.

It was a picture of Adrienne. Bound and gagged with tears rolling down her cheeks. She wore the dress Maddie had seen her in only an hour earlier.

Beneath the photo were the words:

Come to the cliffs. Alone. Tell anyone and your friend will die. THE RING will be gone forever . . .

The Ring? Another movie reference? Maddie could only assume the sender was talking about her engagement ring.

That jewelry meant nothing to her in comparison to Adrienne's life, however.

Maddie's heart raced.

Going to the cliffs would be stupid. Most likely a death wish. Especially since the sun would disappear beneath the horizon at any time.

But if she didn't go then Adrienne would die.

She couldn't let anything happen to Adrienne because of her either.

She glanced at the ceiling before closing her eyes. *What should I do? Tell Detective Kalani?*

It seemed the only smart thing to do.

Then, almost as if the perpetrator of these crimes had read her mind, her phone buzzed again.

If you don't come, the detective will see this after Adrienne dies. Check your earlier messages.

Her earlier messages? What did that even mean?

Maddie scrolled down, and a gasp escaped.

Text messages had shown up on her phone between her and Adrienne.

Texts that made it appear the two had a fight. That made it appear Maddie had asked her to meet on the cliffs.

That made it look like Maddie was behind all of this.

Who had done this? These messages hadn't been there earlier.

Even if she deleted them, she had a feeling whoever was responsible could make these magically reappear.

This person was forcing her hand. And if the sender was capable of making messages appear on her phone, what else was this person capable of?

———

Maddie had no choice but to do this. Or maybe she did have other choices but none she could conjure at the moment.

If she went to the cliffs, maybe she could save Adrienne. If she didn't go, Adrienne could die, and Maddie might be blamed for her death.

If Maddie told the police . . . there was no guarantee Detective Kalani wouldn't think she was guilty anyway. Especially now that Kalani knew she had a record from her juvenile days.

She knew what she had to do.

Instead of leaving through the main exit, Maddie followed the hallway down to the opposite end of the resort and took the door leading to the parking lot. From there, she could skirt along the edge of the resort and hopefully avoid running into anyone.

Was everyone still at the gala? What had happened after that video played? Had they tried to wrap things up and somehow place a nice pretty bow on it, pretending like it wasn't a big deal? Had the board members realized Josh's character and decided they'd made the wrong decision?

What a disaster. An utter disaster.

It was getting dark as she reached the cliffs near Shipwreck Beach.

When she'd first met Bree and Fowler, the two of them had been hiking these cliffs early in the morning. They knew this area better than most.

Could they be behind this? As far as Maddie knew, Fowler hadn't been found yet. Was that because he had disappeared on his own and set all of this up?

So much still didn't make sense.

These cliffs covered a large area. Exactly where was she supposed to find Adrienne?

Maddie wasn't sure, so she started up a sandy path through some trees until she reached a rocky area closer to the water. The cliffs waited up ahead.

Maybe if she walked closer to the edge she could spot someone. However, she also needed to stay far enough from the drop-off that she wouldn't be taken by surprise.

She was so out of her element right now. Yes, she had taken a life before. But she'd vowed to never do it again.

However, if push came to shove . . . she couldn't turn a blind eye to an innocent person being harmed.

She paused and cupped her hands around her mouth before calling, "Hello?"

No answer.

Swallowing hard, she kept moving. The sun finally sank on the horizon, leaving the area bathed in a grayish, pinkish haze. Soon, it would be inky dark.

These cliffs would be even more dangerous.

As Maddie climbed over several large rocks, she came to a new area.

Someone knelt on the ground ahead of her.

A woman with her hands bound behind her.

The breath left Maddie's lungs. "Adrienne!"

She glanced around and saw no one else.

This might be her chance.

Maddie rushed toward her.

It seemed too easy that she might be able to untie her friend. That the two of them might get away. That no one was here to stop them.

Where was Adrienne's captor?

Maddie would figure that out later. She needed to act now while no one was close.

Frantically, she untied the gag around Adrienne's mouth. Finally, it loosened enough to slide down to her neck.

Adrienne gasped in several shallow breaths. "You found me."

"Are you okay?"

"I am now." Her words came out raspy with anxiety. "You've got to get me out of here."

"Let me get your hands and feet free."

Maddie worked the knots at Adrienne's wrists until

finally they loosened. Then they both began to work on the ties at her feet.

When Adrienne was free, Maddie helped her to her feet.

"Who did this to you?" Maddie asked as she began to pull her toward the brush, away from the cliffs toward some cover.

"You'll never believe it. It was—"

"Madison! I don't know where you think you're going."

She froze. She would recognize that voice anywhere.

It was Josh.

Was he behind all of this?

LIES, Cecilia realized. There had been so many lies.

Had anything Garrick told her been the truth? It didn't seem like it.

A month had passed.

A month without Garrick.

A month since Cecilia had told him about the pregnancy.

A month since he'd accused her of stalking him and being a rejected escort.

A month since he'd completely shut her out of his life.

Well, maybe not completely.

She'd found ways to gather information. She'd watched Garrick. Maybe even followed him a few times.

He was indeed engaged to a beautiful woman who looked like everything that could be expected of someone who was going to marry the CEO of a company.

Everything Cecilia hadn't been able to be for him.

She'd finally gone to the doctor and found out she was four months along.

She could already feel the baby bump growing, and she couldn't wait to feel the first flutters of life.

But she still had no idea how she would make ends meet.

Panic wanted to seize her every time she thought about it.

A single mom in New York City. It just wasn't going to work. There was no way she could make ends meet.

Now she knew with certainty that Garrick would continue ignoring her calls. Ignoring her. Shutting her out of his life.

Her heart ached at the thought of it. This wasn't the way things were supposed to be.

But she needed to accept it.

She could track Garrick down and demand something from him. But she had no money for that. In all honesty, she didn't have the emotional bandwidth for it either.

He clearly wanted to continue on with his life and pretend like his little rendezvous with her didn't exist.

That woman Cecilia had heard him talking to in the bathroom that time? Probably his fiancée.

The woman she'd seen with him in his office? She *wasn't* his fiancée.

Which probably meant that Garrick had done this with other women also.

He was a pig disguised as Prince Charming.

What a total jerk.

She would move back home, she decided. She would forget that Garrick Harding had ever happened . . . which would be hard considering she was carrying his baby. But getting stressed out was bad for her child. She didn't want that.

Mama didn't have a lot of money either. But at least Cecilia would have someone to help her.

Coming to New York City had been a mistake.

A huge mistake.

Now she was carrying a daughter inside her.

One day she would teach her daughter not to make the same mistakes she had.

MADDIE PUSHED ADRIENNE BEHIND HER, shielding her from Josh.

This wasn't Adrienne's battle. She was an innocent bystander.

"What are you doing here?" Josh appeared above a cluster of rocks. His tie had been loosened and he'd ditched his suit jacket.

Maddie couldn't see his face well enough to read his expression, but his voice sounded exasperated. How had he done all of this? He'd been on stage up until thirty minutes ago.

Her head throbbed as she tried to think it through. Was he working with someone?

That had to be it.

"Don't play dumb, Josh." Maddie continued to take steps back, slowly easing away from him. "You told me to come here."

"Why would *I* tell *you* to come here?" His words almost sounded accusatory.

What kind of twisted game was he playing?

Whatever it was, it wasn't funny.

"Stop acting dumb," she muttered.

"I'm not playing dumb." His words came out faster than usual. "I got a text telling me to come here."

"So you listened to the sender and left the gala where you were just named CEO?"

His story didn't even sound believable.

Adrienne had never said who did this to her. She was about to when she'd been cut off.

She lingered behind Maddie now, her breathing rapid with fear.

"Everything was cut short." Josh's voice hardened. "The whole thing was a disaster, and now the board wants to reconvene one more time. You had a criminal record, Madison? For murder?"

"It's not like that," Maddie explained. "I didn't mean to kill that man."

"Sure you didn't," Josh mumbled as he inched closer.

"I didn't. I was only fifteen when I walked in to visit my Poppy, and this aide—his name was Kevin MacDonald—was manhandling him. I'd seen the bruises on Poppy for weeks. No one at the nursing home could explain the marks—nor did they care."

Maddie drew in a deep breath as that horrible day

flashed back into her mind. She never talked about it. Everything was too painful.

Despite the tension across her chest, she continued. "That day, I realized exactly what had been happening. I tried to stop Kevin." Maddie's voice cracked at the memories. "I pushed him away, and when I did, he fell and his head hit the corner of the counter. He hit it hard. I . . . I never intended to kill him. I was just trying to keep him away from my Poppy."

"So that's why you got that job helping other elders who were abused." Josh pressed his lips together, appearing apathetic at the realization. "I guess it all makes sense now."

This didn't seem like the time or the place to be having this discussion.

This conversation was distracting her from more important issues.

She leveled her gaze with Josh again. "Why did you text me?"

"I'm telling you, I didn't tell you to come out here. I got a text saying *I* needed to come or more of my secrets would be exposed. I made up some flimsy excuse to the board members who were cross-examining me about my love life and came right away."

Maddie knew the truth. Josh had done so out of desperation to save face. He didn't want any more secrets revealed.

But Maddie still had more questions. "You didn't know a camera was in your room?"

He eyed her. "Of course, I didn't. Did you?"

"No, but I found one in my room last night. I didn't even consider there could be one in your suite also."

Josh squinted. "So what exactly is going on? Why are the two of you out here? Why are there ropes on the ground?"

Before Maddie could answer, something hard pressed into her back.

Her muscles tightened as reality hit her.

She'd misjudged this situation, hadn't she? Seriously misjudged it.

"I really just need both of you to stop talking," a voice growled. "Now."

SIXTY-TWO

MADDIE KNEW EXACTLY who the voice belonged to.

Adrienne.

She didn't dare move. She couldn't chance setting the woman off.

"What are you doing?" Josh demanded, an air of entitlement to his voice.

Maddie hoped his sharp words didn't get them both killed.

"I'm doing what's only fair."

"What's that supposed to mean?" Josh asked. "What's fair about you holding me and Madison at gunpoint?"

"She hates the name Madison. It's Maddie, you idiot! And you really don't have any idea what's going on, do you?"

"I'm pretty sure you've lost your mind, but that's not what you're referring to, is it?"

Maddie pressed her eyes shut. "Josh . . ."

Didn't he have more sense than this? This was no time to set Adrienne off.

"No, let him ask questions," Adrienne said. "I would be more than happy to explain things."

"I'm all ears," Josh said.

"Yes, you kind of are, aren't you?" Amusement lilted in Adrienne's voice. "I think you got those from your dad."

His gaze darkened. "Did you bring us all the way out here so you could insult me?"

"No, I didn't. But isn't it kind of funny that we have the same ears?"

"What?" Josh's forehead wrinkled.

Maddie sucked in a breath. What was she talking about? Was she implying . . . ?

She shifted and glanced over her shoulder.

The woman still had the gun raised, but with her other hand, she touched a ruby necklace at her throat.

"Adrienne?" The word croaked from Maddie.

All the amusement left her gaze. "I don't expect you to understand because you weren't a part of this whole mess. You were just a bystander here."

"You've lost your mind," Josh said. "You need to let us go."

Maddie really wished he would stop saying things like that.

"Thirty years ago, your dad fell in love with a beautiful woman named Cecilia who worked in a department store in New York City."

"No, you're wrong. He married my mom thirty years ago."

"Exactly. That was part of the problem."

Maddie glanced at Josh and saw some of the cockiness disappear from his face, replaced by surprise.

"I don't understand."

"Of course, you don't," Adrienne snapped. "You've never been as smart as your dad, and you know it."

"I'll have you know, I graduated at the top of my class from MIT."

"Maybe. But that still doesn't make you your dad. I think you know that. You knew you were at risk of not taking over his company because you weren't good enough."

"I'm so confused," Maddie said. "Some woman named Cecilia dated Joshua's dad thirty years ago." Then the realization hit. "Wait . . . is Cecilia your mom?"

She grinned.

"In other words, his dad had an affair," Maddie continued. "You're Josh's half-sister, aren't you?"

"Bingo!" Adrienne nodded. "Finally, somebody gets it."

"You're my half-sister?" Josh repeated, practically gawking.

"Look at him. He had no idea. Go figure. Not very astute, are you? I told you that you weren't that smart."

Now that Adrienne mentioned it, Maddie could see a slight resemblance.

"Okay," Josh said. "So you're my sister. I had no idea that you existed. It's not as if I was trying to ignore you or pretend we weren't related. I didn't know."

"I know. I don't really care about any kind of relationship with you. Don't be ridiculous. You're so pretentious that being around you is worse than being stuck on a boat in the middle of the ocean full of people with the runs."

In other circumstances, Maddie might laugh at that. But not now. Not with her life and Josh's life on the line.

"So why are we here?" Josh asked.

"Because I'm the oldest child," Adrienne said. "And guess who is supposed to be first in line for Dad's company? Me."

Joshua's face went paler. "There's no way you are going to get that job. There are clauses in the contract. My dad wasn't just going to hand this over to someone who wasn't qualified. He was too savvy for that."

"You mean *our* dad? Either way, I'll never stand a chance if you're still in my way. That company belongs to me."

"Why in the world would you even say that?"

"You never had Dad's smarts, but I do. I know your new product is going to fail."

"No, it's not!" Josh insisted.

"It's why you've looked so nervous all week. This is the big launch, but it has a lot of problems. A battery that doesn't need to be recharged or replaced for three years is a brilliant idea. But I know in tests you've had problems—problems you've tried to cover up. That battery also explodes."

Maddie's eyes widened.

Was Adrienne correct?

Josh didn't argue her point.

"Is that true?" Maddie asked. "You were launching a faulty product, and you didn't say anything so you could be promoted? What if it hurt someone?"

"We just had a few bugs to work out!"

"Josh . . ."

"You have no idea how much pressure was on me! Without this new battery, we would have lost our investors. I would have been out at the company. I had to do whatever was necessary to see that it succeeds."

"You've always been entitled, though, haven't you?" Adrienne continued. "This project is no different. You liked the prestige and the luxury of the company our father started. I know all about your extravagant lifestyle. Then there was me and my mom. We lived in a two-bedroom house with my grandma. My mom and I had to share a room, and we barely scraped by."

"I'm sure if my dad knew he would have helped."

"No!" Spittle flew from Adrienne's mouth as she said the word. "Father had no interest. He pretended like he didn't know my mom. Pretended like I didn't exist."

"Then why didn't you go to court and fight him?"

"Because my mom believed that life would be better without him attached to us. Once she saw his true colors, she wanted nothing to do with him."

"That's not my fault." Josh raised his hands. "I still had nothing to do with this."

"My mom was too nice of a woman to fight for what she deserved. She died two years ago of cancer. If she had been married to your father, I'm sure she could have gone to all of the best treatment centers out there. Maybe she could have even been cured. But we didn't have that kind of money or resources."

"I'm sorry for your loss," Josh said.

"Don't be sorry for my loss. Be sorry for yourself!" Her voice cracked with anger.

"What are you going to do with us out here, Adrianne?" Maddie asked.

Adrienne pointed her gun at Josh. "Walk."

He looked behind him, and his eyes widened. "I have nowhere to go. There's a cliff right here with a thirty-foot drop into the ocean."

Adrienne's eyes lit with malice. "Exactly."

MADDIE HAD TO DO SOMETHING.

If Adrienne got her way, Josh would be forced at gunpoint to jump off this cliff. She didn't have much hope he would survive.

Then what did Adrienne plan on doing with Maddie afterward?

Maybe she could buy time. It could simply delay their deaths.

Or it could give someone the opportunity to figure out what was going on and help them.

She prayed it was the second option.

"So you were the one sending me those notes and texts?" Maddie asked. "The one who killed Jared and Logan?"

"That's right." The gun didn't even tremble in Adrienne's hand as she held it toward Josh. "I got here early and made an excuse as to why I needed to get into your rooms. Said I was your assistant, and nobody seemed to question it. I left those cameras there, hoping I could catch something juicy. You guys delivered."

Maddie's cheeks burned as she remembered that video being played for everyone to see.

"As I was leaving, Jared caught me. He realized I was up to something and tried to extort money from me. Can you believe the nerve of him?"

What Maddie couldn't believe was the nerve of Adrienne, who'd gone through all this trouble just for money. There were other ways to handle this besides murder.

"Then Jared contacted me anyway," Maddie said. "He was going to sell you out."

Adrienne's gaze darkened. "I couldn't let him do that. We had a meeting arranged, right before yours. Jared's scheduling skills weren't that amazing. He apparently didn't consider that our times might overlap —though I have to admit that I had no idea he'd contacted you until later. Anyway, one thing led to another, and . . . I think you know the rest of the story."

"And Logan?"

"Logan saw me using my work computer to create that little presentation for tonight. Though she didn't know what I was doing, she would have put things together. So I made a clone of Josh's phone and texted her, pretending to be him. I wrote that they needed to meet, that it was urgent and that she shouldn't tell anyone. I knew she'd take the bait. You should have seen her surprise when I showed up."

"Did you kill Fowler?" Josh asked.

"Fowler?" Adrienne scrunched her nose as if the question were stupid. "No, I have no idea what happened to that man."

Then another thought hit Maddie. It was probably a bad time to be thinking about something like this, but she did it anyway.

If Adrienne had lied about all of this, then she had probably lied about Brody also. She probably had asked him here under the guise of a psycho ex-husband stalking her. But Maddie had a feeling none of that was true.

Had Adrienne made that up just to get Brody here? Just so she could try and get back with him?

It made sense to her.

To think that Maddie had sided with Adrienne. Had thought her side of the story made more sense, especially considering Maddie's history with men.

Now she might not ever have the chance to apologize to him.

"Why are you pulling Maddie into this?" Josh asked.

Maddie's lips parted in surprise over the fact he was actually considering someone other than himself.

"She's the perfect scapegoat. She liked you, which made me dislike her. Initially, at least. As I got to know her, I realized she was nothing like you. I started to feel bad for a while, but business is business. That's what you always say, isn't it, Josh?"

"Are you the one who tampered with my water heater in New York? Who messed with my tire pressure?"

Adrienne's grin was all the answer Maddie needed. "Just having a little fun and testing the waters. If something had happened to you then, it would have just been a bonus."

"And you knew how to set up the hot tub?" Maddie continued. "Who was that intended for?"

"Either Josh or Nico would have worked. I was a pool girl for a summer at this nice hotel in Jersey. I actually saw that very thing happen to one of the guests there. I thought it was brilliant. It didn't take much research for me to figure out how to set things up."

"Your brilliance really could be put to good use, you know," Maddie said. "Instead of plotting all of this destruction."

"It was really quite fun. Slashing the tire on your side-by-side when no one was looking. Loosening the bolts on the balcony. Sending those notes . . ." She grinned again. "Each time, the look on your face was priceless. Truly, it was."

"You don't have to do this," Josh murmured.

"Enough talking!" Adrienne snapped, appearing irritated that Josh thought he could speak again. "I came here for a reason, and I'm not leaving until it's accomplished. Now Josh, you're going to start walking. And you're going to jump off that cliff."

"And if I don't?"

"Then I'm going to make Maddie push you."

ADRIENNE WAS FAR MORE cunning than Maddie could have ever guessed.

She was going to do whatever it took to become CEO of this company.

Maddie could see it playing out. Josh dying. Adrienne stepping forward to take over her rightful position.

It was clear she'd gotten her father's smarts—only she'd hidden that fact. Meanwhile, she'd secretly learned to hack. To program. To create digital chaos.

How was Maddie going to stop this woman?

"Adrienne, there's a better way to handle things," Maddie said, even though she knew the words sounded lame and cliché.

"Don't even try to talk me into changing my mind. It's made up. You can draw this out to be painfully long and suffer more or you can just do what I tell you."

"What are you going to do with me after he jumps? Besides make it look like I did it?"

"After somebody"—Adrienne cleared her throat—"releases information that you're a murderer to the entire company, people are going to think you're capable of anything."

"Those records were sealed. How did you find out?"

"I'm pretty good at hacking systems to find out whatever I need. It comes easily to me. Must have gotten that from my dad. So when I looked into your background, I saw your juvenile record. I felt like I'd hit the jackpot."

Maddie's jaw tightened. This woman was determined to get what she wanted and wouldn't let anything stop her.

"Anyway, I've been going around randomly mentioning to people that you've had erratic behavior and that I caught you doing drugs. I may have even planted some paraphernalia here and there. I also may have set up some text messages on your phone. I'm really good at making things like that look real. Like, really good."

"You didn't?" Maddie muttered.

"Oh, I did. So Josh is going to jump. I'm going to drug you. Put the gun in your hand. And when I run from these cliffs and try to find help after I witnessed what happened, who do you think people are going to believe? Me? Or you?"

"So Josh is just going to happen to die, you're going to witness it, and then you're going to step up to rightfully claim your place in the company and people are going to think that's a coincidence?" Maddie asked.

Adrienne's eyes narrowed. "I'll have some time pass, of course. Then I'll make it look like a surprise. You don't think I'm that stupid, do you?"

"I never said you were stupid. In fact, I think you're very smart. Too smart to kill someone."

"Well, it's too late for that. I already have two murders under my belt. Three if you include my ex-husband."

Maddie's eyes widened. This woman really had lost it. She had no scruples whatsoever.

Considering the fact she had a gun and they didn't, that would make it hard to have the upper hand in the situation. Adrienne wasn't going to want to keep talking for much longer. Maddie knew that.

Adrienne glanced back at Josh. "So what's it going to be, my spoiled younger brother? Are you going to make this easy or hard?"

He peered down the cliff before stepping back, his head wobbling as if he was woozy and his balance unsteady.

"I can come forward with the company," he pleaded. "Say that you rightfully deserve to be the CEO. There are other ways to go about this."

"You and I both know that's never going to happen.

You can say it all you want now, but as soon as you're off of this cliff, you're calling the police and telling them everything I just said." She paused, something hardening in her gaze. "So walk."

"What if I don't push him?" Maddie asked. "Are you going to shoot both of us? Because it's going to kind of be hard to pin all of this on me if I have a gunshot wound."

"Unless I make it look as if it was self-inflicted."

She really had thought this through. "You don't have to do this."

"But I do." A grin curled across her lips. "You know what? I said I'd only killed three people. But it's actually four."

Adrienne smirked. She'd waited to share this part, hadn't she? She was getting a kick out of it. But why?

"Who else did you kill?" Maddie's voice trembled as she asked the question.

"I actually went to talk to Josh's father once I found out that he was my father too," Adrienne said. "He could care less about the fact I was his daughter. In fact, he dismissed me. That made me very angry."

Maddie's gaze swung back to Josh. His eyes widened as he stared at the gun in Adrienne's hands.

"I watched our father die," she continued. "I was there as the life drained from his eyes. Then I left, and I waited for his assistant to find him in the morning. Do you know what else? I didn't even feel bad about it."

"You little . . ." Josh began to lunge at her.

As he did, Adrienne stepped forward.

Before Maddie realized what was happening, Adrienne's hands hit Josh's shoulders.

He screamed as he flew backward. Then he disappeared on the other side of the cliff.

MADDIE SCREAMED as she watched Josh disappear.

Then, in an instant, Adrienne turned toward her, gun raised. The malice still remained in her eyes.

"Now to take care of you." Adrienne reached into her pocket and pulled out something.

A needle.

No doubt full of drugs of some sort.

"You don't want to do this." Maddie took a step back, careful to head away from the cliff.

"But I do." Adrienne smiled, her eyes gleaming with hatred. "Haven't I made myself clear yet?"

"Adrienne . . . there are better ways."

"Not everyone is a Goody Two-shoes like you are," she said. "And look where it's gotten you? Nowhere. You're the laughingstock of everyone here. At first they thought you were a prude. Now they think you're a killer."

Maddie tried to glance over the cliff. She expected to hear Josh hitting the rocks below.

She hadn't.

What if he had caught onto a branch or a ledge? What if there was still a chance he was alive?

Maddie stared at Adrienne's gun. Then at the needle.

Could she take Adrienne?

She wanted to think that she could. But she wasn't sure.

Maybe she should at least try. She couldn't go down without a fight. If there were scratches or cuts or bruises on her body, then the police would probably ask more questions.

Adrienne would probably tell them that Maddie and Josh had gotten into a fight and that was what they were from.

Still, she had to do something.

She swung her leg out and kicked the gun.

Only it didn't fall out of Adrienne's hand. She held the weapon too tightly.

But the barrel did swing away from her.

When it did, Maddie lunged at her. Tackled her to the ground.

Adrienne was surprisingly strong. She flipped over until she was on top of Maddie.

The malice in her eyes turned into a fiery hatred. "You weren't supposed to do that, nice little Maddie."

Adrienne let out a guttural, primeval sound.

Then she raised her fist and jammed it in into Maddie's jaw.

Pain ripped through her.

She closed her eyes, wanting to disappear from this moment.

But she couldn't.

She had to fight until the end.

But Adrienne had her fully pinned down.

Somehow, the woman had managed to grab that syringe again.

Maddie tried to move. To get from beneath her before she could plunge that drug into her system and Maddie lost control of her thoughts and actions.

But she couldn't move.

Something about the way Adrienne had her pinned rendered her immobile.

Even as much as she wiggled, it did no good.

Adrienne raised the syringe. "Say goodbye to life as you know it, princess."

Then she swung the needle down, ready to plunge it into Maddie's skin.

RIGHT BEFORE THE needle touched her skin, something—or someone—flew through the air and collided into Adrienne.

Maddie scooted back on her hands and feet, desperate to get away. Once at a safe distance, she pushed herself to an upright position.

Then she blinked, trying to comprehend what was happening.

Someone had grabbed Adrienne. Had her arms pinned at her sides. Even as she struggled against this person, he held her tight, controlling her.

"Brody . . ." Maddie whispered.

What was he doing here? Had he followed them?

However he'd found them, he'd gotten here just in the nick of time.

Adrienne thrashed as she tried to get away. But Brody was too strong.

He locked Adrienne's arms at her sides and lifted her off her feet. "Calm down. You're not going anywhere."

"I'm a victim here!" she shouted. "You need to be restraining her." Adrienne threw a glance at Maddie.

"We all know that's not true," Brody said. "So drop the act."

Adrienne let out another half grunt/half cry as she tried to find one last burst of energy.

It didn't work.

Brody had successfully subdued her.

Maddie let out a breath, desperately wanting to believe that the danger was truly over.

Brody glanced at her. "Are you okay?"

"I—I'm fine," she murmured.

She snapped back to reality. What was she doing just standing here? Shock had frozen her in place.

"But Josh . . ." She darted to the edge of the cliff and looked down. She prayed that she might see him hanging on for dear life.

But she saw nothing.

It was dark. Maybe there was something that she couldn't see.

She couldn't be sure.

"How did you know?" She glanced at Brody.

Adrienne still struggled against him, but she was no match for his strength.

Footsteps hurried toward them as well as flashlights.

Maddie turned to see the police had surrounded them.

An officer took Adrienne from Brody, and she yelled out her made-up story. "They tried to kill me. I'm so glad you got here when you did."

"Save your lies for someone else," Detective Kalani called.

Maddie turned toward him, never so happy to see the man.

"Josh . . . he went off the cliff."

"I've already alerted the Coast Guard, as well as search and rescue. They should be here anytime now."

"I've looked over the cliff. I couldn't see him." Panic laced her voice.

"These cliffs . . . they're dangerous."

"I know . . . I know." Maddie's voice cracked as she said the words.

The reality of everything that had happened crashed on her.

She'd come so close to death.

Even though she didn't want to marry Josh, she didn't want to see his life end this way.

Just as her knees started to buckle, arms reached around her.

Brody.

But he wasn't subduing her as he had Adrienne.

No, he held her up.

This time, she didn't resist.

Maddie buried her head in his chest as her muscles went totally limp.

———

Two hours later, Maddie and Brody were still on the cliffs.

Someone had put a blanket around them. Paramedics had checked her out. Police had arrested Adrienne.

And the search party was still out there trying to find Josh.

How could he just be gone like that?

She'd heard someone say something about a strong undercurrent tonight.

Had the ocean pulled him out to sea that quickly?

When everyone left them alone for a minute, Maddie turned to Brody. "How did you know?"

"I thought something might be up, so I tried to follow Adrienne. But I lost her. I kept wandering around, and I finally found you guys."

Gratitude filled her. "I'm so glad you came when you did. If you hadn't shown up, it would be an entirely different situation right now."

"I'm glad I got here when I did."

She pressed her eyes closed as she realized all the things she needed to say to him—the apologies she needed to make. "What you told me about Adrienne was the truth. I'm so sorry I questioned you. Adrienne told me the two of you were still together and made it sound like you were a player."

"It was a lot to take in," he murmured. "Adrienne . . . she has some issues. It's why we broke up. She was sweet when I met her the first time. But as we got to know each other, something about her didn't seem right. It seemed off, you know?"

"Like what?"

"She would just go ballistic over seemingly minor things. When one of her friends got the apartment that Adrienne had also been trying to get, I caught Adrienne trying to sabotage her friend by charging up her credit cards so she'd have bad credit. That's when I knew we were done."

She soaked in everything he said. "So why did you come here with her?"

He let out a long breath. "A year ago, my sister was killed by her husband. It was right before Adrienne and I met. It tore me up knowing what had happened to her. Knowing I hadn't been able to stop it."

He paused and Maddie gave him a minute to collect his thoughts. Moisture glimmered in his gaze.

He licked his lips and continued. "Adrienne mentioned to me that she'd been married before and that her ex-husband had been a bad man. So when she called me and told me he was threatening her, I didn't want to leave her on her own, not if I could do something to protect her. I agreed to come on this trip with her, but I set some very firm boundaries because I didn't want her to think too much of it."

That sounded exactly like Brody.

She squeezed his hand. "You came here to watch out for her."

"But I should have known better. She wanted to get back together. I didn't know that until a few days into the trip. I think she was still determined to find a way to get back with me. Coming was a mistake . . . except I got to meet you."

Her heart lurched into her throat.

She was grateful they'd met also.

But this didn't seem like the time to tell him that, not when there were so many other things to talk about.

"Brody . . . she mentioned something about killing her ex."

"What?" His eyes widened.

Maddie nodded. "She said she'd killed four people. Jared. Logan. Danny. And Josh's father. Who also happened to be her own father."

He ran a hand over his face. "I knew she was off-balance, but I didn't realize she was that off-balance. I can't believe that."

"At least she's been arrested. I have a feeling she'll be going away for a long while."

"I have a feeling she will be too." Detective Kalani appeared. "I'm glad you're safe, Ms. Waters."

"I'm glad I am to." She turned toward him, but still held on to Brody's hand. "It was iffy there for a while."

"Our island is usually peaceful. I hope you'll give it another chance."

She considered his words a minute. "I'd like to give it another chance sometime. Just not at a Sunny Days retreat."

She and Brody exchanged a look. They still had a lot to talk about. Maddie had more questions for him.

But there would be time for questions later.

For now, she needed to process everything that had happened.

And maybe there would be an update on Josh soon.

CHAPTER
SIXTY-SEVEN
ONE YEAR LATER

BENCHMARK WAS NOT HAVING their retreat in Kauai this year.

But Maddie had returned.

Things in one year could change so much. Coming here felt cathartic.

She checked herself one more time in the mirror. The lovely peacock-blue sundress she wore fit her in all the right places. She smoothed her hand down the skirt before giving herself an approving nod in the mirror.

Then she left her room and started outside for the beach. A rainstorm had just passed through a few minutes ago, but now the sun peeked out.

All too well, she recalled being here a year ago and all the horrible things that had happened.

She'd tried to put most of those behind her.

Just as she'd wanted to do, she quit her job with the

charity and went back to being an investigator with social services. She'd decided not to stay in New York, but she hadn't moved quite yet. She was still trying to figure out where exactly she wanted to put down roots.

She was open to almost anywhere—other than the big city.

Josh still hadn't been found, a fact that bothered her. It meant she had no closure.

But maybe the ocean truly had pulled him into its depths never to emerge again.

Adrienne had been sent to jail and now faced many charges, including murder. Her trial would start in a few months, and Maddie would be one of the witnesses.

Though she didn't want to rehash all that had happened, she would.

Adrienne needed to pay for everything she'd done. She needed justice.

From what Maddie understood, the woman really had been Garrick Sr.'s biological daughter. Those parts of the story had been true.

Adrienne had been dealt a bad hand in life. But that didn't justify everything she had done. The police had retrieved Maddie's engagement ring.

She'd sold it and given the money to the charity she worked for right before she quit.

Last Maddie had heard, Nico had taken over Benchmark. He'd put the long-lasting battery on the back shelf until they worked out more issues, and it still hadn't been released. But from what Maddie understood, the company was still doing well.

Fowler had finally been located. Bree was with him. They'd been working together to steal information from Benchmark.

Fowler had gotten his hands on the last piece of information and had tried to flee.

When he'd climbed that ridge to go to the bathroom, he'd kept walking. When search parties had come near, he'd hidden. Then he'd continued his trek through the mountains.

When the coast was clear, so to speak, Bree had rented a car and gone to pick him up. The two were going to wait things out, and when everyone with the retreat left, then they'd planned to return to the continental United States.

The money they'd get as a payout from Blue would have been enough to start a new life under new identities. Part of Maddie wished they had given those plans to Blue, and that Blue had rushed to make a faulty battery. It would have served them right.

Thankfully, the two of them had been caught, and they were also facing serious charges.

Maddie paused at the beach, her thoughts going back to that dreadful day when she'd seen Jared calling for help in the waves.

Little did she know when she'd tried to save him that it would set in motion a deadly chain of events.

"Hey, you," someone with a deep Texas drawl said behind her.

She grinned as she turned around and saw Brody standing there.

He looked as handsome as ever, and his grin, as always, was enough to knock her socks off.

He reached for her hand and squeezed it. He didn't let go as they faced each other.

For the past year, they'd been keeping in touch with each other, talking via phone and text. They'd met for dinner a few times.

They'd both agreed that they needed time, and that jumping into things too quickly would be a mistake.

But now, a year later, Maddie felt as strongly about the man as ever.

"You look gorgeous," he murmured.

"You don't look too bad yourself." She stepped closer and straightened the collar of his white button-up shirt. Not that it needed to be straightened. Maddie just wanted another excuse to touch him.

"I had a brief fear you wouldn't show up," he said.

"I've been counting down the days."

They shared a grin.

With one more glance at each other, they both turned to face the ocean. Brody put his arm around her and pulled her close.

Maddie let out a gasp as she looked out.

"What is it?" he asked, concern filling his gaze.

She couldn't blame him after everything that had happened.

She pointed at the sky. "Look. It's a rainbow. I searched everywhere trying to see one of those the last time I was here. I never did, and I couldn't help but think that was a sign—not that I really believe in signs. But the idea did seem rather poetic."

"I agree. The rainbow in the Bible was a sign of brighter days to come. Maybe this rainbow can be the same thing for you. For *us*."

Maddie turned toward him and, when Brody wrapped his arms around her waist, she didn't hesitate to rest her hands on his chest. "I like that. I like it a lot."

As the breeze swept over them, their gazes locked. He leaned closer as if he might kiss her.

But before their lips met, the sound of nearby laughter pulled them from the moment.

They glanced over as two couples walked down the beach toward them.

Maddie's throat tightened when she saw them.

They looked so nice, like her kind of people in their casual outfits and with their hair flying unpretentiously in the wind.

Brody pulled her closer. "What do you think? You want to make some vacation friends?"

She groaned and closed her eyes shut as she remembered how excited she'd been to meet everyone on her last trip here.

But she already knew the answer to that question.

It was a definite no.

She didn't need to make new friends here.

She was perfectly content just to hang out with Brody . . . not just now, but hopefully for far into the future.

~~~

Thank you for reading **Vacation Friends.** If you enjoyed reading this book, please consider leaving a review.
~~~

ALSO BY CHRISTY BARRITT:

YOU ALSO MIGHT ENJOY: TRUE CRIME JUNKIES

<u>Just the Nicest Person</u>

Strangers—each with their own secrets—are thrown together after the murder of a beloved true crime podcaster.

Disgraced attorney Andi Slade is seeking justice for the killer who destroyed her reputation and her career. But going undercover as an ice road trucker in Alaska to find answers is just the tip of the iceberg. A brutal snowstorm, a handsome stranger, and an unsolved cold case send Andi's plans into a tailspin.

Former CID investigator Duke McAllister refuses to give up searching for his fiancée who disappeared two years ago on the Dalton Highway. When he rescues a woman on the side of the road, he knows just how much danger she's in. Stranded together and butting heads, they discover a common interest: true crime.

When their favorite local Alaskan podcaster goes radio silent right before revealing the name of a cold case killer, they dive in to investigate only to make a terrifyingly frigid discovery. Can these strangers work together to find answers before the biting, dangerous cold claims their lives? Or even worse . . . before the killer comes looking for his own brand of justice?

He Walks Among Us

With a killer walking among them, no one is safe . . .

When the newly formed Arctic Circle Murder Club meets in Fairbanks, Alaska, to investigate the mystery of the Missing Women of Dalton Highway, their plans take a gruesome turn.

Upon the group's arrival at the hotel, three women's frozen bodies are pulled from the nearby river. When a friend of one of the victims pleads for help finding out who's behind the murders, how can they say no?

The club must detour from their original plan and dive into the recesses of a killer's mind before another victim is claimed. As they seek the truth behind the murders, opposition hits them at every turn. Shocking revelations from the past along with brimming conflict threaten to end the group just as they've started.

Can this group of true crime podcasters uncover someone's dark secrets before one of their own plunges into an icy grave?

Never Happen to You

Crime is something that happens to strangers. Until it's not.

As women continue to vanish in Alaska's Far North, the Arctic Circle Murder Club meets again to combine their skills and search for the truth. Only the evidence isn't adding up. The case of The Missing Women of Dalton Highway has gone cold, and every new possibility leaves them with frostbite.

Duke McAllister's and Andi Slade's personal investigations point them in new directions, and they're left with more questions than ever. But there's one thing they—and the rest of the true crime podcasters—know for sure: whoever is behind these disappearances will keep taking women until he's caught.

Will the team find answers and expose the truth before this madman strikes again? Or will the secrets of the infamous Dalton Highway remain as isolated as the landscape surrounding them?

The Dead of Night

A woman disappears in the dead of night as a haunting crime from the past comes to life again.

When a mysterious email leads true crime podcaster Mariella Boucher to southeast Alaska on a quest for the truth about her past, she never expects to plunge head-first into danger. But when a stranger with a troubled history saves her life, she's drawn into a five-year-old cold case that leaves her chilled to the bone.

Jason Somersby has been living in the shadow of suspicion ever since his girlfriend was murdered five years ago. When another woman disappears under similar circumstances, everyone in town looks at him with accusation—and to demand answers he doesn't have.

Mariella brings in the other members of the Arctic Circle Murder Club to help find the killer and clear Jason's name. But the more the team digs, the shakier the ground becomes. When it becomes clear one of their own is the next target, they must scramble to stop the killer before he claims another victim.

Leave the Lights On

First the lights go out . . . then they die.

The body count is rising. Six murder victims. The only connection? An X carved into the dead person's chest. When the family of one of the victims asks the Artic Circle Murder Club to investigate, the team dives into their toughest case yet.

Stopping the murders isn't the team's only challenge. When Duke McAllister sees his teammate Andi Slade dodging the cops, he knows she must be in deep trouble. But Andi isn't the only one on her team on thin ice. Trouble seems to be following them all.

With more murders making the headlines, the threat

level reaches an all-time high. The end game has begun. The clock is ticking, and disaster looms near. Will they stop the killer before the deadly grand finale? Or will the lights go out one final time?

The End of the Road

With the future of the Arctic Circle Murder Club teetering on rocky ground, the team members have scattered. But it's not long before they realize some bonds can't be broken.

Fearing an adversary from her past will find her, Simmy Samuels runs, determined to find a new place to hide. But Ranger Garrett isn't about to leave Simmy out in the cold and alone. He's determined to both protect Simmy and to search for his daughter, whom he thought was dead.

As Ranger and Simmy set out to find his little girl, danger follows them into the vast wilderness of Alaska. Challenges meet them at every turn: unyielding danger, truth that feels more like fiction, and reality blurred by deception.

Will they survive long enough to set things right? Or will this be the end of the road for the murder club?

The Secrets She Kept

In the Land of the Midnight Sun, secrets cast long shadows.

Former Army investigator Duke McAllister remains determined to uncover the truth behind his fiancée's mysterious disappearance two years ago. Joined by his friend and podcast teammate, Andi Slade, Duke delves into Celeste Dawson's past and soon uncovers a mind-bending conspiracy.

When a shocking news report names Celeste as a suspect in a series of murders, Duke must grapple with the mounting evidence that his fiancée may not be the person he thought she was. The stakes rise to terrifying new heights when bodies start piling up and the podcast team becomes a target.

Duke and Andi must navigate a labyrinth of secrets, betrayal, and murder to unravel the web of deceit that reaches far beyond anything they ever imagined. Will they find the answers before it's too late? Or will the secrets Celeste kept destroy them all?

Most Likely to Die

When a plane goes down in the Alaskan wilderness, so does the senator onboard . . .

With voting for the proposed oil drilling project only days away, former defense attorney Andi Slade knows what happened to the senator was no accident. It was a calculated and ruthless attack by Victor Goodman, the man who ruined Andi's reputation and career.

As Andi and her friends, members of The Round Table podcast, join forces to put an end to Victor's destruction once and for all, the stakes rise to a new level.

The team has had their share of differences in the past, but they can all agree on one thing: justice comes with a price. As they fight for their lives in a killer's twisted game, one question remains . . . who will be the most likely to die?

ABOUT THE AUTHOR

USA Today has called Christy Barritt's books "scary, funny, passionate, and quirky."

Christy writes both mystery and romantic suspense novels that are clean with underlying messages of faith. Her books have sold more than four million copies and have won the Daphne du Maurier Award for Excellence in Suspense and Mystery, have been twice nominated for the Romantic Times Reviewers' Choice Award, and have finaled for both a Carol Award and Foreword Magazine's Book of the Year.

She is married to her Prince Charming, a man who thinks she's hilarious—but only when she's not trying to be. Christy is a self-proclaimed klutz, an avid music lover who's known for spontaneously bursting into song, and a road trip aficionado.

When she's not working or spending time with her family, she enjoys singing, playing the guitar, and exploring small, unsuspecting towns where people have no idea how accident-prone she is.

Find Christy online at:

www.christybarritt.com
www.facebook.com/christybarritt
www.twitter.com/cbarritt

Sign up for Christy's newsletter to get information on all of her latest releases here: **www.christybarritt.com/news letter-sign-up/**

facebook.com/AuthorChristyBarritt
x.com/christybarritt
instagram.com/cebarritt